"A top-notch milita[...] [...]us-
pense, and action. [...] Galdorisi continue to
make the Clancy brand shine."   —*Booklist*

"Intricate plotting, plenty of action . . . will leave you
sleep-deprived."   —*Defense Media Network*

"Op-Center attempts to pull off a daring, skin-of-the-
teeth operation . . . Exciting."   —*Publishers Weekly*

OUT OF THE ASHES

"The U.S intelligence agencies have spent billions since
9/11 learning how to 'connect the dots.' But what if there
are only one or two dots? *Out of the Ashes* is a smoothly
written story by two authors who understand the inner
workings of U.S. intelligence, government, and the military, and tell a frightening and exciting tale about a
very new, but also a very old threat."

              —Larry Bond, *New York Times* bestselling
              author of *Dangerous Grounds*

"Thriller addicts like me devoured every Tom Clancy's
Op-Center tale. Now they are back, intricately plotted,
with wonderfully evil villains and enough realistic

military action and suspense to ruin a couple of nights' sleep. Highly recommended."

—Stephen Coonts, *New York Times* bestselling author of *Pirate Alley*

"Fans of the original Op-Center series created by Tom Clancy and Steve Pieczenik will welcome this solid continuation from Couch (*SEAL Team One*) and Galdorisi (*Coronado Conspiracy*). . . . This thriller procedural packs plenty of pulse-raising action. The open ending promises more to come." —*Publishers Weekly*

"Op-Center is back with a vengeance! *OUT OF THE ASHES* isn't just a reboot of the Op-Center series; it's one of the best techno-thrillers to hit the shelves in a long time. Dick Couch and George Galdorisi have just raised the bar for military adventure fiction. Suit up, strap in, and hang on, because you're in for one hell of a ride."

—Jeff Edwards, bestselling author of *The Seventh Angel* and *Sword of Shiva*

TOM CLANCY'S OP-CENTER NOVELS

ALSO BY GEORGE GALDORISI

NONFICTION

FICTION

Tom Clancy's
OP-CENTER
SCORCHED EARTH

CREATED BY
Tom Clancy and Steve Pieczenik

WRITTEN BY
George Galdorisi

St. Martin's Paperbacks

This is a work of fiction. All of the characters, organizations, and events portrayed in this novel are either products of the author's imagination or are used fictitiously.

TOM CLANCY'S OP-CENTER: SCORCHED EARTH

Copyright © 2016 by Jack Ryan Limited Partnership and S&R Literary, Inc. Excerpt from *Tom Clancy's Op-Center: Dark Zone* Copyright © 2017 Jeff Rovin and George Galdorisi.

For information address St. Martin's Press, 175 Fifth Avenue, New York, NY 10010.

ISBN: 978-1-250-13022-8

Our books may be purchased in bulk for promotional, educational, or business use. Please contact your local bookseller or the Macmillan Corporate and Premium Sales Department at 1-800-221-7945, ext. 5442, or by e-mail at MacmillanSpecialMarkets@macmillan.com.

Printed in the United States of America

St. Martin's Griffin edition / August 2016
St. Martin's Paperbacks edition / August 2017

St. Martin's Paperbacks are published by St. Martin's Press, 175 Fifth Avenue, New York, NY 10010.

10   9   8   7   6   5   4   3   2   1

This book is dedicated to my family: first and foremost, my wife, Becky; our son, Brian, and his wife, Annie; our daughter, Laura, and her husband, JT; and their three sons—our grandsons—Jack, Larkin, and Davis.

Writing takes you away from the people who you care most about—often for countless hours. Having a family that can power through those times and offer constant encouragement and support makes the writing process infinitely more joyful.

ACKNOWLEDGMENTS

There are many people who helped make the new Op-Center series, and this book, *Scorched Earth,* live up to the expectations of readers of the previous Op-Center books—as well as those of our new Op-Center readers. Many thanks to the following who contributed their time and talent to this effort: Mel Berger, Bill Bleich, Larry Carello, Wanda Clancy, Ken Curtis, Melinda Day, Geoff Dick, Jeff Edwards, Hannah Fergesen, Herb Gilliland, Robert Gottlieb, Kate Green, Kevin Green, Denny Irelan, Brad Kaplan, Pete Kissel, Krystee Kott, Carl LaGreca, Robert Masello, Laurie McCord, Scott McCord, Kevin McDonald, Madeleine Morrel, Rick "Ozzie" Nelson, Bob O'Donnell, Jerry O'Donnell, April Osborn, Norman Polmar, Sheila Sachs, Curtis Shaub, John Silbersack, Charles Spicer, Matthew Shear, Scott Truver, Matt Vernon,

Sandy Wetzel-Smith, Ed Whitman, and Anne Wilson. I am in your debt, and Op-Center's readers will silently thank you as these books take them into the world of the future.

AUTHOR'S INTRODUCTION

The setting for this novel is the greater Levant. The term Levant is typically used by historians and archaeologists with reference to the prehistory, as well as the ancient and medieval history, of the region encompassing the countries we now know as Egypt, Iraq, Israel, Jordan, Lebanon, Syria, and Turkey. However, the term has made a recent resurgence. Indeed, there have been fresh attempts to reclaim the notion of the Levant as a category of analysis in the political and social sciences. The reason for this resurgence is due to the phenomenon sweeping the region—the Islamic State of Iraq and Syria—or ISIS.

Few would argue against the statement that ISIS (or ISIL—the preferred term used by U.S. national security officials—the "L" standing for Levant) presents a profound threat to the West. As President Obama said in a widely watched speech in September 2014,

"Our objective is clear: We will degrade, and ultimately destroy, ISIL through a comprehensive and sustained counterterrorism strategy."

Almost two years later, U.S. national security officials remain perplexed as to how to deal with ISIS. No one is talking today, in 2016, about *defeating* ISIS, only *containing* it. What is happening in the greater Mideast in areas where ISIS roams freely will not resolve itself in the next several years. For Western nations, and especially for the United States, today's headlines are looming as tomorrow's nightmare.

ISIS will remain a threat to the West—and especially to the United States—years into the future because America has not come to grips with how to deal with this cancer. As Jessica Stern and J. M. Berger describe in their best-selling book *ISIS: The State of Terror*, and as Michael Weiss and Hassan Hassan describe in their best seller *ISIS: Inside the Army of Terror*, the very nature of ISIS makes attempts to deal with it by employing the conventional instruments of national power all but futile. Here is how Michiko Kakutani framed the challenge ISIS presents in her *Books of the Times* review of these two books:

> The Islamic State and its atrocities—
> beheadings, mass executions, the enslavement
> of women and children, and the destruction
> of cultural antiquities—are in the headlines
> every day now. The terror group not only

continues to roll through the Middle East, expanding from Iraq and Syria into Libya and Yemen, but has also gained dangerous new affiliates in Egypt and Nigeria and continues to recruit foreign fighters through its sophisticated use of social media. Given the ascendance of the Islamic State, it's startling to recall that in January 2014, President Obama referred to it as a "JV team," suggesting that it did not pose anywhere near the sort of threat that Al Qaeda did.

In this novel, *Scorched Earth*, we believe life will imitate art for years to come. We're certain the challenge ISIS presents today will remain fresh and relevant for years. Indeed, the issues driving what makes the greater Levant the center of enormous strife today guarantee that it will remain this way in the near-to-mid future. Simply put, from our point of view, as well as that of political officials, military leaders, historians, and many others, the Mideast will remain a petri dish, spawning and regenerating cancers like ISIS for as long as any of us can see into the future.

It took President Obama only eight months to elevate ISIS from "a JV team" to an organization that the United States was committed to "degrade, and ultimately destroy." And since the normal instruments of national power the United States can bring to bear cannot begin to degrade—let alone destroy—ISIS, this president, as well as future presidents, will have only one card to play. The president will need to call on the National Crisis Management Center, more commonly known as Op-Center, to protect American lives and freedoms.

CHAPTER ONE

March 3, 0930 Eastern European Time

Alan Burton's head slammed into the overhead of the Humvee with eye-watering force. Nearly stunned by the impact, he dropped back into his seat, feeling his scalp for signs of blood. "Damn. That hurt!"

General Bob Underwood suppressed a smile and held out a Kevlar battle helmet to his aide. "Try this. It's harder than your skull."

Burton accepted the helmet and put it on, just in time to cushion his head's next collision with the roof of the heavily armored vehicle.

The ride in the army truck was rough as it stormed across the Syrian farmland that lay hard by the Euphrates River and close to the Iraq border, en route to the Syrian city of al-Bukamal. Their convoy had crossed the unguarded Iraqi-Syrian border a half hour ago. One Humvee led the one Underwood and his aide were riding in, while one trailed them. A total of eight special operations Rangers from the 75th Ranger Regiment provided security for Underwood and Burton.

While Underwood and his aide were attired in much the same way as their Ranger Regiment escorts—Interceptor body armor bullet-resistant vests, MICH TC-2000 Kevlar Advanced Combat Helmets, M9 Beretta side arms and the rest—there was one distinct difference. Underwood had last hung up his Marine Corps uniform almost two years ago when he retired as the Commander of the United States Central Command—or CENTCOM.

Now, he was back on familiar territory as the special presidential envoy for the Global Coalition to Counter ISIL—the Islamic State of Iraq and the Levant. In his six months in this assignment, Underwood had spent time in Iraq, Jordan, Lebanon, Syria, Turkey, and Yemen. He was in Syria again because the Syrian refugee crisis was worse now than at any time since it began in the wake of the 2010 Arab Spring uprisings. The president had dispatched him to Syria to try to broker a cease-fire between the Syrian government and the forces opposing it—Hezbollah, ISIS, the Free Syrian Army and a number of fringe rebel groups. Underwood didn't fancy his chances of success forging an agreement between and among the warring parties. Still, to Underwood, a presidential order was a presidential order.

"How much longer until we get to al-Bukamal, Sergeant?" Underwood asked the driver.

"About fifteen minutes, General."

"Thanks. Ask our lead vehicle to slow down after

we make the next turn. Last time we ran this route we almost took out a herd of cattle."

"I remember, sir, and wilco."

Underwood returned his attention to the ruggedized Panasonic CF-29 laptop as his aide scrolled through their agenda for the meeting. "General, here are the players from the Free Syrian Army we'll—"

The sound of the rocket-propelled grenade hitting the side of their Humvee was ear-splitting and shook their three-ton truck violently. Flames shot along the side of their vehicle. Underwood and his aide hung on as their driver tried to steady the burning Humvee.

Seconds later, there was a deafening sound as an improvised explosive device detonated under the lead vehicle. Underwood and his aide both looked up in horror as the lead Humvee leapt into the air just yards ahead of them and crashed down on its side and then rolled over on its back. Fire began to consume that truck as thick black smoke billowed into the air.

Their driver immediately started to take well-rehearsed evasive action and gunned his V-8 turbo-diesel engine as he tried to drive around the destroyed truck in front of them. Suddenly, Underwood's aide cried out, "Look out!" as an AMZ Dzik "Wild Boar" infantry military vehicle barreled straight for the right side of their Humvee. It was too late. The Polish-designed truck the Iraqi Army once owned hit them square-on as Underwood and his aide tried to grab on to any available handhold.

Gravity took over and their vehicle teetered—then landed on its left side with a sickening thud. The last thing Underwood remembered before passing out was their driver's head hitting the bulletproof glass on the left front door, his helmet popping off, and blood gushing from his skull as it rebounded from the glass before hitting it again.

The Rangers in the trailing vehicle did precisely what they'd been trained to do—they converged on Underwood's Humvee, dismounted, and quickly deployed in a protective ring around it, their gun muzzles pointed in different directions, searching for threats.

"Command, this is unit Mike-Hotel, taking fire from unknown hostiles approximately one-five klicks southeast of al-Bukamal!" the senior man in the trail vehicle shouted into his Motorola XTS5000R secure UHF radio. "One vehicle destroyed, one disabled. Hawk down, repeat Hawk—" the first lieutenant, the senior Ranger still alive, started to say. But his voice was quickly silenced as well-aimed shells from Browning M2HB heavy machine guns, fired from converging American-made M1117 Guardian armored security vehicles, ripped through him and also cut down his fellow Rangers.

With all the Americans in the lead and trail American trucks dead or dying, the men in the attacking vehicles converged on the Humvee carrying Underwood.

"Major, I just got a radio call from Mike-Hotel, the 75th Ranger Regiment element providing security for General Underwood. Sir, it was a partial transmission—"

The watch commander cut him off in midsentence. "What did you hear, Staff Sergeant?"

"Sir, he said they were southeast of al-Bukamal and that Hawk was down—"

The Army major standing the duty watch at the former Victory Base complex near Baghdad International Airport converged on the staff sergeant's console and immediately barked, "Play it back now!"

Every man and woman in the command center stood transfixed as they listened twice to the frantic call from the convoy.

The watch commander turned to another man and said, "Call CENTCOM Headquarters on the command net. Tell them Hawk is reported down and request air cover."

"Yes, sir. Major, where should I request they get the air cover?"

"Just tell 'em, damn it!"

But the watch team knew there would be no air cover. The United States had pulled out of Iraq years ago. A skeleton U.S. military force remained in Iraq to train the Iraqi Army as well as provide security to people like the special presidential envoy for the Global Coalition to Counter ISIL. However, they had little more than a few dozen vehicles like the now-destroyed Humvees, a handful of helicopters, and a few crew-served weapons in addition to their personal weapons. The Americans in the convoy were on their own.

As soon as Underwood tried to move, he realized his left arm was broken. With the Humvee on its left side, his brain was in overdrive as he hung suspended by his lap belt and harness and looked out the smoke-blackened right-side windows of the smashed truck. What had just happened? They were attacked—but by who? He thought he knew, but he tried to banish the thought from his mind.

"Sir, are you okay?" Burton said as he struggled to free himself from his belt and harness and come to Underwood's aid.

"I . . . I think so, Alan. Our driver is dead. What about the Ranger in the front passenger seat?"

His aide looked into the front seats and replied, "I'm afraid they're both dead, sir."

"My arm's bunged up; help me unstrap. We've gotta get out before this truck explodes," Underwood said, as he groped for his Beretta with his right hand.

Just then, they heard loud voices and felt heavy thumping on their Humvee. They jerked their heads and looked as the right-side back door was yanked open. Several pairs of arms reached into the vehicle as first Underwood, and then Burton, were lifted out of the truck and roughly dropped to the ground. Other men grabbed them and dragged them a short distance away from their broken vehicle.

A crowd of men surrounded the two Americans and began kicking them while shouting in a language neither understood. Suddenly, another man pushed his way to the front of the group and stood over Underwood. He held a tablet in his hand. He looked at Underwood, then looked at the tablet, then looked at him again.

"That's him," the man said, drawing a pistol from his belt, as the other men nodded in agreement.

Underwood looked on in horror as the man raised the pistol, took aim, and put a bullet in Burton's forehead.

The special presidential envoy recoiled in horror as blood, bone, and brain tissue from his aide's shattered skull landed on him. Then he looked up at the flag flying from the nearest Guardian armored security vehicle. It was the unmistakable black flag with white Arabic writing. It was the flag flown by ISIS.

Underwood cried out in agony as two of the men grabbed him, bent both his arms back, hog-tied him, and threw him into the Guardian ASV. Then the ISIS vehicles sped away.

"The special presidential envoy?"

"Yes, sir!"

"His convoy was attacked?"

"Yes!"

"Where?"

"Southeast of al-Bukamal, Syria."

The Air Force colonel conducting the interrogation was the watch commander at the CENTCOM command center at MacDill Air Force Base in Tampa, Florida. The report by the Navy chief petty officer manning the command net on their watch floor was far from complete. She knew only as much as the sketchy report she'd heard from the soldier at the former Victory Base Complex in Baghdad. It was still well before sunrise in Tampa and they were two of only five watchstanders in the command center. The partial report was enough to rouse the colonel to action.

He turned to the Army master sergeant at the console on his left.

"Call Beale. We need eyes-on at that location—*now*! Tell 'em to get a Global Hawk moving in that direction. We'll give 'em updated position information when we get it."

The rest of the watch team sprang into action as chat windows opened and questions—but few answers—streamed back and forth between Baghdad and Tampa. Meanwhile, flash messages rocketed up several chains of command. Soon, other watchstanders, those manning the National Counterterrorism Center, the National Military Command Center, the White House Situation Room and other command centers processed what they heard and began to notify key seniors. In the Sit Room, the National Security Council senior staffer leading the watch team picked up the phone and called the president's national security advisor, Trevor Harward.

Bound and gagged and with a sack over his head, Underwood tried not to let the sheer terror of the moment overwhelm him. As a Marine Corps first lieutenant he had led men in combat in Operation Desert Storm. He had served in other conflicts in the ensuing decades and had numerous tours as a commander in Iraq as well as in Afghanistan. He had never feared his enemy—but he feared those holding him now.

The Guardian ASV bounced along near its maximum speed of sixty miles an hour. Underwood tried to keep track of time to somehow gauge how far he was traveling but random large bounces shot shards of pain into his broken arm that almost overwhelmed his senses. He became almost numb to the pain and tried to think through what over three decades of military training had taught him about how to react in a crisis.

It was morning in Washington, D.C., when Trevor Harward entered the Oval Office. He had called President Wyatt Midkiff in the family quarters shortly after the president's normal wake-up time and told him the news, promising to bring him up to speed in the Oval later that morning.

The president had worked with Harward long enough to know his national security advisor was giving him every detail he knew, but the lack of information about the situation still frustrated him. And there was a personal element. Midkiff had worked closely with Underwood when the general commanded CENTCOM and was especially cheered when he had accepted the position as special presidential envoy for the Global Coalition to Counter ISIL. He knew Underwood had dedicated his life to the Marine Corps, had served almost continuously in the Middle East and South Asia for the latter third of his career, and was a devoted family man who looked forward to spending more time with his wife, his children, and his grandchildren when he retired and came home to Great Falls, Virginia. But the man's unique credentials made him the consensus choice to serve in this capacity and the president and his wife had courted the Underwoods—especially Mrs. Underwood—to entice the general to take on this assignment. Now he was missing and very likely kidnapped.

"Trevor, I've listened to what you told me over the phone and I read your memo. I'm less interested in what's happened than I am in what we're going to do to find Bob Underwood."

Harward paused. He knew what the president wanted to hear: that the U.S. national and military intelligence agencies had located Underwood's position and that a combat search and rescue mission was being mounted to snatch him away from his captors. That was not the case—far from it.

"Mr. President, we got eyes-on with a Global Hawk about two hours ago. General Underwood's convoy was ambushed in what appears to have been a well-orchestrated attack. All of the vehicles in the convoy are still there and are either damaged or destroyed. There were ten personnel in the convoy counting General Underwood and his aide. The Global Hawk picked up what we think are six bodies surrounding the vehicles."

"But we can't see inside the Humvees, right?"

"Right, Mr. President. We have two channels working to try to do just that—"

"How . . . how will we do that?" the president interrupted.

"We have operatives working with the Free Syrian Army. The closest ones are in—" Harward paused to look down at his secure iPad, "—Deir ez-Zor. It's about one hundred and thirty kilometers—eighty miles—north-northwest of al-Bukamal. Our people there don't have air assets, so they're driving toward al-Bukamal, but it's rough terrain and slow going.

"The other channel we have is with the Iraqi Army," Harward continued. "The CENTCOM commander is working with the Iraqi military to try to get some of our 75th Rangers aboard Iraqi helicopters and get to the site ASAP—"

"Iraqi helicopters?" the president interrupted again. "Don't we have any American helicopters there?"

"We do, but they're attack helicopters, with very little space for troops. We need bigger birds that can haul more men out to the site."

"All right, I get it. But you said, 'working with' the Iraqi military. Are there any issues? With all the damn blood and treasure we've poured into that country and the way we're still propping them up now, they'd better treat this like a five-alarm fire and give us everything they've got. Do I need to call the Iraqi president?"

"No sir. I made it clear to General George that if he needed our help he'd get it. The Iraqi military has a pretty good inventory of American, French, and Russian helicopters. It's just a question of picking ones that can make the two hundred-plus mile round trip carrying the Rangers and all their gear."

"I want to know immediately when those helos are en route."

"Yes, Mr. President."

"Anything else you need to tell me about this mess?"

"There is one more thing. We won't know this for certain until we have eyes at the site; the Global Hawk can only pick up so much detail. But we think there's an ISIS flag planted in the ground at the ambush site."

The normally controlled president lost it. "Damn it!" Midkiff shouted, "Find Bob Underwood. I don't care how we do it, just do it!"

"Roger . . . Aaron?" Chase Williams said as his intelligence director and the intel director's networks assistant appeared in his doorway. Op-Center's director was reading a report and sipping his Sumatra dark roast coffee from his Navy mess-decks mug. Williams put the report aside and motioned the two men to sit down.

Now in his third year as the leader of Op-Center, Williams had helped his president deal with crises across the globe, as well as at home. He was recruited—hard—by Op-Center's former director, Paul Hood, when the president decided to reestablish the organization.

Williams brought just the right qualities to the job. A retired Navy four-star, he was a former combatant commander for both Pacific Command and Central Command. He had proven his mettle in uniform, and now, as director of the National Crisis Management Center—as Op-Center was officially known—Williams enjoyed the president's complete trust and confidence. He had saved American lives at home and abroad and used his international and domestic Op-Center assets as precision instruments.

Roger McCord began, "Boss, you've read our reports and have likely seen the network news feeds, so you know the convoy carrying the special presidential envoy was attacked. You also know there are at least six KIA and the CENTCOM commander is trying to get eyes-on the ground to see if General Underwood is there."

"Bob Underwood's a good man," Williams said. "He did a phenomenal job at CENTCOM under tough circumstances—much tougher than I ever faced. What else we got?"

McCord, a former Marine who previously commanded the Intelligence Battalion at the Marine Special Operations Command, or MARSOC, had been one of Williams's first hires when he took over Op-Center. With a PhD from Princeton, magna cum laude in international affairs, McCord was a former infantry Marine who transferred to Marine Corps intelligence when he was wounded in Ramadi. He was in many ways Williams's alter ego. Williams trusted him without question, but what he liked best about McCord was that his intelligence director never guessed and always gave it to him straight.

"Aaron has mined ISIS's social media and also hacked into the transmissions bouncing off some of the cell phone towers near their compound in Mosul. I'll let him tell you more, but from what we can figure, it looks like ISIS has General Underwood and has taken him well away from the ambush site."

Williams had suspected as much, but hearing it from McCord caused him to sag in his chair. "Aaron?" he asked.

Aaron Bleich's official title was Intelligence Directorate, Networks Assistant. But that title so understated his role in the organization that Williams kept asking McCord to change it. Widely regarded as the intelligence director's MVP, Bleich had been recruited through a gaming company front at the annual Comic-Con International convention in San Diego, California. "Chief hacker" sounded like a too-judgmental title, but that was the long-and-short of what Bleich did so well.

Bleich was the architect behind the data mining and anticipatory intelligence programs that made Op-Center hum and that put its analysis abilities on a level above—likely far above—any other intelligence collection efforts in or out of government. Bleich ensured that Op-Center had access to all the information collected by each of the sixteen U.S. intelligence agencies. More importantly, he had carefully built the automated collation and analytical programs to make sense of the mountains of data Op-Center ingested. Big data didn't worry the Geek Tank leader; he embraced it and put it to use. Bleich had built his Geek Tank around machines and people—and the people were the best and the brightest minds, hired away from companies like Google, Amazon, Salesforce, and eBay.

"It's like this, sir," Bleich replied. "ISIS has only dribbled out a little bit into social media, but they've been burning up the cell phone circuits. They definitely have General Underwood. We're all but certain he's out of Syria and into Iraq. Beyond that, there's not much more we can say with any certainty."

"But what's your anticipatory intelligence suggesting?" Williams prodded.

Bleich looked toward McCord before continuing. He had overstepped his bounds with his immediate boss before and had been gently nudged back into line. McCord just nodded, so he continued.

"Well, the special presidential envoy for countering ISIL is a prize for any terrorist organization, but perhaps more so for ISIL because his very existence suggests we intend to take the fight to them. Most of the cell phone conversations we're picking up are carefully worded—we suspect ISIS is well aware of our monitoring capabilities—but my . . . umm . . . our analysis suggests there's little drama in their calls. It's more like whoever has him is just reporting in to someone at the top of their food chain."

"Mabad al-Dosari is still their leader," McCord interjected.

"You're saying the ISIL fighters who snatched him aren't operating independently. You think they've grabbed him at al-Dosari's behest and are bringing him to their compound in Mosul?"

"That's right," Bleich added. "And you know that area is no-mans-land for the Iraqi Army. They don't even make a pretense of controlling it."

"Do you think what you're picking up and what you're analyzing will alert us once they have him there in Mosul?" Williams asked.

"We're pulling out all the stops to ensure it'll do just that," McCord interjected. "Aaron will keep us posted on a real-time basis. You want us to send the ops folks in, boss? You thinking of sending our JSOC unit downrange?"

"No, not yet," Williams replied. "Give me a minute to let the president know what we know. Once I do that, we'll get the rest of the staff together and see if there's anything we can do to help."

As soon as McCord and Bleich left, Williams sat in front of his computer and composed one of his short, cryptic memos to the president. It was in the format of Williams's own design for communications that were strictly between him and President Midkiff. The infrequent communiqués were initially labeled, "President of the United States/Op-Center Eyes Only" which Williams later abbreviated to, "POTUS/OC Eyes Only."

CHAPTER TWO

MOSUL, IRAQ

March 5, 1530 Arabia Standard Time

Bob Underwood awoke and tried to clear the cobwebs from his head. The last thing he remembered was the men holding him down and one of them injecting something into his right shoulder. Then it all went black.

He saw he was in some sort of hospital bed. He looked down and could see his left arm was in a cast. The pain was all but gone but he attributed that, as well as his grogginess, to pain medicine they must have injected him with before setting and casting his arm.

Underwood tried to move but realized his hands and feet were bound by restraints. He pulled against them with all his might but he was tied tight. He was about to drift off into sleep again when the door to the room burst open and four men entered.

"Well, what *do* we know?" General John "Jack" George asked as his ops deputy finished briefing him and telling him, again, that they didn't know where the special presidential envoy was.

"General, our operatives with the Free Syrian Army got to the site about six hours after the ambush. They confirmed nine KIA and saw no signs of General Underwood. There were vehicle tracks leading off in a northeasterly direction. They followed the tracks up to the Iraq border but didn't cross it."

"What about our Rangers that the Iraqi Army was supposed to fly in from Baghdad?"

His ops deputy paused before responding, worried that what he was about to tell his commander would set him off. He steeled himself and then said, "Ah, General, they had cascading maintenance problems and couldn't muster two birds to fly our Rangers in."

"Dammit!" George shouted.

His ops deputy waited for more, but George remained silent. That worried his staff—a lot. They knew he was simmering. After an extended silence the man plunged ahead until he had told the CENTCOM commander everything he knew.

"Yes, I knew all that *yesterday*," George said in almost a whisper. "What I want to know is what our intelligence has turned up and what we've extracted from the three-letter agencies."

The CENTCOM commander hadn't slept in the forty-eight hours since Underwood was kidnapped. It was on his watch and on turf for which he was responsible. But he couldn't do anything because he didn't know all he needed to know to take action. It was frustrating beyond words. He knew his staff was trying, but it wasn't enough.

George tried to bring his thirty-five years of military experience to bear to take action—any action—that would rescue Underwood. He inventoried what he had learned in the last two days. The intelligence agencies had confirmed the attack was well planned and executed with precision, and that suggested it was directed from ISIL headquarters, maybe by Mabad al-Dosari himself. The collective assessment told them Underwood was most likely in ISIL's hands in central Mosul.

But it got worse. ISIL had consolidated its power in Mosul after the American-led coalition had finally pushed them out of Raqqa, Syria. While the United States had overhead assets that could focus on Mosul, the city of over a million was so densely packed these high-tech eyes in the sky could tell them little. And ISIL's control of the city was so complete that it could move its headquarters at will. His staff's collective assessment was that if they tried to mount a combat search and rescue op with what little intelligence they had, they'd be setting up another "Blackhawk Down" scenario.

After digesting all the bad news, George, trying to find some way, any way possible, to rescue the hostage, asked, "I get it, but what about the Iraqi government, can't they help? Without us, they'd have collapsed by now. Surely they can do something to help find him."

The ops deputy could tell George was just venting now. He knew the Iraqi government had yielded control of central Mosul to ISIL years ago, and American-backed attempts to retake the city had been futile. It was no-man's-land.

"Their intel isn't any better than ours, General. The best we could hope for is that they'd stand aside if we mounted a CSAR effort, but until we know where General Underwood is, we can't even begin the process."

"I know—I know. And I know our intel directorate is in overdrive trying to help. Tell my aide to set up a call with the director of national intelligence. I need to know everything he knows."

"Mr. President, turn on CNN now!"

Harward never burst into the Oval like this. The president's antenna went up; he could see the alarm in his national security advisor's eyes.

Midkiff reached for the remote and turned on the flat screen television hanging on the right side of the Oval Office. He toggled until he found CNN. The American network was broadcasting a direct feed from Al Jazeera.

Both men moved close to the screen. There, to their horror, they saw ISIL leader Mabad al-Dosari standing behind the kneeling Underwood. The American was attired in an orange jumpsuit with his head bowed. Al-Dosari was reading a long diatribe against the West, and Al Jazeera was broadcasting the English translation in a feed across the bottom of the screen:

> I am back, Midkiff. I am back because of
> your arrogant foreign policy toward the Is-

lamic State, and because of your insistence on continuing your bombings in Mosul, despite our serious warnings. You, Midkiff, have but to gain from your actions but another dead American citizen. So just as your missiles continue to strike our people, our knife will continue to strike the necks of your people. We take this opportunity to warn those governments that enter this evil alliance of America against the Islamic State to back off and leave us alone.

I take great pleasure in slitting the throat of this man, your so-called special presidential envoy for the Global Coalition to Counter ISIL. You insult us many times over. You refuse to use our proper name, the Islamic State. Burn that name in your brain, Midkiff. And you dare to call for a global coalition to fight us! No coalition can defeat the caliphate we now have established here.

We roam freely anywhere we want to go and soon we will be on your shores and we will slay you, Midkiff. You send this man and a few soldiers here to do what—to be sacrificial lambs because you are too much the coward to come here yourself? He is paying the price for your cowardice and your stupidity. I hope his family spits on you, Midkiff. You have made his wife a widow and his children fatherless—

Suddenly, al-Dosari stopped talking, yanked Underwood's head up by his hair, pulled a large knife from his belt, and held it under Underwood's neck. The ISIS leader paused a moment while his fighters behind him cheered and shot their weapons in the air. Then in one motion, al-Dosari ripped the knife into the American's throat. Blood gushed as al-Dosari held Underwood's head under his armpit, and the camera zoomed in as he bore down and carved until the American's head was completely severed from his neck.

The president and his national security advisor gaped in horror. Harward turned away, too sickened to look any longer, but the president just stood mesmerized.

"You bastards!" Midkiff exclaimed at the horrific image on the screen. "Bob!" he shouted. "They can't be doing this, look!"

Harward turned around to look at the screen. The video zoomed in on the ISIS fighters as they kicked Underwood's head around in an improvised soccer game. Harward turned away again and retched on the carpet of the Oval Office.

The president remained transfixed on the television for a small eternity as the ISIS fighters continued their gruesome game. Then abruptly, the screen went black.

The president turned to his national security advisor, who was trying to clean himself up, and ordered, "Get Defense and the Joint Chiefs chairman over here immediately."

Six hours later, at CENTCOM headquarters at Mac-Dill Air Force Base, General George had still not left his office. He had watched the same video the president and his national security advisor had seen. He had then ordered his executive assistant to tell his principal department heads to remain at the headquarters until further notice.

The call from the chairman of the Joint Chiefs of Staff had come as he had anticipated it would. But the chairman had not asked the question George expected to be asked: what forces were on station in his AOR—the CENTCOM area of responsibility—the question usually asked so higher headquarters could evaluate options. Instead, he was told to prepare to strike ISIL in Mosul in the next forty-eight hours with the full force of everything he could bring to bear. All the chairman wanted to know was how soon George could make that attack happen.

Calls had gone out to his Army, Navy, Marine Corps, Air Force, and Special Operations component commanders. Those commanders and their staffs, in turn, fed what they had back to the CENTCOM staff. Now it was evening, and his senior staff was assembled in his conference room.

"General, we've received inputs from all our component commanders," his ops deputy began. "We've sent you briefing memos over the last few hours with the details, so I'll just surf the wave tops in this brief."

"Good, quicker is better. I'm overdue with an answer to the chairman," George replied.

"Yes, sir. The *Theodore Roosevelt* strike group was in the southern Arabian Gulf just east of Qatar when this crisis broke. Fifth Fleet started them moving north as soon as we called. They'll be in the northern Gulf in," he paused to look down at his tablet, "about eight to ten hours."

The briefing continued with his military staff describing the precision bombing packages the *Roosevelt* strike group would use to hit urban areas in central Mosul. His staff anticipated he would ask about Iran—the 800-pound gorilla in the Gulf—and that their commander would want to know what they were doing to ensure Iran didn't feel threatened as they surged the strike group into the northern Gulf. Their answers weren't perfect—but they were good enough to leave George satisfied that Iran wouldn't interfere with the strikes. After answering several questions, his ops deputy was finally finished.

"If there's nothing else, General, I'll turn it over to the pol-mil advisor to answer those other questions you had."

"What do you have for me, Joan?" George said, turning to his political-military advisor.

Joan Hszieh had been the general's pol-mil counselor for almost five years, first in his two previous commands, and now here at CENTCOM. He had lured her away from a full professorship at Georgetown's School of Foreign Service, where she had been the deputy director of the Center for Contemporary Arab Studies. She had served him well in his previous assignments, but now she was really in her element working for him at CENTCOM.

"General, as you're well aware, it's crucial we

stress-inoculate the Iraqi government before we conduct these strikes. They'll be extremely sensitive to civilian casualties—that's why we've dropped leaflets warning civilians about previous strikes in Mosul. But as you know, every time we've done that, ISIL has simply picked up and moved and we've had virtually no impact on them."

"I know. But we're not going to do that this time, are we?"

"No, sir. This is still emerging in real time, but I'm told the president has directed the secretary of state to contact Iraq's foreign minister and tell him there will be no warning when we strike. We know their government will protest vehemently, but secretly, they're desperate for us to help degrade ISIL and keep it from taking over wider swaths of the country."

"Right, but I know they'll never say that publicly. What about the Iraqis helping if any of our pilots get shot down in these strikes?"

His ops deputy jumped in and he and Hszieh reminded George of what he already knew: The Iraqi government had no combat search and rescue capability. But what Hszieh's furious negotiating had accomplished was that *completely* off the books, the Iraqis would let U.S. Air Force CSAR birds stage out of an abandoned military airfield due west of Nasiriyah and also let them refuel at Al Muthana Air Base—the military side of Baghdad International Airport—en route to and from Mosul.

Satisfied his staff had planned for every contingency,

George turned to his EA and said, "I'll be in my office. First I need you to place a call to the chairman. Then we need to raise the Fifth Fleet commander on the secure net. I'll need to tell him we're go for these strikes."

Early the next morning, Chase Williams sat at the small conference table in his office with his operations director, Brian Dawson, his planning director, Richard Middleton, and his intelligence director, Roger McCord. McCord had asked for a meeting based on recent intelligence his Geek Tank had uncovered.

Williams often referred to the three men as his "thoroughbreds." Together they brought more than a century of national security experience to the table. While Williams prided himself on the fact that he ran a flat, largely egalitarian, organization, he had to admit that when he had a tough operational problem, he sought out the advice and counsel of these men above all others.

Dawson and Middleton sat next to each other, and it occurred to Williams that no two people on his small Op-Center staff could be more different—yet still be in his circle of close advisors.

Dawson was military through and through, even out of uniform. He was a West Pointer, former 5th Special Forces Group commander, accomplished linguist (Arabic, Dari, Pashto, and others), and perhaps most importantly for Op-Center, an *operator* with massive contacts in the Pentagon, at State and in the most important three-letter intelligence agencies. Put a current-day Special Operations superstar in civilian clothes, and you had retired Army Colonel Brian Dawson.

Middleton, on the other hand, was—with the exception of Bleich's self-named misfits in his Geek Tank—the most unmilitary person on the Op-Center staff. An Amherst graduate and blue blood, he had marched against the Vietnam War when he was in junior high. He went to the CIA after a tour at State and found his niche as a covert operator. There, he excelled and became one of the best. He rarely considered doing anything by the book, but was so successful accomplishing what his seniors wanted and needed that he survived numerous attempts to cashier him.

With a nod from Williams, McCord kicked off the meeting. "Boss, gents, as you all know, we're on the verge of strikes against ISIL in retribution for the kidnapping and killing of General Underwood. Aaron's Geek Tank has cracked something that's been stumping us for several days. ISIL is good, but they're not ten feet tall. I asked him to walk it back, and try to find out how ISIL was able to finger the location of the general's convoy in spite of all our efforts to keep the location of his meeting in al-Bukamal secret."

"We pulled the string on that with the IC," Dawson added, referring to the intelligence community. "They say this meeting—let alone the route General Underwood's convoy would take—was extremely close-hold."

McCord continued his intelligence assessment,

reminding them that after having to deal with a Saudi prince in an operation several years ago, Bleich's Geek Tank had kept a keen eye on what the Saudis did, and especially what their intelligence services were up to. They all knew Saudi Arabia saw ISIL as a buffer against Iran and that they continued to do a great deal covertly to aid ISIL.

What Bleich's team had recently discovered was that ISIL's leader, Mabad al-Dosari, had a free hand to reach directly into the Saudis' General Intelligence Directorate. Given the suffocating electronic blanket Saudi Arabia had over its territory, as well as that of its neighbors, it was all but certain the Saudis had sniffed out the meeting and passed that information to al-Dosari once he'd decided he wanted to go after the special presidential envoy.

McCord finished his assessment, and there was silence—but only for a moment.

"Our so-called allies," Middleton huffed . . . then caught himself. "I know you had to deal with these assholes when you were the CENTCOM commander, boss; but they really are making themselves the friends we love to hate. And how much military gear have we sold them in the last five years?"

"North of sixty billion," McCord added.

"All right, I've got it," Williams said. "Roger, tell Aaron and his team well done. I'm assuming we're the only ones who know this—even the IC is still in the dark?"

"Right, boss, and we won't share it unless you direct it. It answers an important question, but I'm not sure what else we need to do with the information right now."

"I need to let the president know we've found a leak we may need to plug later. For now, we'll have to wait to see if we strike ISIL."

CHAPTER THREE

March 7, 0430 Arabia Standard Time

In the early morning darkness, the glow from the secure iPad lit up the port side of USS *Theodore Roosevelt*'s (CVN 71) flag bridge. Seated in his bridge chair, the commander of Carrier Strike Group Twelve, Rear Admiral Jay Bruner, was flanked by *Theodore Roosevelt*'s commanding officer, Captain Rocky Wilson, and *TR*'s air wing commander—or CAG—Captain Bruce Michaels.

"Admiral," Michaels began, scrolling through the pages of the tablet he held in front of Bruner, "here's the execute order from Fifth Fleet to conduct these strikes on Mosul. Nothing's changed from the rough draft their staff shared with us last night. Still no Tomahawk strikes laid on, and no Air Force strikers."

Bruner had been through this with his CAG already; but he knew if Michaels was raising it again he owed him a professional response. "Look fellas, I know we get paid to give our seniors the best possible professional advice. And when we first got the alert order from Fifth Fleet, we recommended a comprehensive strike package with plenty of Tomahawks launched from our Aegis ships, as well as Air Force strikers flying out of Qatar."

"That would have been the best plan to take out the target with minimum risk to our pilots," Michaels replied.

"You're right, but this decision was made way above our pay grade. Step back and think about it—while we can call it 'politics,' it might do us some good to walk in our seniors' shoes."

Bruner had served tours in the Navy's office of legislative affairs, first as a commander and again as a captain. Rumor had it he was the odds-on favorite to return to Washington when his tour as the *Roosevelt* strike group commander ended in a few months and take the top job at OLA as chief of legislative affairs. But while Wilson and Michaels knew Bruner understood the political landscape, they respected the fact that he had made his bones as a fleet aviator and continued to set the example for *Theodore Roosevelt*'s pilots. The admiral flew several times a week with the air wing's eight squadrons. They trusted his operational instincts and recognized he had the big picture they sometimes didn't see.

"Remember how the president's predecessor was criticized for using only Tomahawk missiles in various crises? And you know how drone strikes backfired on us in the past," the admiral continued.

Wilson, whose ship would be the only combat asset employed under the current plan, chimed in. "We remember that, Admiral, but that doesn't make it any easier to understand why we're holding back now."

"Yeah, and remember, the president served in the Surface Navy after he graduated from Naval ROTC. He knows that Tomahawk is accurate—but often not accurate enough—especially when striking an urban area. I can see why he doesn't want to go that route."

For a moment, the three men were silent. They shared the same frustration regarding the lack of Air Force participation. Saudi Arabia and the rest of the Arab Gulf states—Kuwait, Qatar, Oman, and the rest—looked at ISIL as their strongest defense against having a Persian-dominated Gulf. In spite of major arm-twisting, at the end of the day none of those countries would host U.S. Air Force strike planes on their territory. Iran was the threat they feared most, not ISIL.

"There's one other thing," Bruner continued as he looked around to ensure the three of them were alone on the flag bridge, "and this information is at the highest level of classification, so it doesn't go beyond the three of us. There's anecdotal—but compelling— evidence that Saudi Arabia and maybe some of the other Arab Gulf states are assisting ISIL. It adds up since ISIL is the proverbial 'enemy of their enemy,' Iran. If we base U.S. Air Force strikers in any Arab country and then launch a strike from their territory, it's virtually certain they'll tip ISIL off. If they do that, ISIL will just move again as they've done many times before, and we fail in our mission. Keeping this an all-Navy show is our best chance for success."

Bruner had a way of putting things that didn't make Wilson and Michaels feel like they were being scolded. Rather, both senior captains understood they were being let in on inside information the admiral didn't have to share—but elected to reveal as a professional courtesy to them.

Michaels continued, holding the iPad in front of Bruner. "Yes sir. We've got it. Here's the lineup for our first launch . . . "

The CAG went through the intricate particulars of how they were going to employ a large portion of their sixty-plus aircraft to deliver the planned strikes. These were details Bruner was well familiar with, but this was a case where there was no such thing as too much planning. Michaels explained how they would get the SAR helo up first, then two Rhino—or F/A-18E/F Super Hornet—tankers to give the strike package a drink before they went "feet dry." Five minutes after those aircraft were airborne the attack package launch would begin. The E-2D Hawkeye would launch first, followed by the attack aircraft—the Super Hornets and F/A-18C Hornets—and finally the EA-18G Growler electronic jamming aircraft.

The admiral nodded as CAG continued to lay out the plan. This was to be a precision strike, so it would be a small strike package, but the air wing would have armed backups on alert. Michaels explained—and Bruner agreed—that this would give them redundancy while still making it a surgical strike.

Their strike group had been given barely enough time to plan these attacks as they steamed north at thirty knots to get into position in the northern Gulf, approximately fifty miles southeast of Kuwait City. There was reasonable—if not generous—sea room for Wilson to steam *Theodore Roosevelt* into the wind and get all the aircraft off the deck in one run.

Bruner paused before speaking. "I think we've got a good plan. It's a little over twelve hundred miles from here to Mosul and back," he said. "Has the Air Force checked in with us yet to let us know their tankers are heading to station?"

"They reported on station about twenty minutes ago," Michaels replied. "There are two KC-135s orbiting just east of Baghdad to service the ingressing and egressing strikers. Our Rhino tankers will give our planes a drink before they go feet dry, so even if one of the Air Force tankers goes down, we'll be fine. We'll put our own gas in the air again once the strikers come off target and run a Rhino bucket brigade—"

"Admiral?" Michaels asked as Bruner arched his eyebrows.

"Not counting on the Air Force to pull their weight, CAG?" Bruner asked, suppressing a smile.

"Oh, I trust them okay, Admiral. It's just that we look at all of Iraq as Indian country. If the gas doesn't show up for any reason, that means our guys have to land in Iraq. Then it becomes a question of whether we can get them before ISIL does."

"Hard to argue with that logic. No quibbles from me

if you have as many Rhino tankers as you feel you need meet the strikers on the back side."

"Launch time skipper?" Bruner asked, turning to *TR*'s captain.

"The OPORDER says 0530, Admiral."

"Well in that case, you'd better get your Air Boss busy."

As *Theodore Roosevelt*'s captain and the CAG left the flag bridge, Bruner had a moment to reflect. His two-plus decades as a career naval aviator had prepared him for a moment like this, unleashing the power of a U.S. Navy carrier strike group on his nation's enemy. Bruner was one of those people who had known he wanted to fly since he'd been a toddler. Once he had earned his Navy wings in Pensacola, he'd tried to stay in the cockpit as much as possible—and had largely succeeded. Now he was sending his pilots into harm's way.

His CAG and *Theodore Roosevelt*'s skipper had valid points regarding putting this mission solely on the backs of *Theodore Roosevelt*'s aviators. But Bruner had been there and done that and had flown with probably half the pilots in his air wing. He knew they were up to the challenge. He was broken out of his reverie by the familiar voice of *Theodore Roosevelt*'s Air Boss as the 5MC—the flight deck announcing system—came alive:

> Now on the flight deck . . . all hands ensure
> you're in the proper flight deck uniform. Let's

get cranials on and buckled, sleeves rolled
down. Excess personnel clear the flight deck.
Aircraft launch in thirty minutes. Let's look
sharp. Now clear the flight deck.

Satisfied he had done all he could to get his carrier,
his air wing with its sixty-plus aircraft, and the five
thousand men and women aboard the Big Stick—her
crew's name for *Theodore Roosevelt*—ready for these
strikes, Bruner lifted himself out of his flag-bridge
chair and headed for *TR*'s O-3 level. He wanted to
make one last pass through his air wing's ready rooms
and talk with his pilots.

In the two days since he'd decapitated President Midkiff's special presidential envoy, Mabad al-Dosari had
focused on two things. First, he had one of his lieutenants make several calls to the Saudi General Intelligence Directorate, trying to tease out anything they
might have learned about possible American retaliation. Thus far, they had nothing to tell him. Second,
he worked to ensure ISIS's social media campaign got
maximum leverage from the fact that the United States
couldn't even protect the individual they had made the
point man in taking the fight to the Islamic State.

But what kept him up at night was the fact that his
war against the West was a war of attrition, and he
wasn't winning. At best, he had fought Western, and
now Persian, interests to a draw. More nations were
aligning with the United States to fight ISIS everywhere in the Levant. And now Iran was filtering more

and more "volunteers" into Syria and especially into Iraq to attack his fighters.

In the past, he had hundreds of recruits from the United States, Canada, Europe, and especially the United Kingdom simply get tourist visas to Turkey, Iraq, or Syria and then stay and join the cause. But the Western nations had turned the screws on this process, and now these potential fighters were stuck in their home countries, unable to join the fight on the ground in the Levant. He had told his number two, Shakir al-Hamdani, to find a way to use these men—and a few women—in a different manner. The man owed him an answer soon.

Moments before, *Theodore Roosevelt* had launched its MH-60S helo to take up a SAR station on the ship's starboard side. Captain Wilson had then turned and steadied on "Fox Corpen," the course that headed the 100,000-ton supercarrier directly into the wind. At precisely 0530, the F/A-18F Super Hornet on *TR*'s cat one went to full power, its two General Electric F414 engines sending searing heat into the JBD—the jet blast deflector—that rose behind the jet to keep it from frying everything aft of it on the flight deck. Seconds later, the pilot flipped on his external lights, signaling he was ready to launch. In a flash, the hold-back fitting attached to the nose gear broke and released the shuttle, which then drove the Super Hornet the 325 feet down the track, going from zero to one hundred and fifty-five knots in four seconds, as the jet leapt into the pre-dawn sky.

Seconds later, the Super Hornet on cat three went through the same minuet, roaring down the track and climbing steeply to join up with the lead jet. Soon after that, the JBDs behind cats two and four popped up, the aircraft on those two cats came alive, and another two Super Hornets clawed their way into the air.

No matter how many times he did this—as an aviator in a cockpit or as an onlooker—Bruner still marveled at the precise choreography that took place on an aircraft carrier's flight deck. Ghostly figures stalked the four-and-a-half acre deck, their shapes barely discernible in the glow of the light wands they carried to direct aircraft. Once the Air Boss issued his original order to the flight deck crew, there were no more shouted commands. Instead, the yellow-shirted directors and blue-shirted aircraft handlers went through well-rehearsed procedures that brought aircraft up on deck from *TR*'s cavernous, three-deck-high hangar, loaded them with ordnance, started each bird, taxied them to the appropriate catapult, and then finally thrust them into the air.

More aircraft roared off *TR*'s cats and into the dark sky. Finally, as the last aircraft leapt off the deck and clawed its way skyward, Bruner heard the Air Boss's voice again. He knew he would be respotting the deck and ordering a FOD—or foreign object damage—walk-down to clear the flight deck of any debris that could be ingested into an aircraft's multimillion-dollar engine:

> Now on the flight deck, launch complete. I
> say again, launch complete. Respot the deck.
> All hands get ready for FOD walk-down.
> Now FOD walk-down.

As the last jet—a Growler—disappeared into the pre-dawn sky, Bruner hopped down from his flag-bridge chair and headed for the *Theodore Roosevelt*'s O-3 level and TFCC—his tactical flag coordination center—to track the progress of his strike.

There was a time when what happened aboard navy ships at sea was completely opaque to those ashore, but that was before systems like the Global Command and Control System—GCCS (pronounced "geeks")—and the emerging Joint Information Environment gave commanders anywhere the chance to see exactly what the local on-scene commander saw. Some commanders feared that if higher headquarters could see the same picture they were looking at, they would get unsolicited—and even gratuitous—advice from those senior commanders. But those fears never materialized. In fact, what junior commanders experienced was that when senior commanders could see what they were doing on-scene, their comfort level increased, and they tended to ask fewer questions and also didn't second-guess those closer to the action as often.

The display Bruner saw in TFCC showed the same picture viewed in the Fifth Fleet headquarters in Bahrain, in the CENTCOM command center at MacDill

Air Force Base, and in the National Military Command Center in the Pentagon. In each of these command centers, senior commanders viewed the progress of the strike Bruner had unleashed.

As the last thirsty Super Hornet finished taking a drink from one of the Air Force KC-135s and the strikers formed up to push the final two hundred miles to Mosul, Bruner liked what he saw on the GCCS display. The jets were well beyond *Theodore Roosevelt*'s radar range, but their positions were tracked by the VAW-123 E-2D Hawkeye radar aircraft anchored north of *TR* and just twenty miles east-southeast of Iraq's Bubiyan Island. The Hawkeye's Link 16 piped the picture directly to *Theodore Roosevelt*, as well as to other command centers via the Navy's MUOS—Mobile User Objective System—satellite constellation.

What Bruner saw on the GCCS display was as familiar to him as the position of eleven players on the field was to an offensive or defensive football coordinator. Two mixed divisions, each comprising two Hornets and two Super Hornets, were grouped together and were bore-sighted on Mosul. They were flanked by two sections of EA-18G Growlers and their wingmen providing electronic jamming and offensive EW, short for electronic warfare. Each Growler carried two AGM-88 high-speed, antiradiation missiles. The HARM, as it was known to the Growler crews, had acquitted itself well in conflicts over the past three decades. Designed to home in on electronic transmissions coming from surface-to-air radar systems, the old but reliable HARM was a Mach 2, fire-and-forget weapon that would protect the strikers against any pop-up threat.

When a TFCC watchstander clicked on—or "hooked"—an individual aircraft, that jet's weapons load-out was displayed. For this strike, each Hornet and Super Hornet carried two one-thousand-pound GBU-32 JDAM precision-guided bombs, a FLIR— forward-looking infrared—pod and two wingtip AIM-120 advanced medium-range, air-to-air missiles— AMRAAMs for short—to deal with any jets ISIL might send up to oppose them.

It was just after dawn, and, as was his custom, Mabad al-Dosari and a few of his more senior lieutenants embarked on their walk. They had commandeered a few of the strongest buildings in the Az Zanjili section of the city, hard by the Tigris River, and had moved their close and extended family members into these apartments. From a security perspective, it made sense, but the sheer number of people stuffed into these buildings made their compound in central Mosul cramped and noisy.

With women rising early to cook and children and babies stirring, al-Dosari found this the perfect time to get away from the compound and talk with his closest lieutenants as they walked about. Today, as he had on many previous occasions, al-Dosari's only son asked to walk along with him. The boy was only eleven, but he wanted to follow in his father's footsteps and become a fighter as soon as possible. He thought joining these walks would help him become a fighter sooner. But as he had done every time the child had asked before, al-Dosari had told him no.

Today, they walked toward the Al Shohada Bridge and then turned southeast and walked along the Tigris. Al-Dosari liked walking along the waterfront; it helped clear his mind. Although they had repulsed the Iraqi Army, the Peshmerga, and others who had tried to oust them from the city, it had taken a toll on his forces and damaged or destroyed many caches of equipment his fighters had captured from the Iraqi Army. This morning he would talk with his men about a raid he planned on an Iraqi Army depot northeast of Erbil.

One hundred and fifty miles southeast of where al-Dosari and his men walked, Deputy CAG, Pete "Shooter" Wallace, was leading the fourteen-aircraft strike package that was bore-sighted on the ISIL compound in Mosul. Flying at sixteen thousand feet, Wallace looked at the situational awareness display in his Super Hornet and saw the other jets arrayed around him.

His division of two F/A-18F Super Hornets and two Marine Corps F/A-18C Hornets was in the lead and flying in a wall formation. Thirty seconds behind them was a similarly configured division, also flying in a wall formation. On their flanks were two sections of two EA-18G Growlers, each with a Super Hornet wingman. One section of Growlers was assigned to CAP—combat air patrol—the ingress route, and one was tasked to CAP the egress route.

Wallace hadn't expected to be leading this strike; that was a role typically given to one of the air wing's senior squadron commanding officers. Those more junior officers were better trained and more current with the myriad of sensors and weapons carried by the strike aircraft, but Admiral Bruner was old school and wanted a senior man airborne for this crucial mission.

While he was happy—overjoyed really—to be leading this strike, Wallace wondered about the impact they'd have. It was well known that in the past, ISIL had routinely moved their location in central Mosul just to make themselves immune from targeted airstrikes like this. And it was also generally understood that ISIL periodically threatened to behead Iraqi citizens who tried to leave buildings surrounding their compound. They wanted them there as human shields.

Eight jets, with two GBU-32 JDAM bombs each, seemed like overkill to him—way too much to take out just one guy. But he knew their mission was to decapitate the ISIL leadership, and this was the way his government had decided to do it. He feared there would be civilian casualties, but he also knew why other options to eliminate Mabad al-Dosari had been taken off the table.

While the U.S. military had trained and equipped the Iraqi Army, that army still had military gear Saddam Hussein had purchased from a number of nations over the course of his years as Iraq's dictator. As ISIS ranged freely across wide swaths of Iraq, it captured massive quantities of that equipment. And as United

States and coalition forces continued to try to destroy ISIS from the air, anti-aircraft missiles became some of the terror group's most-prized assets.

The Russian-made SA-15 Gauntlet was one such weapon. Produced in the early 1990s, it wasn't a sophisticated missile, but it had many advantages. It was mobile, completely autonomous, easy to operate, and was a highly reliable system capable of surveillance, command and control, and missile launch and guidance from a single vehicle. It was the perfect weapon for a crew with minimal training to man and operate.

Mabad al-Dosari considered these SA-15s some of his most valuable possessions and had his three remaining Gauntlets deployed around his compound in Mosul. His instructions to his crews were simple and straightforward—don't wait for orders or ask permission—shoot down any aircraft that approached their compound.

Back aboard *Theodore Roosevelt*, Jay Bruner was camped out in TFCC with CAG Michaels. As strike commander, it was Michaels's job not just to plan and order the strikes, but to also determine BDA—battle damage assessment—to ensure that the mission was successful. Michaels had his ops officer by his side and the man had a secure iPad with a chat window open with the Air Force's 13th Intelligence Squadron at Beale Air Force Base north of Sacramento, California. The 13th IS was part of the 548th Intelligence Group and operated the RQ-4B Global Hawk. Soon after the strikers were on their egress route, he'd tell the pilots in their air-conditioned spaces at Beale to fly their unmanned aerial vehicle—UAV for short—over the compound to determine BDA. If the first strike didn't destroy the target, the air wing would have to conduct another attack on the compound.

The Tigris River is the eastern member of the two great rivers that define the ancient land of Mesopotamia, the other being the Euphrates River. The river flows south from the Taurus Mountains of southeastern Turkey, through Syria and Iraq. The Tigris and Euphrates, with their tributaries, form one of the most prominent river systems in Western Asia. And the land they irrigate is some of the most fertile in the world.

None of that mattered to Shooter Wallace at the moment. What *did* matter was that the Tigris presented a perfect navigation aid to guide him and his strikers directly to Mosul's Az Zanjili neighborhood. Wallace was no throttle-jockey—far from it—he had a math degree from Cal Poly, San Luis Obispo. But say what you will about the high-tech wizardry the U.S. military had available: GPS—global positioning system—satellites, inertial navigation computers, high-fidelity data links and the like, following the river that pointed at the ISIS compound like a dagger gave him the kind of assurance he needed to be completely certain he was headed for his target.

Wallace and his flight streaked north at Mach .85—almost six hundred and fifty miles per hour—following the Tigris. They would arm their weapons systems when they were twenty miles from the target. The mission was proceeding as planned.

At the southern end of Mosul's Az Zanjili neighborhood, the Gauntlet vehicle commander, system operator, and vehicle driver were bored senseless. They were assigned to man their Soviet-designed anti-aircraft vehicle for 24-hour watch shifts—one day on and one day off—for weeks at a time. Each one of them cursed their luck. They'd much rather be ranging freely across Iraq and Syria with their fellow fighters, destroying everything in their path.

The vehicle commander, a forty-five-year-old veteran of Saddam's army who had been trained by the Russians to operate the SA-15, was one of the few ISIS fighters who understood this system well. He knew he was doomed to be chained to the Gauntlet until some coalition airstrike destroyed his machine as they had so many others.

Suddenly, the sensor operator cried out, "I have something!"

"What?" the vehicle commander asked.

"Right here, see? I have multiple aircraft coming from the south; they look like they're following the Tigris and are headed straight this way."

"Wait until they get into range, and then prepare to fire on my command! I'll alert the other batteries!" the vehicle commander shouted.

The veteran of many campaigns did some quick mental calculations. The SA-15's H-band Doppler radar could pick up targets at up to twenty-five kilometers and could effectively track them inside twenty kilometers. But the Gauntlet had a range of only twelve thousand meters and could reach up to an altitude of only six thousand meters. Waiting until the aircraft got close—uncomfortably close—was their only option.

Within minutes, the radars on the other two SA-15 batteries were also searching the sky for the approaching aircraft.

Wallace's wingman was the first to pick up the screaming alert from his radar-warning receiver—the RWR. There on his UFCD—the up-front control display—was the unmistakable indication of a targeting radar. "Dealer One-One, Dealer One-Three, I'm spiked, bearing zero-one-five!"

DCAG looked down at the bottom of his instrument panel, right in front of his control stick. There on his MPCD—the multipurpose color display—was the moving map with the threat info just where his wingman had said it would be. Wallace recalled the intel brief they had gotten in *Theodore Roosevelt*'s CVIC—the carrier's intelligence center—less than two hours ago. There had been no mention of an anti-air threat.

"Dealer One-One, Dealer Two-Two," came the call from a Super Hornet in the second division. "I'm spiked, bearing zero-one-zero."

Twenty years of flying and fighting let Wallace make an instantaneous decision. "Dealer Two-One and flight, detach and climb, return to Tango-Golf," he began, using *Theodore Roosevelt*'s daily changing call sign. "Dealer One-Three and One-Four, you do the same," he continued. "Dealer One-Two and I will make this a one-section attack, over."

In the severely abbreviated vocabulary of naval aviation, no further words were needed. The division comprising the second wall of aircraft began a high-G turn and climb, and the two Hornets in Wallace's flight did so as well. As they did, the two Growlers assigned to cover the ingress picked up the same threat on their displays, lit off the AN/ALQ-198 low-band jamming pods, and began to jam along the threat axis.

Shooter Wallace wondered—but only for a moment—if he was being too cautious in telling six of his eight attacking aircraft to break off the engagement while he pressed the attack with only two jets. He knew his mission was important—but so was the safety of his junior pilots. And he was confident the sophisticated systems on his aircraft and that of his wingman were more than up to the task of taking out a single terrorist.

"We're being jammed!" the Gauntlet sensor operator shouted.

"Where?" the vehicle commander asked.

"From the south. Just where we picked up the approaching aircraft."

Like Shooter Wallace, the vehicle commander was a veteran with years of training. He reacted instantly. "Fire along the bearing line."

"Dealer One-One, Dealer One-Two, I've got a target acquisition radar on the nose!"

"Looking," Wallace replied, as he searched for the unmistakable sign of smoke from an ascending missile.

He didn't have to look for long. Wallace jinked hard to the right in an effort to break lock and his wingman followed. Training kicked in as the section began to execute a bow-tie pattern, long called a "SAM weave," designed to keep an anti-air missile from getting a good lock, or if it did manage to lock on, to force it to deplete its energy before it could rise high enough in its trajectory to hit them. Their MPCDs showed them descending as they loaded up their jets to four Gs.

"I see smoke, one o'clock!" Wallace's wingman shouted. Time stood still as they watched the SA-15 climb toward them.

Wallace jinked left and his wingman followed, pulling even more Gs as they tried to defeat the deadly missile.

As they continued their SAM weave, jinking hard while craning their necks to keep an eye on the threat, Wallace watched the faint trace of smoke as the missile reached the top of its parabolic arc, hesitated for a split second, and then, its energy depleted, began to fall back to earth. No words needed to be exchanged as they broke off from their SAM weave, climbed, and once again headed north along the Tigris.

"Look!" one of Mabad al-Dosari's men shouted as he pointed at the smoke trail of the SA-15 Gauntlet as it streaked up into the sky.

The ISIS leader followed the smoke and searched the sky for threats. He saw none.

"It looks like one of our batteries fired at something," one of his lieutenants said. "Or maybe they just got spooked and shot at ghosts."

"I don't know," al-Dosari replied. "But we can't wait to find out. We need to return to the compound."

With that, the small group of men began running toward Mosul's Az Zanjili neighborhood.

"Reload, reload!" the vehicle commander shouted.

The other two men scrambled to comply, but they all knew that in the time it would take to load another SA-15 on the launcher, the aircraft they were aiming at would be long gone. It was up to the other two Gauntlet batteries now.

As al-Dosari and his men ran toward their compound, they instinctively scanned the sky to the south—the direction that first one, and then another, smoke trail headed. They knew that previous air attacks against them had all come from the south and it was the most likely route enemy aircraft would take.

"Look!" one of his men shouted as he pointed to two small shapes in the sky high above the Tigris River. "They look like military aircraft."

Al-Dosari and his men broke out into a dead run. There was little doubt in their minds about what was happening.

As they scanned their MPCDs for more missiles and steadied out on their attack course again, Wallace and his wingman armed their weapons systems and saw the word "JDAM" displayed on their HUDs—the Super Hornet's heads-up display. On their flank, the two Growlers continued to jam. The Super Hornet pilots monitored the moving maps on their MPCDs as the target came into range.

As they screamed north toward their target, the two pilots simultaneously launched their four one-thousand-pound GBU-32 JDAMs. They felt the weight of the bombs leave their jets with a jump, and then the section jinked right and began a tight turn.

The GBU-32 JDAM, or joint direct attack munition, is one of the most sophisticated air-to-ground weapons in the U.S. military inventory. Simply put, the JDAM is a guidance kit that converts "dumb bombs" into all-weather "smart munitions." JDAM-equipped bombs are guided by an integrated inertial guidance system coupled to a GPS receiver, giving them a range of up to fifteen nautical miles. When installed on a bomb, the JDAM kit is given a guided bomb unit—GBU for short—nomenclature.

Wallace understood all the technical attributes of the GBU-32 JDAM and knew how to use it operationally. But what mattered to him most was the fact that he could put the JDAM precisely where he wanted it—when he wanted it there. As his flight jinked right, he checked the time-of-flight indicator in his cockpit to see how long it would take the JDAMs to fall from sixteen thousand feet and hit their targets. As the section continued to turn to the south, both pilots looked over their shoulders and saw the flash from the explosions. Then they looked at their FLIR displays and saw those screens had "gained out" as the white-hot heat of the explosions overwhelmed the FLIR with energy.

The ISIS leader and his men were about five hundred yards from the eastern edge of the Az Zanjili neighborhood when the JDAMs hit. They saw the first flash, and then, seconds later, heard the deafening booms as the four bombs hit their compound. Instinctively, they dropped to the ground until the shock wave passed, then got up and looked at their leader.

"Faster, faster!" al-Dosari shouted as the group of men broke into a sprint and headed directly for their compound.

The report from Wallace to CAG Michaels was like most conversations between naval aviators—brief and to the point. "Tango-Golf, Dealer One-One, four away. Enemy anti-air observed in the vicinity of target. Tron 11 and 21 flights employed HARM, assess ADA to be neutralized," Wallace said, using the general terms for the Growlers and for air-defense artillery respectively. "Two strikers egressing along planned route."

Michaels relayed the message to Bruner and the admiral allowed himself a small smile. They had completed their mission, and just as importantly, all his aircraft were returning.

"I'll have Beale bring in the Global Hawk for BDA, Admiral," Michaels said as his ops officer typed instructions into a chat window he had opened with the Air Force controllers over nine thousand miles away. The controllers, in turn, steered their bird, which had been doing lazy circles at 58,000 feet northeast of Mosul, directly to the coordinates of the target.

As al-Dosari and his men approached the rubble of what was once their compound, they saw smoke everywhere and small fires here and there around the skeleton of the large building they'd left a short while ago.

A man in tattered clothes with a soot-stained face was crawling out of the rubble. They heard groans and cries for help coming from the pile.

"No!" al-Dosari cried as he made straight for the still-smoldering pile. One of his lieutenants tried to grab his arm and restrain him, but he yanked it away.

Soon, all the men were pushing through the rubble and making their way into what remained of their building. Al-Dosari was out ahead of the group, and he was singularly focused on getting into one section of the smoking ruins.

Several minutes later, while his men made their way into various areas of what was once their compound, Mabad al-Dosari emerged.

Once on top of the target, the Global Hawk began streaming video back to Beale via a secure satellite connection. Air Force photo-imagery analysts who had been brought in especially for this mission poured over the BDA video. There was no need for much analysis. The targeted buildings were little more than skeletons and piles of rubble.

Had the Global Hawk cameras had a bit more fidelity, they would have seen a man crawling out of the rubble holding the limp, broken body of a young boy. And if they had had facial recognition capabilities, they would have seen that the man was Mabad al-Dosari. And if they had known all they wanted to know about his family, they would have seen that the boy was al-Dosari's only son.

CHAPTER FOUR

March 8, 0700 Eastern Standard Time

In the wake of the strike against the ISIL compound in Mosul, American intelligence agencies anticipated a response from the Islamic State on social media. What they didn't know was when and how it would come. While their central compound was destroyed, ISIL could launch its social media campaign from anywhere. One fighter with a cell phone and a Twitter account was all that was needed.

The words "Central Intelligence Agency Open-Source Center" (commonly called the CIA OSC) sound counterintuitive. For the CIA, long known as the nation's most secretive intelligence agency, and the one that dealt with information at the highest levels of classification, to mine open—meaning unclassified—sources of information seemed to be a waste of time and resources.

Since the early 1990s, several congressional intelligence committees, as well as independent groups such as the 9/11 Commission, had recommended that the intelligence community—the IC—create an open-source intelligence entity. These external pressures were one thing, but most IC insiders attributed the ultimate creation of the CIA OSC to one factor. In spite of access to the most sophisticated technology and human intelligence analysis, the IC was completely surprised by the May 1998 Indian nuclear tests. Had the IC been more focused on open sources instead of the highly classified material they typically dealt with, they might not have missed the fact that one of the pledges of the Hindu nationalist Bharatiya Janata Party in its 1998 election campaign was to add nuclear weapons to India's arsenal.

The charter of the CIA OSC was to collect information available from: "The Internet, databases, press, radio, television, video, geospatial data, photos and commercial imagery." In addition to collecting openly available information, its mission was to train analysts to make better use of this material. Therefore, it was no surprise that after the attack on ISIL's Mosul compound, the CIA OSC was on the forefront of the effort, not just to ingest whatever the Islamic State pumped out into social media, but to mine it and analyze whatever it could reveal on two fronts: how successful the U.S. strike had been and what, if anything, ISIL intended to do next.

Melinda Patterson—MP to her friends and

coworkers—was one of the youngest GS-15 analysts at the CIA OSC and was assigned to lead the team pulled together to answer these two questions. MP took the assignment on one condition: No one on her team could be older than thirty-five. She had her team keyed in on all the normal social media feeds, as well as some that were popular primarily in the Mideast. MP knew her team wouldn't disappoint her or her bosses at the Open Source Center or higher up in the IC.

While the sixteen agencies comprising the U.S. intelligence community leaned forward to analyze whatever ISIL threw into the social media mix, Mabad al-Dosari and his key lieutenants were finishing their message. Not only had the U.S. strike failed to take out al-Dosari or any of his top lieutenants, but by killing al-Dosari's only son, as well as many family members of his closest comrades, they had driven ISIL to call for a new and more comprehensive global jihad against the United States and other Western interests. What they were about to pump out into social media would be the leading edge of that call.

ISIS's use of social media was sophisticated enough that it could be timed to hit Western countries—and in this case, specifically the United States—when its citizens were first awake and getting their initial news for the day. It was no surprise to MP and her team at

the OSC—or to any of the other analysts elsewhere in
the IC—when their Twitter feeds came alive shortly
after 0700 Eastern Standard Time.

"MP, over here, look what just popped up on
Twitter!" one of her analysts yelled.

She took the tablet he handed her.

*You think you have taken the fight to us but once
again U are so wrong. Ha! U know where to look and
see what will happen to U now, don't U?*

"What do you make of it?" MP asked.

"They use Twitter more than any other social
media, so I think this is the first alert that they'll be
hitting us with a more comprehensive message."

"Looks like they used all one hundred forty characters by my count."

"You're right, but I think the 'U's are more than just
abbreviations for a personal pronoun—"

She stopped him in midsentence. "YouTube!

"Who's monitoring YouTube?" MP shouted across
the room.

Two of her analysts came on the run, both holding
their tablets. As they huddled around MP, the ISIL
video popped up. A large pile of rubble was in the
foreground, and the video was silent—eerily silent.

"This looks like the ISIL compound in Mosul," one
of her analysts said.

"It is," MP replied. "We've seen it from a number
of angles with the Global Hawk video feed. I've looked
at it more times than I care to remember."

As they continued to stare at the pile of rubble and

fiddle with the volume control on their tablets to see if the sound was set too low for them to hear, one of her analysts noticed a tiny figure at the far end of the rubble. "Look MP, there's a man, right there."

The solitary figure began to walk toward the camera and suddenly the sound came alive:

> Midkiff, are you disappointed to see me? You sent your puny planes to kill me and my fighters and look what you have done. You have not killed me. See, I am very much alive. I know you are angry that your assassins have failed in their mission to destroy me and eliminate the threat to you and to your people.
>
> But look around at what they have done. Look. You have destroyed the homes where our women and children live and killed many of them where they are still buried under this rubble. You accuse us of killing innocents? These are the innocents, and among those you massacred are my own flesh and blood. You and your cowardly pilots are responsible for this!

As his diatribe continued, the all-black-clad figure continued moving forward and one of MP's analysts said, "That looks like al-Dosari; I'm almost certain it's him. I'm sending this over to our facial recognition people for confirmation."

"Good," MP replied as they all continued to listen.

> So, Midkiff, you wonder what will happen?
> The jihad has just begun. Don't try to protect
> your women and your children. They are
> no longer safe anywhere, even in your cursed
> nation. We are coming for them and we are
> coming for you!

As he finished with a flourish, al-Dosari was now just a few feet from the camera. A hand thrust out and handed him the all-too-familiar black flag with white Arabic writing. Al-Dosari waved the flag violently from side to side and began chanting something in Arabic. Then the screen went black.

"Have what he said interpreted and analyzed!" MP shouted, but her team was already rushing out to do just that.

Within minutes of the ISIS video appearing on You-Tube, McCord and Bleich were in Williams's office. The Op-Center director was just finishing his morning meeting with his deputy, Anne Sullivan. Williams beckoned the two men to join them at the small conference table.

"Got something for me? ISIL finally pop its head up on social media?"

"They sure have," McCord replied. "Aaron, prop your tablet up here so the boss and Ms. Sullivan can see it."

Bleich did so and played the YouTube video. As the

video finished playing, the four of them were silent for a few moments. Finally, Williams spoke.

"Aaron, I think I know you well enough that you're already ramping up our intelligence collecting and analysis of everything ISIL is putting out. This is pretty strong stuff—even for them."

Bleich just nodded and looked toward McCord.

"Aaron and his team will stay on top of this," McCord said.

"I know you will," Williams replied.

"Do you want me to get Brian and Rich in here? Are you thinking of alerting either our JSOC team or the folks down at Quantico?" McCord asked.

"I don't think we're ready for that step yet, Roger. Let's let Aaron's folks churn for a while. Once we have a bit more intel, then maybe we'll be ready to move."

Not far from the rubble of his former headquarters, Mabad al-Dosari met with his number two. They had driven out the residents of a six-story building in Mosul's Al Mawsil al Jadidah neighborhood and were now moving their families into the structure.

Al-Dosari used al-Hamdani as his primary conduit to the Saudi's General Intelligence Directorate. He wanted the man to know precisely what he expected him to do. Yes, the Saudis had helped them before, but al-Dosari didn't trust them as far as he could throw them.

Al-Dosari wanted revenge, but he wasn't blind with

rage. He wanted to extract payback on those who did this, but he wanted to succeed in what he did, not expend resources on something that wouldn't work. There had been too many revelations about foiled attempts to kill important Western leaders. He couldn't fail this time.

Nor did he think the Americans would make it easy for him, as they had when they sent their special presidential envoy to areas where his fighters roamed free. No, he wanted to take out his revenge on a high-profile figure who was directly responsible for the strike that killed his son and so many others. All he knew was that death had come from the sky. He told al-Hamdani precisely what he wanted him to find out from the Saudi's General Intelligence Directorate. And now he waited.

Eight time zones from where al-Dosari was giving these instructions, five young Muslim men in Minneapolis, Minnesota, were walking home from evening prayers at the Masjid Omar Islamic Center. They were all second-generation Americans who lived in the same lower-middle class neighborhood. Each of them enjoyed a relatively comfortable life their parents had secured for them through hard work and trying to live the American dream.

Each twenty-something man had a good—if not lucrative—job in one of the twin cities, owned a car or borrowed one from his parents, had a circle of friends, and two even had steady girlfriends. And they all shared one thing in common—they all wanted to leave the United States and join the fight with the Islamic State. But each had been denied a visa by American authorities. They knew they needed help if they were going to wage jihad—they just didn't know where that help would come from.

CHAPTER FIVE

At first, there had been twice-daily meetings, then once a day, then three times a week. Now the director of national intelligence—or the DNI as he was more commonly known—only called these meetings once a week. His staff had just finished subjecting him to death by PowerPoint, detailing how they were continuing to mine ISIL's social media for some sign of a specific threat against the United States. But this week's report was the same as the week before, and the week before that—there was no actionable intelligence on any specific threat.

A similar scene was playing out at most of the sixteen agencies that comprised the IC, as well as in military commands with any stake in the fight against terrorism. Even the best analysts had been forced to eat crow. They had all predicted that Mabad al-Dosari would carry out his threats to take the fight to the American homeland and maybe even to the president within days of posting his YouTube video. But nothing had happened, and while ISIL continued to pump venom into social media, no threat had materialized in the three months since al-Dosari had climbed atop that pile of rubble in Mosul.

Even at Op-Center, in spite of the enormous brain power and all the technical wizardry Bleich and Geek Tank brought to bear on the problem, they knew as little as anyone else. And while Williams was cheered by the fact that no news was good news, every professional instinct he had told him ISIL would strike—and strike hard.

In Minneapolis, the five friends met in the basement of the home one of the men shared with his parents and two younger sisters in the Powderhorn neighborhood, hard by I-35W. His parents ran a local gas station and convenience store near Powderhorn Park and worked seventy hours a week. Unbeknownst to his parents or to the parents of the four other young men, they all were trying to obtain visas to leave the United States and join ISIS.

One of the men suggested engaging a forger he knew to have him fabricate false credentials so they could leave the United States to take a "vacation" in Turkey and then slip across the border into Syria to join the fight. The peer leader of the men, Amer Deghayes, told his friends that the imam had explained—because they lived in Minneapolis and were Muslim—they had likely been identified by the Department of Homeland Security as possible ISIS sympathizers. He said the imam had also told him that they might even be under surveillance by U.S. immigration and other officials determined to staunch the flow of potential ISIS recruits from the United States. Amer told them that, even with forged papers, they would likely be stopped if they tried to leave the country. The imam wanted them to be patient—their time would come.

In Springfield, Virginia, in a scene 180 degrees out from the unhappy one playing out for the five young men in Minneapolis, Rear Admiral Jay Bruner was having breakfast with his wife and two teenage daughters. Bruner, now the Navy's chief of legislative affairs, was enjoying his first shore duty in years after successive sea-duty tours, most recently as a carrier strike group commander.

"Dad, you gonna be able to come to my soccer game tonight?" Amber, their oldest daughter, asked.

"Who you guys playing, honey?"

"West Springfield."

"Bad news for West Springfield, huh?"

"Yeah, right," Amber mumbled.

"Amber's just made the starting team, Jay," his wife, Meagan, added. "And now she's playing midfield, the same position Dale played when we were first stationed in D.C."

The mention of the Bruner's oldest, their only son, Dale, brought a smile to his face. While he loved their two teenage daughters dearly and unconditionally, Dale had always been his favorite. And the son had followed in his father's footsteps in the Navy—to a point.

Growing up, Dale had never been interested in the military. Maybe it was the fact that even though his parents did everything they could to make their frequent change-of-station moves seem normal and routine, they were anything but. Every move meant he and his sisters had to make new friends, find a way to fit in with a new social group, and try to get up to speed in their studies in a new school with a different curriculum. The three Bruner children survived the family's constant moving, and even thrived in a situation that often challenged children in military families.

But toward the end of his college career, Dale became motivated to serve. He wasn't sure what triggered it. Maybe he finally came to the realization that having to cope with being Navy brats actually strengthened him and his sisters. He decided to join the military and also to put marriage on hold. He wasn't sure he had the skills his parents had to raise normal children while moving a family around the country—let alone possibly having to move them to overseas postings in Asia or Europe. However, Dale found a different calling from naval aviation. Growing up in the wake of 9/11, he had decided to join the part of the

Navy he felt was taking the fight right to the enemy—he joined the Navy SEALs.

"Well, sweetie, I promise I'll try to make it," Bruner replied. "You know I'm swamped at work, but I'll be there if I can. What time is it?"

"Eight o'clock. You may actually have to leave work while it's still light out." Amber was pouting now, and her younger sister piled on.

"Dad, my softball game is *Saturday*; you're not going to work again this Saturday, are you?" Katherine asked.

"Girls, your dad is doing the best he can," their mother said.

"It's okay, I get it and I deserve it. I promise I'll try to make it to both games." Bruner added, "And now that Dale's finally on shore duty in San Diego, maybe he can fly back when your teams make the playoffs."

All three women rolled their eyes as the ever-competitive Bruner got up to leave and get into his new BMW to join the many thousands of military people who get into their cars to go work in the Pentagon every day. While chief of legislative affairs was a coveted job among U.S. Navy officers, for Bruner it could never be as satisfying as going to sea. He'd make the best of it, and maybe one more sea-duty tour—serving as a U.S. Navy numbered fleet commander—was somewhere in his future.

Meagan Bruner accepted the peck on the cheek from her husband. She knew he loved her and their three children and would try his best to make it home for their daughters' games. But she knew she shouldn't count on it. She didn't like the fact he was working twelve-hour days any more than their daughters did.

CHAPTER SIX

June 22, 1515 Central Daylight Time

Amer Deghayes was only one year older than the next oldest of the five Minneapolis friends who were stymied in their attempts to join ISIS in Syria and Iraq. But for that reason, as well as the fact that Amer's parents had a large basement where they allowed the men to meet, he had become their peer leader.

Amer had texted his friends earlier that afternoon to tell them he had exciting news to share with them. They knew that while he wasn't a bit more religious than any of the rest of them, the imam at the Masjid Omar Islamic Center had taken a shine to Amer and had agreed to help him—and by extension his friends—in their efforts to achieve the goals they so desperately wanted to attain: leave the United States and fight with the Islamic State in Syria and Iraq.

The men assembled in the Deghayes basement and said prayers, as was their custom whenever they met. Then they listened as Amer began to share his news.

"You know that Imam Maher has always had our best interests at heart—"

"How do you figure?" one of his friends interrupted.

"Hear me out," Amer replied.

He couldn't help himself as he paused for effect. "Imam Maher told me today that a benefactor has provided a generous amount of money and that we'll receive scholarships to American University in Washington, D.C., soon." The room fell silent; he now had their attention. None of their parents could afford to send them to college, so these scholarships were a start.

"But that does nothing to get us visas and help us travel to the Mideast to wage jihad," another of the friends groused.

"The imam knows that, but he says this is just the first step in the process," Amer replied.

Amer didn't disagree with his friend; he wasn't certain what the imam was offering was going to get them to their ultimate goal. But it was better than sitting around in Minneapolis and doing nothing. He didn't like having to act like a salesman to get them to accept what was clearly a generous offer—a once-in-a-lifetime opportunity.

He patiently explained to his friends that the imam had told him that American University had several study abroad programs in the Mideast. If they signed up for one of those once they got to the university, they could travel out of the United States without the kind of scrutiny they would get if they applied for tourist visas. Then he explained that if they applied to American right away and mentioned this specific scholarship, they could enroll for the summer semester. Finally, he could see his friends coming around to his way of thinking; maybe he was a better salesman than he thought he was. He saved the best news for last.

"There's more. Come over here and look in the alley."

The four friends followed Amer up the few steps to the alley behind the Deghayes home. There was a late-model Honda van sitting there.

"What's that?" one of the men asked.

"That's our van, courtesy of our benefactor. That will be our transportation to Washington, D.C. The imam has a friend there who manages rental units for students. He'll find us a place to live."

The men all looked at Amer, and each allowed himself a small smile. They were finally beginning their journey.

Just over a thousand miles as the crow flies, east-southeast of where Amer was sharing this exciting news with his friends, Rear Admiral Jay Bruner was on familiar turf on Capitol Hill. The chief of legislative affairs for the Navy didn't typically testify before congressional committees—his job was to facilitate more senior officers doing that, as well as to prep them for their testimony. Beyond that, working the back-rooms and bargaining with these senators and representatives to defend the Navy's budget—especially its procurement budget for ships and aircraft—was also part of his role as chief of legislative affairs, and Bruner was good at it. And because of his prior tours with OLA, the admiral was a well-known quantity with congressmen and senators—and especially with their personal and professional staff members. Because of his reputation, he was on call to testify at the drop of a hat.

The hat had just dropped. Senator Sonny Enfield was the senior senator from the Commonwealth of Virginia and the ranking member of the powerful Senate Armed Services Committee Subcommittee on Seapower. Part of the Navy's budget request this year was for money to procure another of its Ford-class supercarriers, carriers built—not coincidently—in the massive Huntington Ingalls shipyard in Newport News, Virginia. Tens of thousands of jobs—and at least that many votes—revolved around keeping the production of those carriers going strong. Enfield knew he would keep returning to the world's most exclusive club only as long as the grateful voters of the Commonwealth knew that he was protecting those jobs.

Enfield's committee had heard from "all the usual suspects" as he so inelegantly called them—the secretary of defense, the secretary of the Navy, the chief of naval operations, the Naval Sea Systems Command program manager for aircraft carriers—and a host of others. They had all fed him the same sop—convincing sop—that he, his committee, and especially the voters from the Commonwealth of Virginia watching the hearings on C-SPAN, wanted to hear. They all spewed the party line: If the dedicated workers at Huntington Ingalls shipyard didn't keep churning out Ford-class aircraft carriers as fast as they could, the United States would be defenseless against a host of foes around the globe.

But Enfield saved the best for last. He wanted his committee and the voters to hear from a man who had actually *used* a nuclear-powered aircraft carrier to carry out the work of the republic in waging war against the enemies of the United States. And he wanted them to hear from someone he knew he could count on to say what he wanted him to say. While familiarity bred contempt for some, for Enfield, it bred assurance that the man sitting at the table in front of him would say just the right words.

The statesmanlike Enfield had let his colleagues on the Seapower Subcommittee question Bruner first, and now that it was early evening and C-SPAN had its maximum audience, Enfield began questioning him. "Admiral, thank you for taking time from your demanding duties as chief of legislative affairs to testify before the committee."

"It's always a pleasure, Mr. Chairman. The Navy appreciates all you and your fellow senators do to ensure our Navy continues to be a global force for good."

Enfield smiled. Bruner was on-script. "Indeed, Admiral, and that's precisely why we—and you—are here this evening. And you also know we in the Congress have been, I'm sorry to say, less than diligent in moving forward on the president's defense budget request." Then, contorting his face in a gesture of resignation, he continued, "And that's precisely why we'll not recess until we vote on this bill."

"Yes, Senator, I understand," Bruner replied.

"Now, Admiral, I want to take you back to earlier this year when the terrorist Mabad al-Dosari, the leader of the scourge we call ISIL, brutally murdered the special presidential envoy, General Underwood. The general was a native of our great Commonwealth of Virginia," Enfield added with a flourish, looking directly at the C-SPAN camera.

"Yes, Mr. Chairman, that was a tragic event indeed."

"It certainly was. And I want to take you back to two days ago when the secretary of defense testified that when our commander in chief sought to extract retribution and go after the ISIL leader, he said, on the record, and I'm quoting now, 'Our carrier strike group operating in the Arabian Gulf provided the fastest and most lethal way to go after al-Dosari.'"

"Yes, Mr. Chairman, I'm familiar with the secretary's testimony."

"Just so, Admiral. But the secretary wasn't there on scene; he was thousands of miles away in his Pentagon office. So for the benefit of this committee, and for the American taxpayers who fund these supercarriers that are on station day in and day out to provide the 'fastest and most lethal way' to deal with our enemies, we want to hear from you. You were the man who was on scene. Please tell us, from the moment you received the execute order originated by our commander in chief, just how you carried out these strikes."

Enfield looked directly into the C-SPAN camera as he concluded his question, but then the camera shifted immediately to Bruner.

Bruner knew it mattered not one whit to Enfield that the strikes he directed didn't actually take out the ISIL leader. This was theater, pure and simple. Speaking with no notes, he began a long and detailed recounting of the events of March 7 as the C-SPAN audience drank it all in.

CHAPTER SEVEN

Even in early July in southern California, the morning marine layer chilled the air with a heavy mist. For the thirty-six Navy SEAL candidates of Class 318 who had spent the last twenty minutes in the surf, it seemed even colder. Class 318 had begun with 175 men—men carefully screened for Basic Underwater Demolition/ SEAL training, or BUD/S. Thirty-eight from that class had made it through "hell week," but two were too battered to continue. Past experience said that not all of the thirty-six survivors would make it through the six-month BUD/S ordeal or the seven months of SEAL Qualification Training.

"You've been here two years, Chief. How does this class stack up to the others you've worked?" Lieutenant Dale Bruner asked.

Chief Petty Officer Josh Anderson paused before replying. Bruner was his boss, and would be until

Anderson's three-year tour at BUD/S was up next June. The lieutenant was new to the Naval Special Warfare Command training component and was assigned as the Phase One training officer. "Well, sir, I think they're a lot better prepared than when you and me went through BUD/S, but some of them still come for the wrong reasons. I think that fella over there," he said, pointing to an officer trainee struggling to do one more pushup, "he's gonna ring the bell before the day's over. The rest, who knows? Most of 'em should be good to go. They're tough enough to get through the next few months. We'll see if they're smart enough."

As if on cue, the struggling trainee stood up and walked over to a brass ship's bell lashed to a stanchion outside the BUD/S training office. He made no move, but just stood there staring at the bell.

"You had enough of this, Mister Cavanaugh?" Anderson asked in a neutral tone. There was no response. "Look, sir, it's like this," he continued. "You either want to do this or you don't. Either ring the damn bell or get your sorry ass back out on the grinder and start pushing them out."

BUD/S candidate Cavanaugh looked at Anderson, then Bruner, and then Anderson again. There was no sympathy or encouragement in the face of either. He shrugged, and then grabbed the braided lanyard tied to the bell's clapper.

CLANG! CLANG! CLANG! And so ended the attempt of yet another physically—but maybe not mentally—capable young man to become a Navy

SEAL. Head down, he turned and walked off the grinder.

Ringing the bell was the way a SEAL trainee let Anderson and the others know he'd had enough of the torture that was Navy SEAL training. That was why the shiny brass bell sat in a prominent place on the grinder, within easy reach of any recruit who wanted to quit. This would probably not be the last trainee from this class to ring out. Bruner and Anderson watched dispassionately as Ensign Cavanaugh departed. Then Bruner turned to his chief.

"You may be right, Chief, but the operational teams need these men. I know your reputation and that you won't coddle these guys, but our job now is to help 'em succeed."

"Copy that, sir," Anderson replied. He knew Bruner had done his homework even before coming here and checked out the reputations of all the BUD/S instructors who were part of his training cadre. In the small, close-knit SEAL community, it wasn't that difficult to learn about another man's reputation. Nor was it difficult for Anderson and the other BUD/S instructors to learn about their new phase officer. All it took was a few phone calls to chief petty officers in the operational teams.

All the officers coming to the SEAL training command were combat veterans, but few had more trigger time than Bruner. He had done several tours in Afghanistan with SEAL Team Three and had fought through some desperate situations. He was a gunfighter, and he led from the front. But what Anderson and the others found most interesting about their new lieutenant was the independent streak he'd demonstrated in several ops. While other officers might have paused to check with the next level of command to help weigh options, once Bruner had decided how to pursue a mission and had talked it over with his squad, he was good to go. And the fact that he had pulled off some missions his seniors might well have vetoed—and not lost any of his men in the process—impressed Anderson and the other senior enlisted instructors in the training cadre.

Growing up as a Navy brat, Bruner had moved from city to city as his naval aviator father advanced through his career. Even during grade school, whenever his dad left for a deployment, he felt it was his responsibility to look after his mother and his two younger sisters. Nothing was ever said, and his mother was a strong, independent woman who didn't need "looking after"—two decades working as an ER nurse had steeled her to deal with just about anything. But the unspoken words between father and son somehow conveyed a sense of responsibility in the younger Bruner. It was one of his earliest memories.

Bruner played a myriad of sports growing up. Many of his friends gravitated to football, and he played running back in Pop Warner leagues. But football simply didn't seem like a team game to him. It bothered him that he got the attention while those who blocked for him received little or none. He eventually found soccer more to his liking and played throughout high school—on three different teams due to his family's frequent moves. He was good, but he never became a regular starter. But on occasion, when an opposing midfielder got a bit too physical with one of their team's smaller players, Dale was sent in to help the opposing player adjust his attitude.

He wasn't a scholarship player at Georgia Tech, but made the team as a walk-on. There, as in high school, he didn't start, but his coaches noticed that he trained and practiced like he would be starting every game. Years of tough practice sessions conditioned him and also refined his sense of team play. He could run and move before he got to SEAL training, and he loved a physical challenge.

There are some SEALs who get through training with few problems, but don't do all that well when they get into combat. Bruner wasn't one of them. He led from the front, but he allowed his senior SEAL petty officers to run his platoon, working closely with them in the planning and execution of SEAL operations. And when his platoon or one of his squads made a good hit, he pushed the recognition down the line to his enlisted SEALs. Yet his combat time hadn't gone unrecognized. When he donned a dress uniform, there was a Silver Star, two Bronze Stars, and two Purple Hearts.

"Here you go, sir," Anderson said as he handed his lieutenant a sheet of paper. Bruner wanted to see what the men they were training would have to cope with when they finished this phase, and Anderson got him just what he needed. "These are some stats on the class that just graduated from SEAL Qualification Training."

Bruner took the sheet and scanned it quickly.

SEAL Class 314 Statistics

Class 314 began with 166 Trainees–men who had completed 8 weeks of conditioning at the Great Lakes Training Center, Illinois, and 3 weeks of precourse conditioning in Coronado prior to beginning SEAL training.

44 men completed Hell Week—5 days, 4 hours sleep.

39 men graduated from the 6-month basic course.

39 men graduated from the 6-month SEAL Qualification Course. (4 men "rolled" into Class 315 from previous classes due to injuries.)

–Each trainee ran approximately 2,000 miles through timed runs, conditioning runs, and required daily running between training venues.

–Each trainee swam in excess of 150 miles.

–Each trainee ran the obstacle course 41 times.

–Each trainee patrolled with a combat load for 150 miles.

–Each trainee conducted 42 dives, spending a total time of 62 hours (2.5 days) underwater.

–Each trainee expended 26,000+ rounds of small-arms ammunition.

–The class detonated over 13,000 pounds of high explosives.

–Each graduate of this 12-month course completed the equivalent of swimming from Cuba to the tip of Florida, then running to New York.

When Bruner finished scanning the sheet, he looked at Anderson and asked, "What's with this Cuba to Florida swim and the run to New York, Chief?"

Anderson laughed. "The public affairs lady put that in. She thought it added a little impact to what we do here."

"Impact, yeah right," Bruner replied, "but the question is, can they fight?"

"That's the big question, El-Tee. If you can figure that out while we're training 'em, all our lives will get a lot easier."

"Roger that, Chief. Until then, it's hard days, little sleep, and cold water."

Bruner watched from the sidelines as Anderson and his fellow trainers rousted their wet and sandy charges and prepared to march them off to breakfast. As they did, Bruner stepped inside the training building.

"Hey, Bruner." It was Captain Pete Cummings, his commanding officer.

"What's up, Skipper?"

"I keep seeing your dad on C-SPAN with these congressional hearings, and I keep noticing those shiny aviator wings. He still ragging on you about becoming a SEAL?"

"Not any more than your old man is still grinding you because you didn't decide to drive boats."

"Yeah, well, I guess we're both misfits."

Bruner just shook his head. You could say all you wanted to about "one fight, one team" within the Navy, let alone the entire military. But there were still tribes. For Cummings and Bruner, they knew they belonged to the best one.

"Oh, one more thing. Check your e-mail. Bonnie sent out an e-vite to the wardroom. We're having a hail and farewell at our house next Saturday night. And fair warning, there's a single gal-pal of hers she's invited. Consider yourself warned."

"Thanks for the heads-up, Skipper. I guess all of us single guys are targets of opportunity."

Three time zones to the east, Amer and his friends would have welcomed the Coronado marine layer. There was no air conditioning in their third-floor walk-up apartment near the intersection of Nebraska Avenue NW and Wisconsin Avenue NW, just south of Wilson High School. The July temperature in the Washington, D.C., metro area was typically in the nineties in July, with the humidity not far behind. But that was not the worst of it for Amer.

He had all but talked his friends into taking this "first step to wage jihad," based on the imam's promises. And Imam Maher had kept those promises—to a point. The van he provided got them to Washington all right, but it was a gas hog and the thousand-mile trip had been an expensive one. And yes, the realtor the imam had connected them with had found them a place to live, but it was a dump. And while the imam told them the realtor friend would also find them jobs, what he didn't tell them was the jobs were the most menial kind, where they had to constantly negotiate with less-than-understanding bosses to balance their jobs and their classes.

He had also neglected to tell them that as "special scholarship students," they were at the end of the queue when it came time to register for classes. The table scraps of courses they were able to register for were hopelessly spread across the week, so their ability to balance work and studies and try to have any time for a social life was a constant challenge.

But the biggest rub was the jobs two of the men had been given. Those two had been told to work for a company that provided packing services to major shipping companies such as DHL, UPS, FedEx, and others. But strangely—even bizarrely it seemed to Amer and his friends—these two men had been assigned to work in a warehouse near the BWI airport. That meant a daily commute of forty miles each way, which could take up to two hours twice a day in the Washington metro area's notoriously gridlocked traffic. And, worse for the other three of them, that meant they had no transportation while their friends took the van to work every day. Life back in Minneapolis began to look better to all of them, even as Amer tried to put a good face on things.

"Hey, Aaron!"

Bleich looked up and saw Maggie Scott standing in his doorway. Even in a group of self-named misfits who didn't look like they had grown-up jobs—let alone looked like they worked for the president's most trusted agency—Maggie stood out. Her flaming red hair—and not a shade of red you'd find in even the biggest Crayola crayon box—sat atop a broad, Goth-clad frame. Scott dominated the doorway. "Whatcha got, Maggie?"

"You know how we've been expanding our search

on the domestic front in the months since al-Dosari threatened the president?"

"Yes, and I appreciate you leading the effort," Bleich replied. Though they never uttered the word "profiling," that was precisely what he had Scott and her small team doing. He knew Maggie had her team crunching mountains of big data and using their anticipatory intelligence to watch for anomalies among young Muslim men who had tried to get visas to Syria or Iraq. But there were hundreds of them and narrowing the field was like pushing a big rock up a steep hill. Maggie explained how they were focusing their search.

"We've targeted a few key cities; Minneapolis is one of them—"

"Top of the list, I bet."

"Yep, and here's the thing. A few weeks ago, five guys on our list up and moved to Washington, D.C.—"

"And they tried to leave the country from there?" Bleich asked.

"No, that's the odd part. They're all matriculated at American University in AU's Middle East studies program, and they all live together near the school. I think we ought to start hacking into their e-mails and other comms, that is, if it's okay with you."

A nod and a smile from Bleich was all that Scott needed.

It was late afternoon when Amer emerged from the Tenleytown station on the Metro's Red Line with a broad smile on his face. He had a spring in his step as he made a beeline for his apartment. He had texted his four friends that it was important—no, urgent—that they meet him at the apartment immediately. They were to make any excuse necessary to leave their jobs or their classes early.

What Amer didn't tell them—he wanted to do that in person—was that the secretive meeting he had been summoned to with no notice had resulted in the best possible outcome. They were finally going to begin their jihad. They would all meet in their contact's home in nearby Bethesda that evening and begin their training. He told them they had much to learn in a short time.

CHAPTER EIGHT

July 17, 2115 Eastern Daylight Time

Night had long since fallen as Jay Bruner got off the Blue Line train at the Franconia-Springfield Metro station. He knew he'd missed another family dinner and wondered when his job as chief of legislative affairs would get easier. Shore duty was supposed to provide an opportunity to spend time with your family again— not to keep breaking promises.

He looked off at the far end of the park-and-drive lot and spied his new silver BMW 534i sedan. It was the nicest car he had ever owned, and he admitted to himself that he felt he needed a "status car" if he was going to have to deal with the political glitterati during his three-year tour at OLA. He had agonized over spending the money, but he and Meagan had finished paying for Dale's college education at Georgia Tech years ago, and it would be a few years before they would have to start paying college tuition for their two daughters. He reminded himself to do what he could to ensure they focused on Virginia schools, where the in-state tuition would make their college bills a bit more manageable.

He didn't so much hear or see anything—it was more like he felt something. Then, instantly, it was all violence. Three black-clad figures grabbed him from behind. A gloved hand clamped over his mouth, and two strong hands pulled his arms behind his back as another hand grabbed the BMW key from his fist. He felt a snap tie going around his wrists, and then a piece of duct tape going across his mouth, and then another piece going across his eyes. He heard the trunk of his car pop open and soon several pairs of hands lifted him off the ground and rolled him into the car's trunk. Then the trunk was closed, and it was black. Seconds later, the BMW roared to life and he tumbled around the trunk as the beamer lurched out of the parking lot. As the car whisked away, a small pile of twenty-dollar bills lay scattered around the parking spot it had just left.

It had taken Annie Jacobson a while to gather up all her shopping bags while exiting the Metro train. She was the final rider getting off at the Franconia-Springfield Metro station, so she was the last to walk out into the park-and-ride lot. As she looked up from her smart phone to spot her white Toyota Corolla, to her horror she saw several men putting another man into the trunk of a car—it looked like a late-model BMW—and driving off at high speed.

Annie looked around to see if anyone else saw what she saw. The lot was empty, save for a half a dozen parked cars. Was she imagining things? She didn't think so. Her fingers trembling, she punched 9-1-1 into her smart phone and then rushed to the safety of her car.

The desk sergeant at the West Springfield police station was the first to field the call from the 9-1-1 dispatcher. Within minutes, one of their patrol cars rolled into the park-and-ride lot at the Franconia-Springfield Metro station. The dispatcher had asked Jacobson to stay in her car with the doors locked. She had complied, and the officers in the patrol car found her Corolla and began their questioning. Soon, another West Springfield police car rolled into the lot, as well as a Virginia State Police car.

Jacobson poured out her story amid a sea of red and blue flashers. She led the police to the exact spot where the BMW had been parked, and a West Springfield police officer carefully picked up the twenty-dollar bills on the ground with a gloved hand and put them into an evidence bag. Soon a BOLO ("be on the lookout") went out for a car-jacked BMW—type and model unknown—and a request went to the credit union that owned the ATM at the station to get the video and see who withdrew money from the machine.

As the other law enforcement officers and their vehicles eventually made their way out of the park-and-ride lot and the terrified Jacobson was told she could go home, two West Springfield police cruisers remained behind and began to manage the crime scene.

"Boss, ready for us now?" Bleich asked as he and Scott stood in the doorway of Roger McCord's office. Bleich had called McCord at home—something he rarely did—and asked him if he could come back to Op-Center immediately. McCord had ridden his Harley in from Reston at a notch above the speed limit. If Bleich called him at home, it was important—and worrying.

"Sure, Aaron . . . Maggie. I got back here as fast as possible. What's up?"

The duo propped themselves up on the credenza across from McCord's desk.

"It's like this," Bleich began. "We've briefed you before on how we've been keeping an eye on the domestic front, looking at ISIL sympathizers here in the United States."

"Yes, you said you all were following a few leads."

"Yep. Maggie got interested in this group of guys up in Minneapolis, except they're not there now; they're here in Washington. We know they're also on the DHS watch list, but . . . well . . . that's all DHS is doing, they're 'watching' them—"

McCord had worked with Bleich long enough to know his Geek Tank leader was looking for a way to tell him the normal channels of U.S. security were creaking along and that he was taking things into his own hands. "Aaron, I get it. You smell something with these guys, and you've all started doing things we're not gonna tell the *Washington Post*."

"Exactly, boss. Maggie has been following these guys—they're all students at AU and work jobs in the District—except for two of them who work up near BWI—"

"BWI?"

"Yep, it gets stranger. I'll let Maggie take it from here."

"Sir," Maggie began. "Like Aaron said, these guys all suddenly arrived here in the D.C. area and started summer sessions at American University. They live in an apartment a bit north of AU and, except for the two who work up near BWI, they all work jobs in the District. They have one van among them, which the BWI duo takes to work every day."

Scott paused, and Bleich nodded for her to continue. "So now I'm trying to connect some dots that may not all connect—but maybe they do. Everybody's pretty sure the Islamic State is still seeking some kind of retribution for the attacks that destroyed their headquarters in Mosul. These five men get here and their e-mails back to pals and girlfriends in Minneapolis are all downers. They're bitching and moaning about school, about their jobs, about the weather—"

McCord kept nodding, his body language encouraging Scott to get to the point.

"Well, here's where it gets *really* strange. About a week or so ago, the tenor of their e-mails completely changes. Now they're happy, life is good, and they start talking about jihad—"

"I know what you're thinking, boss," Bleich interrupted, "they're all matriculated at AU in the Middle

Eastern studies program, they've heard a lecture by some flaming radical, and they're just parroting back what they've heard to impress the yokels back in Minnesota."

"So that's not it?" McCord asked.

"Not at all," Scott continued. "First, we've checked their class schedules and none of them are in the same class at the same time. Second, none of their professors is even a blip on the radical-detection radar. Third, they're talking about specifics, about them doing something—"

"Sorry, I'm still not seeing any dots connecting," McCord prodded.

"Here's where they *do* connect. The guy who's clearly their leader—his name's Amer Deghayes—used his credit card and PayPal to rent a garage four days ago, but not one near their apartment; it's way the hell up near Hyattsville. And here's where it gets really interesting and why we called you—"

"I'm still listening," McCord prodded.

"In one of his e-mails, this Deghayes guy is talking to someone we haven't identified yet and telling him today is the day. Nothing happened all day today until a few hours ago. Then we picked up a BOLO for a late-model BMW that got car-jacked at the Franconia-Springfield Metro station. You know that Metro stop services a number of neighborhoods where tons of DoD employees live—"

"You think these guys are the instrument for what Mabad al-Dosari threatened months ago, and that he's not going after the president. You think he went after someone else, maybe a DoD employee?" McCord blurted out.

"Well, yes, maybe a senior DoD employee who was someone connected to the strike on his compound," Bleich added. "We may know more soon, though. What we picked up on the police networks was that there was a lot of cash on the ground near where this BMW was jacked. The police are probably looking at film from the ATM in that Metro station now. They're thinking whoever is on that video withdrawing money is likely the person who was car-jacked. It shouldn't be too hard matching who's on that ATM video against DMV records."

"Aaron, Maggie, good work. Go after those video and DMV records—but quietly."

"Like church mice, boss," Bleich replied. "You gonna push this up to Mr. Williams?"

"I am. Keep at it and let me know if you get any other leads. I'm camping out here with you all tonight."

CHAPTER NINE

Meagan Bruner was used to her husband working late, and she wasn't a worrywart; but she had finally had enough. He had never been this late before. That, and the fact that he hadn't responded to any of her texts, e-mails, or phone messages set off alarm bells. She decided to do the only thing she could, retrace her husband's steps from the time he left for work that morning. Her two teenage daughters insisted on going with her.

As they pulled into the park-and-ride lot at the Franconia-Springfield Metro station and saw the two West Springfield police cruisers, but didn't see Jay Bruner's BMW, their hearts sank. Meagan's youngest daughter started crying. Something was wrong, terribly wrong.

* * *

The object of Meagan Bruner's worry was at that moment still in the trunk of his car, but he was no longer moving. In fact, the trunk was open and her husband sensed he was in some sort of building. He remained bound and gagged and with duct tape still covering his eyes, but every so often someone came by and shook him and caused him to stir.

Where was he? Who had taken him and *why* had they taken him? And where were they taking him? Was this the final destination? Were they going to do something to him? A gamut of emotions ran through his mind: shock, numbness, fear, anxiety, helplessness, hopelessness, dissociation, anger, and a host of others coursed through his brain. *Pull yourself together, Jay,* he told himself. *They jacked your car. That's all they want. Now they're just trying to figure out what to do with you, then they'll take the car and it'll be over. Right?*

Bruner thought back to his training during his first squadron tour. All naval aviators go through a week of SERE—survival, evasion, resistance, and escape—training in a mock POW camp. It had been a long time since SERE, but the brutal training was seared onto his brain. He had to communicate with whoever had taken him. But he couldn't even see them, let alone talk with them. He fought despair with everything he had.

Amer and the two others sat huddled in the rented garage, as far away from the trunk of the BMW as they could, speaking in hushed whispers.

"You're the only one who's heard the instructions from our contact, and this is all happening so fast," one of the men said. "I still don't know why we have to sit here all night."

Amer paused before replying. Their contact told him he had followed their hostage's movements and decided that Amer and the others needed to grab him at night as the Metro brought him to the Franconia-Springfield station. But they'd need to hold him overnight, since the flight taking him out of the country didn't leave until the next day.

"I told you," Amer replied. "We have our instructions on how to get him out of the country; we just need to follow them."

"So we put him on a plane, then what?" the other man asked. "What does that have to do with what we've dedicated ourselves to do? And what do we do the day after tomorrow? Just go back to our work and our classes? It doesn't make any sense."

It didn't make complete sense to Amer, either. Their two confederates who worked near BWI were going to have to do their part quickly the next day with their hostage and the refrigerated box—that too had been decided and arranged by their contact. And Amer had been told to buy the life-support equipment and send it with those two men. Fine, he had bought exactly what their contact told him to buy, where he told him to buy it; but he was starting to worry about maxing out his credit card. What were they going to do if that happened?

"Look, let's just get some sleep," Amer replied. "This garage is secure; no one knows we're here. But we need to ensure he's alive when we deliver him tomorrow. Give him some more water but be sure to gag him after you do. We'll roll out of here in the van at ten AM sharp."

It was 0500 when they met in Williams's office. McCord, Bleich, and Scott had stayed at Op-Center all night, but McCord had insisted that Williams didn't need to come in until morning. They compromised, and Williams showed up much earlier than he did on normal days.

It had been a busy night for those in Op-Center's Intelligence Directorate, as Bleich had pulled in more of his Geek Tank superstars during the wee hours of the morning. The dots Scott so desperately wanted to connect were now connected. McCord began to lay it out for the Op-Center director.

"At lot came together in the last few hours, boss, thanks to Aaron and Maggie's hard work. We think we can walk this BMW car-jacking all the way back to the bombing of the ISIL compound in Mosul in March."

Williams had both hands clasped around his mess-deck coffee mug and nodded for McCord to continue.

"We've been convinced that Mabad al-Dosari intended to carry out the threats he made after that bombing. He directly threatened the president, but then he likely figured the president was too hard a target. So who would be a good proxy? That's the question no one's been able to answer."

"And you think you may have the answer now?" Williams prodded.

"We do. A little over a week ago, five young Muslim guys on the DHS watch list moved from Minneapolis to D.C. We started keeping an eye on everything they did. We pulled the string on their employment records, and a few of them have jobs that make no sense, and we also noticed they started making rentals that seemed odd. Last night a BMW got car-jacked down in Springfield. Then, a Mrs. Meagan Bruner showed up at the park-and-ride at the Franconia-Springfield Metro station looking for her husband. Turns out that it was her husband and his car that got jacked—"

Williams still looked perplexed. "Boss," McCord continued, "Meagan Bruner is the wife of Admiral Jay Bruner. He's the Navy's chief of legislative affairs now, but he was the *Teddy Roosevelt* strike group commander who led the strikes on al-Dosari's compound back in March—"

"Holy cow! So you think al-Dosari ordered Bruner kidnapped?" Williams asked. "What else do we know?"

"At this point, there's still a lot we don't know. In spite of the BOLO that went out for Bruner's BMW, no one ever spotted it. We know someone has him, likely one or more of the students we've been watching, but we're not certain where they're taking him. But we think the guys who took him will try to get him out of the country—"

"But we don't know how?"

"Our best guess is a flight out of BWI. Aaron and Maggie learned that two of these five men we're watching have jobs working up near BWI, at a packing and shipping company. This company packs shipping crates in their warehouse but also hires out their workers as day laborers when big shippers need a surge capacity. So we're pretty sure the people who jacked Bruner will try to deliver him to these guys, and somehow they'll pack him up in a shipping container and get him on a flight out of the country."

"I don't even want to ask how many flights a day leave BWI," Williams said.

"Ahhh . . . we checked, boss . . . It's north of six hundred flights . . . and over thirty-five tons of cargo a day," Bleich said.

McCord could see Williams sag in his chair and jumped in. "But we do have some leads. We checked the Minnesota DMV records, and we can ID the van they're driving. We also have the make, model, and license number of the car one of their guys rented. Our best guess is that Bruner will be—or already has been—transferred from the BMW to either the van or the car."

McCord walked Williams through their other leads. Scott had done some digging and learned that one of the students on the watch list, Amer Deghayes, had used his credit card and PayPal to rent a two-car garage near Hyattsville—north of where Bruner was car-jacked and on the way to BWI—month to month. While the PayPal transaction didn't specify the location of the garage, the Geek Tank was working to narrow down the options. After an extended conversation, the group was all but certain the hostage was in that garage. McCord and his team had done their staff work, now he wanted to move Williams to a decision.

"Uh, boss, I asked Brian and Jim Wright to come in early," McCord offered. "They're standing by if you're thinking of getting our team down at Quantico engaged. They'd give us our best shot at snatching Admiral Bruner from these guys before he gets spirited out of the country."

As ops director, Brian Dawson was Op-Center's primary conduit for any international or domestic crisis response. But it was Williams's domestic crisis manager, Jim Wright, who would direct any action in the United States and would alert and liaise directly with Op-Center's team at Quantico. Wright was a former member of the bureau's Hostage Rescue Team and had done a tour with the Special Activities Division at the CIA. As Op-Center's "Mr. Inside," with massive contacts in the law enforcement and intelligence agencies, Wright could get it done.

Williams considered this and paused for a long time before speaking. "Roger, Aaron, Maggie . . . you've done a great job pulling this together. I think we've got a damn good chance of rescuing Admiral Bruner. But I'm also mindful about how far our presidential mandate goes—and more importantly, where it doesn't go—"

"Boss, we've got what we need to move now," McCord blurted out.

"I appreciate you all leaning forward," Williams replied. "But you remember how much suasion we had to use to get into the domestic business in the first place, as well as how specific our agreement with Justice and the FBI is. We've got to turn this one over to the bureau."

Williams could see their faces sag and the air go out of McCord. "Roger, get with Jim and have him pass everything you've got to the FBI watch floor. I'll call the director. And once you've done that, ask Brian to come in here. If these guys do manage to escape the dragnet the FBI throws out, then we'll need to get our JSOC team downrange ASAP."

As they all started to stream out of the room to carry out Williams's directions he said, "Aaron, Maggie, stay behind a moment, will you?"

"Yes, sir," Bleich replied.

"You've all done a truly exceptional job. Now I'm going to ask you all to fight a two-front war. Keep feeding the FBI everything you've got, but I need you to be ready to turn on a dime if we launch our JSOC team downrange. They'll need a massive amount of intel, and I'll need you to get it to them in real time."

Bleich was visibly moved. He knew the Op-Center director appreciated and valued what he did, but he'd never been told this directly that Williams *needed* him.

"Boss, we'll yell if we need anything else. And . . . and . . . thank you, sir."

With that, Bleich and Scott made a beeline back to the Geek Tank. Williams turned to his secure computer and began composing a POTUS/OC Eyes Only memo.

CHAPTER TEN

Hyattsville, Maryland, is a city of just over 20,000 residents nestled inside the Washington Beltway in Prince George's County. It is a leafy, semi-urban area comprising mostly small-to-medium-sized houses with modest yards. State Route 1 runs through the heart of this mostly sleepy burg that has a large presence of University of Maryland students and federal government workers, the latter group attracted by the relatively low cost of housing and access to Washington via the Metro's Green Line. The city's motto, "A world within walking distance," as well as the fact that it counts Muppets creator Jim Henson as the most noteworthy person born there, speak to the quiet that is Hyattsville's hallmark.

That quiet was about to be broken. Armed with the intelligence provided by Op-Center, the FBI's Critical Incident Response Group Hostage Rescue Team—the

CIRG HRT—had deployed in the early morning hours and was now staged at strategic locations throughout and around the city, primed to look for the car or the van that might be holding Jay Bruner. With only limited assets and no specific intelligence as to where the rented garage might be in the city proper or its surrounding areas, the FBI HRT vehicles and two helicopters deployed on the northeastern section of the city, near likely routes leading toward BWI.

The watchstanders at the FBI command center had debated whether to call the director and had finally done so at 0330 that morning. He authorized them to deploy and told them he'd be in the office at 0630 to take the call from the Op-Center director. After a detailed discussion with Chase Williams, the FBI director had his HRT deploy additional assets to Hyattsville, but in spite of Williams's urging, stopped short of also bringing in local law enforcement to assist.

Jay Bruner had lapsed into sleep only occasionally during the night. With each passing hour, his terror ratcheted up a notch. Twice, whoever was holding him pulled the gag out of his mouth and shoved a small bottle of water into it. Each time he tried to speak, to bargain with them, to say something, *anything*, his captor shouted "shut up!"

He was able to tell light and dark through the duct tape covering his eyes, so he sensed it was morning when many arms lifted him out of the trunk of his BMW and moved him what he sensed was only a few feet, then roughly deposited him on some surface. It felt like metal, but what was it? He couldn't tell and that only drove his fear and anxiety to another level. His notion that all these people wanted was his car had long since disappeared. Evidently, they wanted him. *But why?*

One question—what kind of surface he was lying on—was suddenly answered when he heard and felt an engine fire off. Seconds later, he heard a creaking and grinding of something opening or closing that sounded like it was coming from the same direction as the engine. Then he heard voices—the same voices he'd heard before—and then whatever vehicle he was in started moving. Jay Bruner began to pray.

Meagan Bruner hadn't slept at all. She willed herself to be strong if for no other reason than to not further alarm her two daughters, both of whom were near panic. Though the West Springfield police officers at the park-and-drive lot at the Franconia-Springfield Metro station had promised to keep her apprised of any new developments, she hadn't heard from them once since she left the Metro station lot.

She was mindful of the three-hour time difference between the east and west coasts so she waited until 1030 EDT to text her son. It was a simple text, only asking him to call her as soon as he could. The text would go unseen for several hours, as at 1030 Eastern, 0730 Pacific, Dale Bruner had been on the grinder with Class 318 for several hours while his phone, wallet, and other personal items remained in his locker at the SEAL training facility.

Amer sat in the passenger seat of their van with a gas station map of the area in his lap while one of the other two men drove and the third man sat in the back of the van with the bound and gagged Bruner. Amer told the driver to keep moving at just under the speed limit. He gave him frequent instructions and constantly checked his watch.

They wanted to stay off main highways until it was absolutely necessary to travel on them. Amer had a timeline in mind for when he was supposed to reach the warehouse where their two confederates worked. He wanted to arrive in ample time so they could put their prisoner in the life-support equipment he had purchased, and then into the refrigerated box his men working for the shipping company were packing up. Their contact had established a front business that shipped fruit overseas. Once the refrigerated box was sealed, it would have tamper-proof locks installed. But Amer didn't want to arrive too early and have the hostage where someone else might see him.

"In a few blocks, you'll come up on Madison Street. You want to turn right there," Amer said to the driver.

"Then what?" the man asked.

His companions were beginning to chafe at the fact that Amer seemed to know everything but elected to share only so much with them. Sure, once they had met at their contact's house that first evening, they all had received the same training. He had taught them how to use firearms, how to use simple skills to subdue and restrain a hostage, and had even taught them evasive driving skills at an abandoned drive-in movie lot. But the contact had clearly treated Amer differently than he'd treated the others during their week plus of training. And he had given Amer the two unregistered handguns and all of the ammunition.

"We'll be on Madison for a little while, then we'll turn north on 43rd Avenue."

"And then?" groused the driver.

"And then," Amer sighed, "we turn east on Oglethorpe Street for a bit, then we'll pick up Route 1 north."

"I'll be glad when we're on a highway. Creeping along on these side streets with this guy in the back of the van is asking for trouble."

"We'll be all right," Amer offered.

At Amer's destination, a warehouse near BWI, their two confederates were ready. The front company, Arnold's Fruits and Vegetables, had contacted the shipping company and asked for a $10 \times 10 \times 6$ foot refrigerated box to ship a large consignment of peaches. Amer's contact had provided an ample supply of fresh peaches to avoid suspicion, and they were packing the box with peaches as they waited for the hostage to be delivered.

For security, Amer and these two men had agreed there would be no communication among them unless the van was going to be delayed. At the warehouse, they had their schedule to deliver the box to the FedEx receiving hangar, where it would be handed over to FedEx employees. Those workers would put the box on their flight leaving that afternoon.

While the FBI director spurned Chase Williams's suggestion to engage local law enforcement in and around Hyattsville so there would be more assets to spot the van or car—"Too many moving parts," he had said. "We have it covered," he added—he did work with local authorities in one helpful way.

Washington metro area commuters are always looking for any edge they can get to discover roads not gridlocked during the early-morning and late-afternoon commuting hours. In addition to government-provided road cameras on federal, state, and county highways, local radio and television networks had deployed a substantial number of traffic cams at important intersections along primary commuter routes. And in the intense competition for market share, as soon as one network put up one camera, their rival popped up one of their own. The D.C. metro area roads were blanketed with thousands of cameras.

The FBI director had his IT people working on getting all those traffic feeds piped into his command center. If they got a hit on the car or the van, they could roll their vehicles or fly one of their two helos and intercept the target.

Some 330 miles south-southwest of where the FBI HRT was deployed to intercept whoever was holding

Jay Bruner, another deployment was underway. Immediately after speaking with Chase Williams, Brian Dawson had called Op-Center's JSOC—Joint Special Operations Command—team at Fort Bragg, North Carolina, at 0615. Major Mike Volner had a brief conversation with Dawson and had issued a recall for his on-call squad. The next call Dawson made was to his right-hand man for international crises, "Mr. Outside," Hector Rodriquez. By 0830, Dawson and Rodriquez were on a Gulfstream heading for Pope Air Force Base. They'd rendezvous there with Volner and his team, and then they all would board an Air Force C-17 Globemaster that would depart as soon as the JSOC team and their gear were safely aboard, but no earlier than 1600 Eastern Daylight Time. Chase Williams and his three thoroughbreds had decided that if Bruner wasn't found by then, he was likely out of the country and they needed to launch downrange.

The kidnappers' van rolled onto Route 1 headed north, and the driver again asked Amer, "So what now?"

"Just drive. You can bump it up to the speed limit. Once we get to the Beltway, we'll take the inner loop and drive until we get to the Baltimore-Washington Parkway. That will take us directly toward BWI. When we get close, I'll call out the exit that takes us to the warehouse."

"Okay, fine. How much longer?"

"Rush hour is over. I'm guessing forty-five minutes maybe, perhaps a little more."

The driver just shook his head and continued to drive.

The FBI command center didn't have systems nearly as sophisticated as those Aaron Bleich had built for the Geek Tank, but they were good enough. The feeds from the hundreds of traffic and news cameras were programmed to trigger on either of two license plates, the one on the car Amer had recently rented or the one on the van that was coregistered to Amer and another individual in Minneapolis.

Suddenly, one of the watchstanders in the command center shouted, "I've got a hit!"

The watch commander was at his side immediately. "Where? Show me. Is it the car or the van?"

"It's the van, and it's right here," the man said, bringing up the shot the traffic cam had taken only seconds before. "It's moving north along Route 1, just north of University Park and south of the University of Maryland at College Park."

"Got it. Alert all units on the secure net. Pull me up a map of where all our assets are deployed."

A few seconds later, a display popped up. Each HRT unit had a GPS transceiver that reported its position in real time. The watch commander studied the display for less than a minute, and then pointed at the screen. "Okay, contact this unit and have them roll onto Route 1 here and pick up a loose trail on the van, and have this one move to intercept them as soon as they get just north of College Park."

"You got it. You gonna call the director?"

"You bet!"

"Think we've got our team ready to head over to Pope," Major Mike Volner's number two, Master Gunnery Sergeant Charles Moore, said as he walked up to the JSOC team leader.

"Thanks, Master Guns," he replied. "This one was really short fused; I appreciate you getting everyone kitted up so fast."

"It's what we do, boss. We're up for any chance to get our beaks wet; it's been a while."

While Volner and Moore grew up in different services, they were simpatico. Major Michael Volner, United States Army, and Master Gunnery Sergeant Charles Moore, United States Marine Corps, had been together for close to three years. Volner had been an Army major for just two years, while Moore was an experienced veteran who had been a Marine for almost two decades. Volner came to JSOC from the 75th Rangers; Moore came from the Marine Corps Special Operations Command. Now they were both part of the JSOC unit that served as Op-Center's force to deal with international crises. They had acquitted themselves well, most recently rescuing the crew of a Navy littoral combat ship who were under siege by North Korean troops.

"Mr. Dawson and Hector gonna meet us at Pope?" Moore asked.

"Already there. The C-17 is inbound. And Master

Guns, how's our civilian analyst feel about being the only woman on the team going downrange?"

"Ms. Phillips? She's got big cojones—sorry boss—she's got the guts of any of our guys. You saw how tough she was when we pulled her out of that pickle in Saudi Arabia a while back. She's good people. How'd we get her at JSOC again?"

"Let's just say Mr. Williams has pull in all the right places."

The subject of their discussion, Laurie Phillips, had been in more than a pickle. She and a Navy helicopter pilot, Lieutenant Sandee Barron, had overflown Saudi Arabia without permission and had been shot down by a rogue Saudi prince while trying to solve the same emerging crisis that Op-Center was dealing with. Volner's team had rescued the two. Barron was shown the door by the Navy for filing a false flight plan and losing a thirty-million-dollar Navy helicopter, and Phillips had been fired by CNA—the Center for Naval Analyses—for being part of the operation.

But the Op-Center director had seen something he liked in both Barron and Phillips. Sandee Barron was now a helicopter pilot with the FBI CIRG, and Williams had pulled strings to have Phillips hired as a government civilian analyst and assigned to their JSOC team at Fort Bragg. Phillips had blended in splendidly in her new role and was a welcome and valued addition to Volner's group.

"We're lucky at that, boss. She's bonded with his

Geek Tank folks. If they have good intel, they feed it to her in real time."

"I suspect she'll more than pull her weight once we get downrange, Master Guns. For now, let's mount up."

With that, Moore marched his troops onto the waiting bus. Their unit, seconded to Op-Center on previous ops in the Middle East and Northeast Asia, didn't know yet where this deployment would take them. For these professionals, it didn't matter.

There was no way to be inconspicuous. The CIRG HRT vehicles looked like the military- or law-enforcement-quality trucks they were. The men in the big black Chevy Suburbans didn't intend to shadow the van they were after for long. Their objective was to intercept it immediately, subdue whoever was driving, and rescue the hostage.

The crew in the trail vehicle pulled onto Route 1 and asked for intel from the HRT UH-60M Blackhawk helo overhead. "How far up ahead is the van?"

"About a half mile," the pilot of the helo replied. "Speed up and take a loose trail. When your partner joins Route 1, you can close in tighter. We'll give the order to intercept."

"Got it."

A mile ahead, the second HRT vehicle waited in a strip-mall parking lot with direct access to Route 1. On signal, it would roar out of the lot and get ahead of the van, then slow and force it to stop.

Both vehicles were getting locating info from the

Blackhawk, which was flying overhead at three thousand feet. The pilots picked that altitude because it was low enough to see the van they were after, but high enough that the van might not notice them. The two veteran pilots, Joe McDaniel and Frank Stang, communicated directly with their two ground vehicles. It was going to be like shooting fish in a barrel.

"There's the sign for the Beltway, I-495; it's just a few miles ahead. We'll turn there and go east to get to the Baltimore-Washington Parkway," Amer told the driver. "Keep your speed up, we don't want to draw attention for going too slow."

As the driver complied, the man in the back of the van said, "Amer, I've been watching out the back windows. I think there's a black truck following us. It looks like a Chevy Suburban. It's just matching our speed."

"Are you sure? Do you see any lights or flashers?"

"No, I don't think so. Should we slow down and see if he goes around us?"

"I don't know," Amer said. "Let's just—"

He stopped in mid-sentence as he looked at the parking lot to his right and saw a second black Suburban barreling out onto Route 1. It looked like it was going to crash into their van.

"Watch out!" Amer shouted at the driver.

The HRT vehicle pulled right out in front of them and started slowing.

"What are we going to do?" the driver yelled.

"That truck behind us, it's closing rapidly. It's right on our tail!" the man in the back of the van shouted.

High above, Frank Stang was at the controls of the HRT Blackhawk and was about to key the mike and talk with his two ground vehicles when he heard his copilot.

"Shit!" McDaniel shouted.

"What?" Stang asked as he kept an eye on the van below.

"Look!" McDaniel replied, pointing at the display on the helo's instrument panel.

"Dammit . . . Master caution light . . . Tail rotor chip light. Reset the master caution and give it a minute to see if it clears."

"I did already," McDaniel answered. "It came back on . . . Frank?"

A tail rotor chip light dictated that they needed to land their bird immediately. The chip light was designed to give the pilots early warning of what could be an impending catastrophic failure of their tail rotor gear box. If that mechanism failed, their tail rotor would stop and the best they could hope for was a semicontrolled crash. Stang wasn't only at the controls, he was the pilot in command, and he should have bottomed the collective by now to get them on the ground—and fast.

"It could just be fuzz. Maybe it'll burn off."

"You know what the procedures say; we've gotta land now!" McDaniel shouted.

"All right, all right," Stang replied. "Call command and tell them to get the other bird up. We can't lose these guys."

"Speed up and go around them!" Amer shouted at the driver. The man needed no further urging, as he punched the accelerator, moved into the left lane, and zoomed around the HRT truck.

"Faster, faster!" Amer urged as they drove in the leftmost lane of the two northbound lanes of Route 1. But as they sped up, the two HRT trucks moved up to stay right behind them and matched their speed.

"See that semi up there in the right lane?" Amer asked. "It must be going only forty-five or maybe fifty. Stay in this lane but slow down and match its speed. Here's what we're going to do . . . "

"Got it, command," the on-scene ground commander in the HRT truck that had just pulled onto Route 1 said. "Any idea when the backup bird will launch?"

"Should be no more than ten minutes. Don't lose this guy."

"Don't worry, we won't," he replied, and then he continued, speaking to the other vehicle. "This guy is slowing down. Should we get out in front of him and slow to a stop and force him to stop too?"

"No, there're too many cars on the road. We don't want to cause a pileup."

"All right, but I'll be damn glad when that second helo is airborne again."

A crisis debilitates some people while it has the opposite effect on others, helping those in that latter category call up reservoirs of clarity and courage they often were unaware they had. Amer Deghayes was in that second group.

He had explained the plan to the driver. The third man had abandoned Bruner and had crawled up to between the van's two front seats and now looked out ahead with Amer and the driver. Their van now rode at about the seven o'clock position behind the semi. The two HRT trucks just continued to follow them. The other traffic on Route 1 was starting to back up behind them.

"Start to slow even more," Amer told the driver.

The van started to slow, and the two HRT trucks matched their speed.

"What's this asshole doing now?" one of the HRT men groused.

"NOW, punch it!" Amer shouted at the driver. The man floored the accelerator and the van leapt ahead. The two HRT vehicles started to speed up too.

Amer hoped he had timed it perfectly. There was a cross street up ahead. The semi continued in the right lane. Their van was in the other lane, beside the semi, and had slowed to match its speed exactly. The two HRT trucks trailed the van, but at a bit of a distance. This clown had slowed abruptly before and they didn't want to crash into him.

"There it is up ahead," Amer said.

"It's going to be close. I don't think we'll make it!" the van's driver cried out.

"Yes we will," Amer said. "Faster, faster; stay right next to the semi."

The driver complied. They were even with the semi's cab, and Amer saw the truck's driver looking down at him. "NOW!" Amer shouted.

The van's driver mashed the accelerator and zoomed slightly ahead of the semi. Then he jerked the wheel violently to the right as they cut in front of the semi no more than fifty feet ahead of its looming grille and headed into the cross street, tires squealing. In the back of the van, Jay Bruner bounced around like a rag doll; his head smashed against the wall of the van, almost knocking him unconscious.

The semi's driver slammed on his brake and simultaneously mashed his horn. The eighteen-wheeler screeched along, smoke billowing out of its brakes.

"Shit, we've lost him!" the HRT on-scene commander shouted to no one in particular. Then to the driver, "Call command, tell them this guy got off at Berwyn Road and we lost him. We'll turn off at the next cross street and double back, but tell them to get that other helo airborne now!"

The van careened east along Berwyn Road as the driver held a death grip on the wheel, and Amer and the other man looked behind them to see if they had lost their pursuers. Bruner continued to bounce around in the back of the van. He braced himself as best he could, fearing the worst: that they might tip over.

Once his heart stopped pounding, Amer reached down on the floor of the van and retrieved his map. He studied it for a few moments, and then said, "Keep going this way. I think we've lost them for now but we can't get back on Route 1. If we head this way for another mile or two, then double back for a few miles, we can pick up the Baltimore-Washington Parkway here," he continued, pointing at the map. But the driver just looked straight ahead and maintained his death grip on the van's steering wheel.

At the warehouse, one of the men looked at his watch as the other continued to pack peaches in the refrigerated box. There was an art to what they were doing, as they needed to avoid suspicion should a supervisor from the company happen to drop in, but they also needed to pack the box in a way that would allow them to easily fit the hostage clad in his survival gear. And they needed Amer to get here on time.

When Dale Bruner finally finished on the grinder and got to his locker, he had a number of texts, e-mails, and phone messages waiting for him. He read and listened to everything on the phone, then prioritized which ones he would deal with immediately. His call to his mother was first on his list.

"Hey, Mom," Dale began when his mother answered. "Sorry I took so long to get back to you. I was out with a class and had all my stuff locked up."

"Dale, oh thank you for calling. It's good to hear your voice. Are you alone right now?" Dale could hear the stress in Meagan Bruner's voice.

"Mom, what's going on?"

"Now I don't want you to worry, but . . . well . . . it seems that your dad's car got stolen, and the car-jackers took him too. I guess a shiny new BMW was just too inviting a target. I'm sure he's okay. The West Springfield police have been very kind, and they have gotten the FBI involved, and I'm certain they'll find him soon. But I just wanted to let you know so you wouldn't worry if you hear something about it—and I just wanted to hear your voice too." Meagan was fighting mightily not to let her voice crack, but it wasn't working.

Amber had sworn him to secrecy, texting him the full details of what was going on. In the Bruner family, there were parental prerogatives, and Jay and Meagan Bruner had made it abundantly clear to their three children that parents were the ones who delivered important news. Her mom would never forgive her if she found out that she had let her brother know about their dad's kidnapping prematurely. Parents made these kinds of calls, not siblings.

Dale knew enough from his sister's text that it was clear to him his mom was putting a good face on things, and she wasn't telling him everything. "Mom, are you okay, and are Amber and Katherine okay?"

"Yes, dear, we're completely fine. I know your dad will be all right. The West Springfield police lieutenant told me these kinds of car-jackings happen all the time—especially with high-end cars late at night in park-and-ride lots."

Dale listened impassively. His mother was trying to spin this as positively as possible, but she wasn't doing a good job of it. "Look, Mom, I've got leave on the books and I've got good people working for me here. I'll make a reservation and get a flight home right away."

"Oh Dale, you don't need to do that. We're all fine. Your dad would flip out if he knew you left your assignment there with no notice to the people you work with."

But Dale Bruner had made his mind up. He would be flying out of San Diego's Lindbergh Field and heading to Washington that evening.

The two men were alone in the warehouse with their mostly filled refrigerated box.

"I can't believe Amer decided that we shouldn't use our cell phones. We have a schedule to meet to deliver this box, but we have no idea where he is now. If we're late, someone will be suspicious."

"I know. I'm getting kind of sick of Amer running the show and not telling us everything. I just want to get this guy into this gear, pack him up, and then we can get the hell out of here. I'll be glad to get another job closer to where we live."

"I've had about enough," the other man replied. "We're not doing jihad here. I'm ready to move back to Minneapolis."

"So am I. Tell me again about why we have to deliver this to the FedEx hangar at a specific time. Why do we have a time slot we have to meet?"

His partner sighed. He had asked the same question and had been told that the union for the trucking company drivers had complained that they were losing time and burning gas waiting in line to make their deliveries to the FedEx warehouse at BWI. At their urging, FedEx corporate made the decision to assign delivery time slots to placate the unions. "It's a stupid rule to keep the unions happy."

"Well if Amer doesn't get here on time, no one's going to be happy. If we miss our time slot, we're screwed. We've got," he paused to look at his smart phone, "less than forty-five minutes to get this box delivered. He's supposed to call if he's running behind, right?"

"Yes, he said he'd call, and I guess he will. But he's probably not that far away by now and remember, he said it was dangerous to arrive too early. Here, have a peach; it will cheer you up."

His companion took the proffered peach. He was sick of waiting, and pretty soon he'd be sick of peaches too.

Frank Stang had been right. It wasn't their tail rotor gearbox about to fail; it was metal fuzz on the chip detector, a common occurrence in most helos.

The other Blackhawk had managed to get airborne from the parking lot of Hyattsville's First United Methodist Church in less than ten minutes—good time, but too late to pick up the scent of the fleeing van.

Their maintenance crew had found the metal fuzz, cleaned the chip detector, and gotten Stang and McDaniel back in the air. They too had lost the scent.

But if anything good came out of this fiasco, it was that the FBI director finally became worried about losing his prey. Maybe two helos and a few ground vehicles weren't enough. At the persistent urging of his on-scene commander in Hyattsville, he authorized him to contact local law enforcement and ask for additional airborne support.

"Do you think we've lost them?" asked the kidnapper who was crouched down between the van's two front seats.

"It's been almost fifteen minutes that we've been off Route 1; I think we're in the clear. Let's start to head north again," Amer replied.

"How do you think that truck found us? It looked like some sort of SWAT vehicle, and I think I saw a bar with lights on the back of the roof. It couldn't have followed us all the way from the garage, could it? And the other one coming on the road ahead of us—how did that happen?" the driver asked.

Amer considered this a minute. "I know we weren't followed out of the garage. I looked repeatedly. And no, these trucks finding us can't be a lucky coincidence. They must have some kind of air support. Maybe a drone . . . or a helicopter. Turn left here," Amer continued, looking down at his map. "We're going to go north up this road, and it'll take us to the Beltway, then we'll continue as planned."

"Are we going to be late getting to the warehouse?" the man in the back asked.

"No, I don't think—"

"Look!" the driver exclaimed. "Right there up above us. It's a helicopter, and it's coming south along this road. It's flying really low. It must be looking for us!"

Amer tried not to panic and swiveled his head left and right. "There, turn left now. This street has large trees; we can get under their canopy."

The driver did as he was told and the highway patrol helicopter never spotted them. But they were now traveling southwest, away from BWI. Jay Bruner bounced around in the back of the van trying not to let panic overwhelm him, but he was losing the battle.

CHAPTER ELEVEN

July 18, 1445 Eastern Daylight Time

The bus carrying Mike Volner and his JSOC team pulled right up to the C-17 Globemaster. As their troops disembarked, Volner and Master Guns Moore walked up to Brian Dawson and Hector Rodriguez, who were loading their gear on the Air Force transport. "Colonel, Hector, good to be working with you two again," Volner said.

"Thank you guys for kitting up so quickly," Dawson replied. "Don't know if this will be the real thing or not, but the boss wants us out in front of this and downrange ASAP."

"I'll sit down with Master Guns and give him the intel we have," Rodriquez added.

Hector Rodriquez was a familiar face to Volner, Moore, and the rest of Op-Center's JSOC team. Rodriquez was born and raised in New York City and enlisted in the Army right out of high school. He came out of boot camp as an infantryman and then joined the 75th Ranger Regiment. He rose to E-7 platoon sergeant in the 75th, and after that, he transferred to the Army's Delta Force. He had completed his active duty—twenty-six years—as the command sergeant major for the Joint Special Operations Command. Rodriquez had been there and done that, and what was more, was a regular visitor to Fort Bragg whenever Volner and his men had a training exercise.

"Thanks, Hector," Dawson replied.

"Colonel—" Volner began, only to be interrupted by Dawson.

"Mike, with all the successes we've had together, getting you to call me Brian instead of colonel is still on my list of failures," Dawson said, breaking out in a false pout.

"I'll work on it . . . ahhh . . . Brian. Do we know where we're headed yet?" Volner asked. He'd received some information by secure text, but not all he felt he needed.

"Not yet, but I think we'll know soon. It's the Mideast for sure, that's why you're in your desert camis. Mr. Williams is still working with the CENTCOM commander to get us where we need to be. My guess is somewhere in Iraq, Balad maybe."

"Right," Volner replied. "But the intel we got says these guys who grabbed the admiral are somehow intent on getting him out of the country and delivering him to Mabad al-Dosari, most likely in Mosul. Don't we need to be within helo-assault range of Mosul?"

"We need to be within striking distance of Mosul;

that's why we're going downrange right now," Dawson replied. "We figure al-Dosari will slit the admiral's throat as soon as he gets his hands on him. The only chance of rescuing the admiral is to intercept him before he reaches Mosul."

"Roger that, sir," Volner replied.

Dawson knew the answer, but had to ask, "Everyone have your full range of weapons and support gear?"

Volner smiled. "We can fight in a back alley or assault a fortified mosque, Colonel—I mean, Brian."

Three hundred miles north of Pope Air Force Base, other men were having a different conversation, but one that also revolved around time. The detours they'd been forced to take to elude the CIRG HRT had thrown their timeline off, so Amer called his confederates packing the refrigerated box. The two men with him in the van heard only his half of a heated conversation.

"No, I told you, we've been running from some law enforcement trucks. Maybe they're CIA, maybe they're FBI, I don't know . . . Yes, we're heading your way now, we're trying to stay off major highways . . . Yes, I know there's a time window for you to deliver that box to the FedEx warehouse . . . I know, I know, but if we get caught by whoever is chasing us then the whole plan falls apart . . . Yes, we need to get off the phone now. Who knows if someone is monitoring us."

Amer and his fellow kidnappers had had their confidence shaken—no, it had been blown apart—when the two CIRG HRT trucks had chased them on Route 1.

And while they had successfully evaded whoever was pursuing them for the moment, the fact that there was at least one helicopter overhead—and likely more—looking for them filled them with dread. Amer held his map as he looked for a way to continue north with the least possibility they'd be seen from above.

"All right, I haven't seen or heard a helicopter for almost ten minutes," he began. "Let's turn right up that street. We'll make another right soon after that, then we'll be on Greenbelt Road; that will take us to the Baltimore-Washington Parkway."

"Isn't that risky?" the man in the back asked. "If they have helicopters, they'll easily see us on that highway."

"I don't think we have a choice," Amer replied, a sense of resignation in his voice. "They can't look everywhere, and this is a popular model van. Maybe we'll just blend in."

The kidnappers made no attempt to talk in whispers, and in the back of the van, Jay Bruner tried to make sense of it all. Going north . . . being chased by law enforcement . . . the BW Parkway . . . someone packing a box in a warehouse? None of it made any sense. One thing he *was* sure of now; this wasn't some low-level car-jacking or even some random local kidnapping. There was an intricate plot in the works and he was the victim. He prayed more earnestly now.

The parking lot and broad lawn at Hyattsville's First United Methodist Church was now filling up. While it might be too little too late, the CIRG HRT had rolled another Mercedes Benz "Sprinter" camper vehicle up from Quantico to function as an additional command post and had called up two more Blackhawk helicopters, as well as a Bell 407 and a Bell 412. The Hyattsville police and Virginia highway patrol had been called upon to block the streets leading to the church to keep "looky-loos" away.

The CIRG on-scene commander called all the command pilots and ground vehicle commanders into the Sprinter to review the search plans for the elusive van that they thought held Bruner.

Three time zones away, Lieutenant Dale Bruner was in his commanding officer's office. "I'm serious, Dale. Take as much time as you need and be with your family. We'll be fine out here," Pete Cummings said.

"I feel bad, Skipper. I'm the new guy, and here I go bailing out on all of you with no notice."

"You forget: You have good people working for you, and you've already gotten them squared away. Family comes first. You flying out tonight?"

"Yes, sir, red-eye out of Lindbergh into Reagan."

"Good. Oh, Dale, don't worry about the little problem back here, I'll take care of it."

"Problem?"

"Yep, we're gonna have to find another single officer to squire around whoever it is my wife invited to the wardroom party."

"Ouch, sir. I'm sure whoever it is will be a better catch than me."

"I doubt it. Take care of yourself—and your

family—and call me if I can do anything." Cummings paused and his look hardened. "And Bruner, I hope to hell they find your dad soon."

"Me too, Skipper."

"You need a ride to the airport?"

"No thanks. I don't know how long I'll be gone, so I'll just park my truck in the long-term lot. Appreciate the offer though."

The object of Dale Bruner's worry was still in the back of the van, but something had changed. Now, instead of twists and turns, slowdowns and speedups, Jay Bruner sensed they were traveling at high speed and in a straight line. And his captors had been strangely quiet for what seemed like the longest time.

It still wasn't making sense to him. What did someone want with him? He was a lowly two-star naval officer. Why would someone kidnap him? For ransom? While he and Meagan no longer lived paycheck to paycheck as they did when he was a Navy lieutenant with three young kids, his family was far from wealthy. He'd done nothing high profile in his career. He was just an ordinary Joe from his point of view.

Things were clarified for him—and not in a good way—as one of his captors spoke.

"Do you think we'll make it in time now?" the driver asked. "We've been on this road for twenty minutes and I haven't seen or heard a helicopter."

"I think we will," Amer replied.

"How long until he gets delivered to al-Dosari?" the man in the back asked.

"Our guys packing the box said the FedEx plane is going to make two stops before it arrives in Mosul, so probably the day after tomorrow, maybe early in the morning."

"Good. When al-Dosari slits his throat—" the driver began to say, only to have Amer put his finger over his lips and shake his head from side to side to silence the man.

Now Bruner knew.

An hour later, in the warehouse, the two men sealed the refrigerated box and then guided it onto the loading dock with a small forklift. They set it down gently on the rollers at the end of the loading dock and then carefully pushed it into the truck. Then they drove toward the FedEx hangar to make their scheduled rendezvous with the FedEx flight departing BWI in less than an hour.

CHAPTER TWELVE

FEDEX FLIGHT 1652

July 18, 1915 Eastern Daylight Time

"How come we keep getting these runs to the Mideast?" the copilot asked.

"Hey, what are you complaining about?" the senior pilot replied. "I know we've had to take these flights to third world shitholes a lot, but we had that cross-country run yesterday, so we'll run out of our crew day once we get to London. I think Baker and Pels are taking over from us there. We'll be 'stuck' in London for thirty-six hours before we pick up our flight heading back to the States. If we can't find a way to enjoy that, then something's wrong."

"Yeah, I get that," the copilot replied.

"Nothing like flying these routes to the sandbox to make you appreciate the good old U.S. of A."

"Amen to that, brother."

* * *

Aboard another flight heading across the Atlantic, four men were engaged in a far more serious discussion than the two FedEx pilots.

Brian Dawson, Hector Rodriquez, Mike Volner, and Charles Moore were huddled around a small, makeshift table in the C-17 Globemaster as it headed east at just over five hundred knots. Their aircraft had just taken a drink from a KC-135 Stratotanker from the 186th Air Refueling Wing of the Mississippi Air National Guard. They had enough gas to make it the rest of the way across the Atlantic, and Dawson had just spoken to the Op-Center director and now had additional clarification about their mission.

"I've just finished talking with Mr. Williams," Dawson began, raising his voice to be heard over the howling of the Globemaster's four Pratt and Whitney PW2000 engines. "He said we're going to do another airborne refueling over the Mediterranean, and then we're going to land at Baghdad International."

"Not Balad?" Volner asked, knowing Balad was closer to Mosul. Dawson just shook his head.

"What then?" Moore blurted out. He knew this mission was important, but knowing so little this close to getting to the area of operations still bothered him.

"Well, we're not sure yet, Master Guns. We're working off anticipatory intelligence we got from the Geek Tank, and for now, it's all we've got."

"I got it, Mr. Dawson; but do we know anything about what happens once we land in Baghdad?"

"All the intel we have tells us that Mabad al-Dosari had Admiral Bruner kidnapped so he could be brought to him in his compound in Mosul. Once he gets him there, we fear the worst, so our goal is to intercept him before al-Dosari gets his hands on him."

"But if al-Dosari is in Mosul, why don't we fly directly into Mosul airport? ISIL doesn't control that any more, does it?" Volner asked.

"You're right, it doesn't," Dawson replied. "The Iraqi Army and our coalition forces pushed ISIL out of the airport two months ago. But ISIL still controls central Mosul, and whatever lines there are between them and the forces trying to push them out of Mosul are fluid at best. It's too dangerous to land an American military aircraft there. This Globemaster would be too inviting a target. Hector, you were in on that part of the conversation, why don't you take it from here?"

"Sure," Rodriquez began. "Duncan Sutherland, who leads our logistics shop at Op-Center, talked with the J-4 folks at CENTCOM earlier today. The CENTCOM commander will have a fleet of Humvees standing by at Baghdad International. We'll take them overland north to the Mosul Airport—it's about two hundred fifty miles over pretty rough terrain."

It was Volner again. "No helos?"

Again, Dawson shook his head. "ISIL has too many listeners out there, and a small column of Humvees draws a lot less attention than helos; so we drive."

Aaron Bleich liked challenges. His director had given him one, and he had mobilized his Geek Tank team to take it on. And while McCord and Bleich ran a flat organization and there wasn't a set chain of command below Bleich, Maggie Scott had the bit in her teeth and was his de facto number two for this operation.

"Okay, show me," Bleich said as he hunched over Maggie's triple-screen monitors.

"The FBI is still trying to catch the van, and we'll know more when we know more, but it's all but certain they're headed to BWI and may even be there already," Scott began. "We figured if the guys who work somewhere up near BWI didn't take the van to work, they must have taken the car this Amer guy rented—"

"But we haven't found that yet, right? Or have you?"

"Well, the bad news is no traffic or other cams triggered on the license plate. But we know many rent-a-car companies have their own LoJack-type systems built into their cars so they can recover them if they're stolen—"

"And this car had one of those?"

"Yes. And I pushed this to Mr. McCord and he had our logistics folks call the rent-a-car company and ask them to locate the car for us. But they got all official—the assholes—and said if the car wasn't stolen, they couldn't give us the info—"

"And?" Bleich asked.

"Well, we could have gone several ways. One would be for Mr. Sutherland to rag on them and try to be more convincing. Or he could have bumped it up to Ms. Sullivan or even to Mr. Williams—or we just could get the info ourselves."

"Maggie, are you telling me you hacked into the rent-a-car company's servers?"

"Yeah, Aaron; I know I should have asked you first.

But you were busy getting Mr. Dawson and the JSOC team the info they needed—"

"You did the right thing. So what did you get?"

"The car is right here," she said, pointing to the far right-hand screen. "And if I superimpose this Google Earth display you can see it's in the parking lot of a warehouse up near BWI. I've got to think that's where the van is taking—or took—the admiral. I think we need to roll the FBI CIRG units north—or have our team at Quantico head up there right now."

"I agree, let's grab Roger and go see Mr. Williams."

In Mosul, one of his lieutenants had just left, and Mabad al-Dosari was talking with his number two.

"Why couldn't we put him on another flight— maybe a DHL flight or another one that would come directly here without stopping?"

The man had been through this with him before, but there was nothing to be gained by telling him that. All al-Dosari was focused on was getting his hands on Bruner and slitting his throat on the Internet. "FedEx is the only cargo carrier that flies into Mosul any more—"

"That isn't true!" al-Dosari shot back. "Just last week there were several Emirates SkyCargo flights as well as at least one DHL flight. Why didn't we use one of those?"

The man could see that the ISIS leader was agitated, so he worked mightily to spin his response in a positive way. "Look, this so-called coalition still says they're going to push us out of Mosul. You and I know that's not going to happen, but the battle rages every day, and the cargo airlines are mindful of who controls the southeastern part of the city near the airport. A few weeks ago, the Iraqi Army had pushed us up toward the northwest—remember how quickly we had to move our base?—and the airport appeared more secure to many. That's why the cargo airlines felt free to use it again. If they can make money and feel they aren't risking getting blown out of the sky, they're going to fly into Mosul."

Al-Dosari considered this for a moment. He knew he had the man's loyalty, but he was still frustrated beyond words. He wanted Bruner in his hands now.

"But you're sure this FedEx flight will land here, even if the others seem worried about the safety of their precious aircraft?"

His number two patiently explained how FedEx had become the world's biggest cargo carrier and how the U.S. military used them because they often found it cheaper to ship that way than to send equipment on a military cargo plane—especially if it was something like a high-priority repair part. He told al-Dosari how their men had learned through social media that FedEx was bringing supplies for American and coalition forces trying to dislodge ISIS from the city. Finally, he told his leader that the flight their contact picked was bringing not only a large number of repair parts and other military supplies for coalition forces, but also other cargo for businesses in the city. He finished his explanation and figured al-Dosari was satisfied. But the questioning continued.

"But this FedEx flight makes several stops, right?"

"Yes, the flight's airborne now. It lands in London, then flies to Damascus, then Mosul, and then on to Baghdad."

"And after the plane lands, what then?"

His number two sighed and continued. He told al-Dosari that FedEx had a small, rented warehouse at the Mosul airport and that all cargo for Mosul would first be brought there. He then explained how FedEx didn't let anyone pick up from their warehouses and how in places where they didn't have their own fleet of trucks—like Mosul—they subcontracted delivery companies to transport everything. Those were the rules, he explained further, but since they were in a "war zone" FedEx let the U.S. military come to the warehouse to pick up whatever they had coming on their flights because the U.S. didn't want ground carriers they couldn't vouch for carrying their supplies. Al-Dosari still wasn't satisfied.

"You're telling me we can't go to the FedEx warehouse and get the box our hostage is in? We need to wait to have it delivered?"

"Yes, but it won't take long. We have control of an import-export business in Mosul. We also operate a local trucking service. A truck will be waiting at the FedEx warehouse and once FedEx does the paperwork, the trucking service will bring the box to the address we specified. It's only about a half kilometer from here. When the box gets there, we'll be waiting—"

"And there'll be no foul-ups?" al-Dosari interrupted.

"Don't worry. We'll be watching the airport when the plane lands. We control more of this area than the so-called coalition force thinks we do," his number two replied, smiling.

Minutes after McCord, Bleich, and Scott had left his office, Williams put in a call to the FBI director. The call was brief and to the point: The search for the van should continue, but CIRG HRT units needed to move and move fast. All their intel told them Admiral Bruner was going to be packed up and shipped out of the country—if it hadn't happened already.

The director responded immediately. He diverted two of his helos searching for the van, had them load up two SWAT teams, and then had them land in the parking lot next to the warehouse the Geek Tank had identified. The car they had been alerted to earlier was gone.

The director watched from a GoPro camera feed as one of his SWAT elements blew the door with a breaching charge, moments before the second team knocked down another door on the far side of the warehouse. Both teams moved quickly and professionally. In the dim light, red IR-gunsight laser dots flashed around the warehouse and the palletized stores. It was a textbook operation, well coordinated and executed with precision. But a quick search by the sensitive-site exploitation teams who followed the assaulters yielded nothing but routine FedEx shipments—palletized and ready for aircraft loading.

Minutes later, the director reported this to Chase Williams. Williams thanked him, but he too had followed the action through the GoPro feed, courtesy of the hackers in the Geek Tank. Williams then called McCord, Bleich, and Scott into his office.

CHAPTER THIRTEEN

July 19, 1630 Arabia Standard Time

The Globemaster pilot threw his four engines into reverse and stopped well short of the midway point of runway 33-right. He taxied the C-17 off into a separate enclave at Baghdad International—Al Muthana Air Base—home to the 23rd Iraqi Air Force Squadron. The U.S. Air Force pilots pulled up next to an Iraqi Air Force C-130 Hercules, and braked to a stop.

Brian Dawson was the first to alight from their aircraft and was met by Captain Jack Larkin of the 75th Ranger Regiment. "How was your flight, Colonel?"

"The best kind, smooth and uneventful."

"Great, Colonel—"

"It's Brian, Captain, I'm a civilian."

"Got it, sir. As soon as your team disembarks, we've got some chow set up for them inside the hangar here," he said, pointing to the closest open hangar at Al Muthana. "This is a pretty active base for the Iraqi Air

Force, especially for their Russian Su-25s working the fight against ISIL, but the CENTCOM commander told us your team was top priority. Once you're all unloaded and fed, we've got the Humvees and gear you requested standing by and ready to go."

"I appreciate it. I knew we could count on you. Rangers lead the way, right?"

"Right, sir. There is one thing. My guys are pretty familiar with the conditions on the ground here, and it's still a hazardous trip up to Mosul. The terrain sucks, and there's always the threat from ISIL on those open roads. The commander wanted my guys to be your drivers, but we needed to be sure that was all right with you all first. We know you have a presidential mandate, so it's totally your call."

"Happy to be traveling with the 75th Rangers, Jack. We packed as light as we could, so it shouldn't take long to load up our gear and yours. Can we be heading north in, say, an hour?"

"You got it, sir; and there's something else. We've been briefed you'll be looking for a human hostage, so we've been instructed to drive one of our Humvees up with your convoy. That truck will be carrying two canines and their handlers. The dogs are on call for disaster relief situations where they're used for finding humans buried in rubble. But the powers that be thought they'd be helpful for what you need to do."

Dawson was used to working with a team with a small footprint—and this was starting to sound big and unwieldy. Nonetheless, he saw the logic in having the canine team.

"Glad to have 'em, Captain. They may come in handy."

Seven time zones away, it was early morning at the Bruner home in Springfield, Virginia. The vice chief of naval operations, an aviator like Jay Bruner who had served with him years ago at OLA, was given the unenviable task of telling Meagan Bruner and her children the news—and it wasn't good.

Based on all available evidence, it was clear that ISIL had kidnapped their husband and father and had successfully gotten him out of the country and that it was likely he was going to be delivered to Mabad al-Dosari. The Bruners had been alerted that the VCNO was going to make this call, and Meagan had steeled herself and her three children—Dale had just arrived earlier that morning—for the news.

Meagan answered the door, "Admiral Oldham, nice to see you again. How's Carol?"

"She's fine, Meagan. And I wish we were meeting under different circumstances."

"I do too. But come and please tell us what you know."

Admiral Eric Oldham walked into their living room, and the surprise on his face showed. He had expected to see the Bruners' two daughters, but not their son, Dale.

Meagan broke the ice, "Admiral Oldham, Dale just completed a sea tour with the SEAL teams. He's on shore duty now at Naval Special Warfare Command.

I told him he didn't need to come home, but his commanding officer insisted."

"Dale, it's good to see you. Your dad tells me you saw some exciting action with the teams. You'll have to catch me up on all that, but perhaps at another time. Amber, Katherine," he said to the Bruners' daughters.

They were all seated in the Bruners' small living room, and four sets of eyes were riveted on Oldham. "What I'm going to tell you is up to date as of about an hour ago," he began, looking at his watch, "but the situation is still fluid. Most of what we know we've gotten from the FBI and from an organization called Op-Center. You might remember Admiral Chase Williams, Meagan; he's the former PACOM and CENTCOM commander. He runs Op-Center for the president."

"Oh yes, I do remember him, Admiral."

Having Meagan Bruner, whom he and his wife knew socially, keep calling him "Admiral" wasn't making this any easier for Oldham. But he didn't have any choice except to plunge ahead.

"I'm afraid the news we have isn't good, but I can tell you that we've got a full court press on to get Jay back just as soon as we can."

With that Oldham poured out the entire story. As he did, first Amber, and then Katherine started crying. Finally he was finished.

Dale Bruner waited for his mother to speak, but when she didn't, he jumped in. "Admiral, if we're sure my dad was smuggled out of BWI a few hours ago, whatever flight he's on must still be airborne. Can't we intercept it and force it to turn around. We can do that, can't we?"

"Your instincts are right, Dale, and that's why I said this is all very fluid. Nailing just what flight your dad might be on is our number-one priority. If we can figure that out, then we can do just what you suggest. But it's what we don't know that's making this difficult. What we do know for sure is that your dad was carjacked at the Metro station park-and-ride, transferred to a van somewhere near Hyattsville, and then the van eluded the FBI HRT and it made it up to BWI. We found the warehouse where they evidently put your dad in some sort of refrigerated box and then loaded him on a plane—likely a commercial cargo plane headed east, probably to the Middle East."

Now Meagan Bruner was crying, and Dale moved to put his arm around her.

"We have our entire intelligence community—as well as the intel assets this Op-Center organization has—focused on nailing down just what aircraft your dad is on. Additionally, and I can share this with you only if you agree it goes no further than the family—"

"Yes, of course, Admiral," Meagan offered.

"This organization, Op-Center—and I have to confess I don't know a lot about them—evidently they can move even faster than our military can and go to places where no one else is authorized to go. They already went downrange and are heading to Iraq as we speak. So if worse comes to worst and we can't intercept the flight as you suggest, Dale, we'll have the Op-Center squad on the ground. ISIL won't get your dad."

The family continued to question Oldham, searching for some shred of information that might give them hope that Jay Bruner would be brought back to them alive. But Oldham's answer to each of their questions only deepened their terror.

Chase Williams insisted that all his principal assistants go home—he felt in his gut this operation was going to be a marathon and not a sprint, and he didn't want them to be burned out. They all had complied except Roger McCord. His Geek Tank was going to keep at it all night until they cracked just where Admiral Bruner was, and if his people were going to be working through the night, he insisted on being there too.

When Williams arrived at Op-Center at 0630, he headed directly for the Geek Tank. Aaron Bleich's world was the most secure space in Op-Center's warren of subterranean offices. Williams placed his hand on the palm-print reader next to the steel door. Then his eyes drifted up above the door. He had looked at it a hundred times, but the sign always made him shake his head. It read: *Abandon Hope, All Ye Who Enter Here.*

Williams could see instantly that his Geek Tank team had pulled an all-nighter. Empty boxes of Thai takeout food as well as Starbucks drink containers, 7-Eleven Big Gulp cups, smoothie drink cups, and other trash littered their spaces. Bleich's self-named misfits looked even more disheveled than usual as some sat in front of computer screens while others chatted in small groups. The Geek Tankers were attired mainly in blue jeans and T-shirts, with an occasional techie wearing Dockers and a sweatshirt. A Sara Bareilles song drifted across the room. It looked more like a student union than the most sophisticated intelligence outfit in or out of government.

Bleich and McCord came up to Williams. "Mornin', boss," McCord began, a small smile showing on his otherwise haggard face. "We know more than we knew last night. Aaron can give you the data dump."

"Go ahead, Aaron," Williams began. "I know your people have been at it all night and I appreciate it."

"Here's what we know," Bleich began. "During the night, we basically played process-of-elimination with flights launching out of BWI and heading east—"

"And there were a lot of 'em," McCord added.

"Anyway, as Mr. McCord said, lots of flights. But before I get ahead of myself, we nailed down *what* the admiral was packed up in. As you know, the FBI HRT raided the warehouse where we spotted the car that this Amer guy rented. There was no packing crate, but there was strong evidence that a box had been packed up with peaches—"

"Peaches?" Williams asked.

"Yes, sir, peaches," Bleich replied. "Seems that Maryland is a pretty big peach-growing state, and they export peaches worldwide, and evidently, especially to the Mideast this time of year. Anyway, we pulsed all the local fruit and vegetable shippers around Hyattsville and found one, Arnold's Fruits and Vegetables, that had contracted for a $10 \times 10 \times 6$ refrigerated box to pack up a load of peaches destined for a company in Iraq—actually one in Mosul—"

"That nails it! Great work, Aaron!" Williams said.

"Well, not exactly, boss. The way this shipping business works . . . umm . . . it's a little weird and is all second- and third-party stuff. All Arnold's Fruits and Vegetables knows is their shipment is going to Mosul to an export-import business there. They just pay to have it packed and shipped, but they have no idea how it gets there—commercial flight, cargo flight, even private carrier—"

Bleich looked up and saw Williams's face sag. "But we know more than that. Armed with the size of the box, the fact that it's refrigerated, and the fact it has tamper-proof locks, we eliminated a lot of possibilities—"

"Go on," Williams urged.

McCord and Bleich walked the Op-Center director through their analysis. The size of the box they believed Bruner had been packed in ruled out any private aircraft like a Gulfstream. Major passenger airlines were eliminated because they had a policy of not accepting locked cargo for security reasons. That left commercial cargo carriers.

Bleich and his Geek Tank had mined ISIL's social media posts, and everything they picked up strongly suggested al-Dosari was going to have the hostage delivered to him in Mosul. And due to the fighting in and around Mosul, most commercial carriers considered it too risky to land at Mosul's airport. But one carrier still flew into Mosul. FedEx had a major contract with DoD to deliver high-priority items—mostly repair parts—to United States and coalition forces fighting ISIL in Iraq. The Iraqi Army and many of the coalition forces fighting the Islamic State had a great deal of American gear, and it was urgent these repair parts continued to flow into the Mosul airport. McCord and Bleich were confident in what their anticipatory intelligence was telling them.

"Everything points to a FedEx plane with Mosul as a destination," McCord offered.

"I'm thinking that if we'd identified a specific flight, you'd have told me already," Williams replied. "So how many FedEx flights, Aaron, at the outside, do we think we have to be prepared to intercept?"

"Six, sir."

"Six? Have any of those six flights reached Mosul yet?"

"No, that's the good news. Every flight that left in the widest possible window that could be carrying that box with the admiral has one stop to make, and some have to make two, en route to Mosul. And not all the routes are the same. The other news, though, is even after Ms. Sullivan and Mr. Sutherland flew to Memphis to make a personal appeal to the FedEx CEO, they couldn't persuade him to divert any of those flights to somewhere where we could intercept them before they landed at Mosul. They tried, boss, but there were too many "what ifs" and "maybes" to satisfy him.

Plus, DoD would be howling for those parts if they were delayed."

"What now?" Williams asked.

"The good news is that Ms. Sullivan and Mr. Sutherland *were* able to convince FedEx's CEO to agree to let our team populate their temporary warehouse at the Mosul airport," McCord replied. "He's providing us with FedEx uniforms, ID badges, the whole works. We know for certain how to identify the box the admiral is in, and we'll meet each one of those six flights as they arrive in Mosul. One of them will have the box with Admiral Bruner, and we'll grab him before the box gets delivered to the target business in Mosul—likely an ISIL front."

"When is the first of those six flights landing in Mosul?" Williams asked.

"In about three hours," Bleich added. "We've spoken with Mr. Dawson and our team will be there, suited up and ready."

"Good work. Keep the press on. I'll be in my office. Ms. Sullivan and Mr. Sutherland back from Memphis yet?"

"Yes sir, they got in a few hours ago. Ms. Sullivan's standing by for your morning meeting."

Twenty-five miles north-northeast of Op-Center's headquarters, in Hyattsville, Maryland, the last of the FBI CIRG command vehicles was pulling out of the parking lot of the First United Methodist Church. The HRT teams all left in a somber mood, disappointed they weren't able to catch the kidnappers and rescue the hostage even after they had them nearly in their grasp.

Before they departed, the FBI director went to their site and had told them they had done everything they could to rescue Admiral Bruner. They had not failed, he emphasized, and now they just had to leave it to others to rescue the admiral. He told them if anyone could intercept Bruner before he fell into ISIL hands, it was Op-Center. Sincere and on-point as his pep talk was, it did little to brighten their mood. They were professionals—this is what they did—but they *had* failed.

The two hundred fifty-mile journey over some of the roughest terrain in Iraq had been bone jarring, but Dawson, Rodriquez, and their JSOC team had arrived at the Mosul airport in good time. Once there, the senior FedEx man on the ground briefed them on the agreement his CEO had made with Op-Center. Within an hour, four members of Volner's team, led by Master Guns Moore, were attired as FedEx workers and were lounging in the warehouse at Mosul airport waiting for the first of six FedEx flights to arrive. Volner and the rest of his team, along with Dawson and Rodriquez, had taken up concealed overwatch positions on a small bluff on the airport perimeter.

Situated in a small tent with the uniformed members of the JSOC team, JSOC civilian Laurie Phillips set up her gear. She would provide the direct conduit back to Op-Center headquarters and to the Geek Tank.

One of the first things Volner had done when Laurie had arrived at Fort Bragg was to take her to Op-Center to meet all the players—and especially Aaron Bleich and his Geek Tank team. She had hit it off with Bleich, and it was clear that his team would always pull out all the stops to provide Laurie and "her" JSOC squad with all the real-time info they could.

"You good to go, Laurie?" Volner asked as he ducked into her tent. The tent was attended by a small generator and a heavily filtered air-conditioning system to try to protect Laurie's gear from the constantly blowing sand.

"Yes, sir. I've got the UHF satellite feed up and running and had a good comms check with the Op-Center watch floor, as well as the Geek Tank. Just so you know, they pulled an all-nighter there to get us what we need—"

"They're good people."

"That's for sure. And thanks for going with my suggestion to use the CENTCOM Global Hawk to provide eyes in the sky for this operation. With ISIL being this close to where we are, we'll need any edge we can get."

"Glad we could make it happen," Volner began. Then smiling, he continued. "It's kind of come full circle for you with these birds since your time as a CNA analyst aboard *Normandy*, hasn't it?"

Laurie Phillips smiled too. It had been Volner and his team that had snatched her out of Saudi Arabia after a rogue Saudi prince had shot down the U.S. Navy helicopter Sandee Barron and Laurie had been flying.

They had tried to get to the bottom of what Laurie had been convinced were false Global Hawk video feeds showing a purported terrorist camp in Syria that was actually a faux camp. The camp had been constructed in Saudi Arabia as part of the prince's plot to have the United States attack Syria. But their decision to take that flight had begun with Laurie's close analysis of Global Hawk video. She'd likely prevented a war—but was cashiered out of the CNA anyway.

"Well, it sure as hell has, Major. But don't worry, I'm not looking to go rogue on you on this op."

Volner considered this for a moment, then hunched down into a squat so he could be eye level with Laurie. "Look, Laurie, we never have really talked about this, so now maybe it's time. I know Mr. Williams was intent on finding a way to get you a soft landing after those idiots at CNA showed you the door. That was 'push' on his part, but there was a lot of 'pull' on our part I suspect no one ever told you about—"

"Pull, sir?"

"Look, Laurie, you were a Marine back in the day so I know you understand how the military works. Given the kinds of ops JSOC gets involved in, we don't have to recruit—we have a constant stream of uniformed and civilian people knocking on our door wanting to join this organization. We have our pick of literally scores of analysts who can do what you do. But none of them have been there and done that like you have, and none of them—and I'll say this carefully—none of them have brass ones like you have. I don't need people standing around waiting for permission—I need people like you who're willing to do what they need to do to get the job done and take their lumps if they need to. I think I've got the right person."

"I won't let you or the team down, sir."

"I know you won't. Okay, I've got to talk with Master Guns. He's down in the warehouse. He's got to get ready to receive the next FedEx flight."

"Nada on the first two flights so far, Major?"

"Zero for two."

Two FedEx flights had arrived in the past five hours, unloaded all their cargo destined for Mosul, picked up some small amounts of freight, and departed. Neither flight had contained a $10 \times 10 \times 6$ refrigerated box with tamper-proof locks. Moore and his FedEx-clad team had inspected every box big enough to hold a human, and the canines they'd brought along proved their worth, sniffing and then turning away from about a dozen boxes each time. Now they waited for the next FedEx flight, due to arrive in about an hour and a half.

Trevor Harward entered the Oval knowing President Midkiff had just finished reading another one of Chase Williams's POTUS/OC Eyes Only memos updating him on the search for Jay Bruner. He knew the president was frustrated, and he had worked with him long enough to be prepared for this meeting.

"Mr. President," Harward began as he and Wyatt Midkiff sat down in the conversational area in front of the president's desk. "Anything new from Chase?"

"No, only that his JSOC team is on station at the

Mosul airport. Two FedEx flights have come and gone and Admiral Bruner wasn't aboard either one. There are four more flights due over the next six hours or so; we're confident they'll get him."

"Chase has good people working for him. If anyone can get the admiral, they can."

"I'm still disappointed our FBI CIRG people lost him after having him in sight."

"We all are, Mr. President. I've spoken with the attorney general already. He knows the FBI director started this op with too light a footprint. It won't happen again."

"It damn well better not."

"It won't, sir."

The president and his national security advisor sat in companionable silence before Harward addressed the 800-pound gorilla looming over them. "Mr. President, what's happening here is unprecedented. A terrorist group on our soil snatching a senior military officer off the streets and getting him out of the country so those they're in league with can assassinate him. It's dreadful, Mr. President."

Harward and the president embarked on an earnest conversation about the implications of what had already happened and how the impact would be even worse if Jay Bruner weren't rescued. The effect on the U.S. military could be profound. Would the U.S. military commander about to strike an enemy stop and think about terrorists on U.S. soil taking retribution on him or her—or their family? Would that cause military commanders to stop and think before they attacked enemies of the United States, or would this concern cause them to start being selective about whom they attacked? The more they talked, the more worried they became.

"I'm counting on Chase's people to get Admiral Bruner back, but I feel we have to do something, anything, to help."

"I know it's not what you want to hear, Mr. President, but for now, all we can do is wait."

Dale Bruner wasn't one to wait. He had spent the morning being with and consoling his mother and sisters and sharing their grief and their dread. Now he felt trapped. He wanted to do something, but before he could do anything, he needed to know more. In the small, tight-knit SEAL community, it wasn't hard to find where people were assigned. He had made the call and the man had agreed to meet with him in his Pentagon office that afternoon.

CHAPTER FOURTEEN

July 19, 1915 Arabia Standard Time

The next FedEx flight was due in less than fifteen minutes, so Moore and the three other JSOC men dressed as FedEx workers lounged casually in and around the FedEx hangar at Mosul airport—or as casually as they could in the 110-degree early evening Mosul heat. Real FedEx workers who had been read into the operation manned two forklifts and would unload the inbound FedEx flight, this one a twin-engine Boeing 767-300 long-range, wide-body jet.

Once all the cargo was moved into the warehouse, Moore and his team would send away the FedEx forklift drivers, close the building's doors, and bring the canines and their handlers out of the room where they were hidden. They'd look for the $10 \times 10 \times 6$ refrigerated box first, but the dogs would sniff out every bit of cargo.

* * *

At Op-Center, Chase Williams met with his deputy, Anne Sullivan. It was their normal morning meeting— but one delayed a bit while Williams parked in the Geek Tank, gathering all the intel he could. Williams and Sullivan had been together at Op-Center from the beginning—she was his first hire.

While Williams had had many tours in Washington during his thirty-five years in uniform, he never considered himself a Washington insider. Each tour in Washington had been brief—usually two years or less—a blessing from his perspective. But the downside was he never had the time, or the inclination, to get into the political minutia that actually made this city run. That's why he had recruited Sullivan—and hard.

Anne Sullivan was from money—old money—and had retired as a GSA supergrade at age fifty-five. She had been content to live out the remaining decades of her life enjoying the art and culture Washington had to offer before Chase Williams—in her words— charmed her into taking the number two spot at Op-Center. They were simpatico but were also yin and yang, as each brought completely different strengths to the job.

Williams and Sullivan sat sipping the dark roast Sumatra blend coffee that seemed to drip endlessly from the coffee maker Williams had installed in his office. His office—by design much smaller than Sullivan's— looked more like a small shipboard office Williams had occupied multiple times during his Navy career as a surface warfare officer. His Krups XP604050 drip coffee machine was the only thing in his office that passed for an indulgence.

Sullivan had just finished debriefing him on her mostly unsuccessful trip to Memphis to try to persuade the FedEx CEO to divert his Mideast-bound flights. Williams could tell his number two was down.

"It's okay. I know if there were a way to persuade their CEO to turn those flights around, you and Duncan would have done it," Williams began. "But you did the next best thing. From what Brian is telling me downrange, he's given us everything we could have wanted—and more—especially using their warehouse as the place we'll grab Admiral Bruner. That's a win in my book."

"Thanks, boss. It'll be a win when we get him back to the States and reunited with his family."

"That's for sure. You said you had something else for me, something you've sniffed out?"

"I do. I've still got friends on the National Security Council, and what they've told me should come as no surprise. But it should reinforce the decision you helped the president make a while ago to allow Op-Center to get involved in domestic counter-terrorism."

"I think we proved that when we thwarted that attack on the U.N. Headquarters a while ago."

"You're right, we did. And based on what my friends on the NSC tell me, maybe after this op is over and Admiral Bruner is brought home, we should lean forward on the domestic side just a little bit more."

"Does this have something to do with the FBI not

being able to intercept the admiral before he was taken out of the country?"

"No, it has *everything* to do with it," Sullivan replied. "My contacts at NSC tell me that the president gave the attorney general an old-fashioned ass-chewing over this and told him to get rid of the FBI director immediately. The best the AG could do was to convince the president to let the director resign on his own for whatever reason he wanted to come up with. But at that, the president said he needed to be out of his office before the end of the week. I heard a search committee has already been formed to find his replacement."

"That's great intel, Anne. I'll talk with Jim Wright and have him broach this with Allen Kim down at Quantico. I'm sure they're talking with the FBI CIRG folks down there anyway, but knowing the president might be willing to let us use Allen and his team more often is valuable. Anything else?"

"Only that there's nothing any of us can do to get Aaron and his team to leave the building until we get Admiral Bruner back. I've had Duncan bring in futons so they can get some sleep, and NGA has been helpful in keeping their gym open twenty-four hours so the team can freshen up and shower," Sullivan said, referring to the National Geospatial-Intelligence Agency that occupied the building above Op-Center's subterranean offices. "If this goes beyond another day, I'll talk with them about keeping a skeleton crew on duty to man their cafeteria at night."

"Hmm . . . from the looks of it, our team does pretty well with take-out."

"Yeah, boss, but we want these kids to grow old gracefully like you and me. They keep eating that junk and their arteries will clog up before they're forty."

Williams just smiled. Anne Sullivan had never married, and given the senior positions she had had during her GSA career, she had rarely spent much time with twenty- or even thirty-somethings. The Op-Center director figured it was the unfulfilled mother hen in her that caused her to take a protective role with the Geek Tank.

"Well, I'm all for that. Let's keep my coffee away from them too."

At the other end of Op-Center's subterranean warren, Aaron Bleich and his team were in overdrive—pumping intel to Laurie Phillips and her JSOC squad downrange. While the FedEx CEO had promised full cooperation and was doing his best to deliver it, the further this instruction had to trickle down the FedEx chain of command, the more it lost in translation.

"Someone" was supposed to provide Op-Center with cargo manifests for each of the six flights that might have Jay Bruner aboard. That hadn't happened quickly enough for Bleich, so he had Maggie Scott hack into their servers—they were more secure than most others, so it took her a while—but she'd done it.

A weary Aaron Bleich looked up from his computer monitor to see the Goth-clad Scott standing in his doorway, right below the sign above his door that read *Senior Hall Monitor.*

"Aaron, this is the one!"

"The one what, Maggie?"

"The FedEx flight that's landing at Mosul in a few minutes is the one with a $10 \times 10 \times 6$ refrigerated box. That's where they've packed up Admiral Bruner."

Bleich leapt up. "Great work, Maggie. You tell our JSOC team yet?"

"Yes, I sent it to Laurie. She said it was timely, as the flight was already talking to the Mosul airport tower."

"Perfect!" Bleich exclaimed. Let's grab Roger and go tell the boss!"

Room 5A524 was one of hundreds of nondescript Pentagon offices far from the building's prestigious "E-Ring." The E-Ring had the only Pentagon offices with windows facing outward toward the green lawns that surrounded the building. That was why the E-Ring contained the impressive, well-appointed workplaces of senior military and civilian officials who oversaw the day-to-day activities of the tens of thousands who came to work in the world's biggest office building every day.

In this tiny office—no more than four jammed-together cubicles with cheap faux-wood desks, far-from-state-of-the-art computers, and phone and computer wires running everywhere in a hopeless tangle—Lieutenant Dale Bruner and Commander Patrick Kissel were having an earnest conversation in Kissel's small cubicle. What passed for a "view" were the perpetually grimy windows and bird-shit-stained walls of an office on the Pentagon's "B-ring." The wall and windows were less than twenty feet away.

Bruner had told his former commanding officer little over the phone, but once seated in his cubicle in the borrowed chair of an absent coworker, he poured out the entire story. Kissel had been more than a commanding officer—he had been a mentor to Bruner during his time with the teams. Now Kissel was doing his "purgatory tour"—as he called it—in the Pentagon as one of the few SEALS on the Navy staff. He was assigned to the innocuous-sounding "Naval Expeditionary Warfare Directorate," N-95 for short. The directorate was an odd duck on the Navy staff in that it was headed by a Marine Corps general. And since SEALs—in spite of their heroics in the field—remained odd ducks in a Navy still dominated by surface, submarine, and aviation "tribes," N-95 seemed the logical place to stash Navy SEALs on the CNO staff.

"Dale, I can't tell you how sorry I am to hear about your dad," Kissel began. "But from what you've told me about the VCNO visiting your home, it sounds like getting him back has everyone's full attention—"

"It may have their attention, Skipper. But I'm not hearing about anyone doing anything to bring him back—at least not in any detail."

"You told me Admiral Oldham said this Op-Center organization was in Iraq and was primed to intercept your dad and bring him home before he falls into ISIL's hands."

"He did, Skipper. And my folks have known Admiral Oldham and his family for years. I trust what he says, but I don't know what this 'Op-Center' is, and I don't know what they're capable—or not capable—of. But I do know we have our own forces in Iraq—hell, we've got fellow SEALs on the ground there advising the Iraqis and other coalition forces. Why can't they be part of the rescue effort?"

"The short answer is, I don't know. But you told me Admiral Oldham said retired Admiral Chase Williams is the director of this Op-Center. I know he finished his active duty before you started yours, so you probably don't know much about him. But I do—"

"You do?" Bruner asked, his face brightening for the first time.

"Yeah, I do. He was the CENTCOM Commander when I was a first-tour SEAL in Iraq. He was the kind of leader who we felt was really one of us. He got the mission done, but took care of his people—to a fault."

"So you're saying Op-Center can get him back?"

"What I'm saying is Admiral Williams is a pro's pro. As much as you, or me, or anyone else might want to help, throwing more bodies at the problem likely won't help—and it might just muck things up."

Bruner paused to consider this. "Well, Skipper, I guess that makes sense—"

"But tell you what. I've been working in this adult day care center long enough to know how to sniff around and find things out. I'll do a little digging and let you know ASAP what I learn, fair enough?"

"Fair enough, and thanks."

"You don't need to thank me; just get the hell out of here and go take care of your mom. I'm married, and I have kids, and I know what it is to fret. Your mom is worried and you need to be with her, copy?"

"Copy, Skipper."

Once the FedEx forklift drivers had finished unloading Flight 1652, Moore and his team quickly closed the warehouse doors and surveyed the cargo. There were almost two dozen boxes of varying sizes on the floor of the warehouse, but most importantly, the refrigerated box that contained Jay Bruner.

"Let's go, this is the one. Bring those cutters over here and snip those two locks now!" Moore said to one of his men.

The man complied, and as the locks fell away, the two of them pulled open the hinged door on the side of the box. They dug into the piles of peaches and began scooping them out, sending them rolling across the floor of the warehouse.

"We need some help here," Moore shouted to his other two men, and soon the four of them were all pulling out thousands of tightly packed peaches. The men worked feverishly, intent on getting the hostage out.

Soon the box was completely empty. "He's not here!" Moore exclaimed, as the other JSOC men looked on in shock.

"Get the canines to sniff each of the other boxes and then let's open each one," Moore said. "Maybe there's been a mix-up, and he's in one of these other boxes."

Twenty minutes later, every box that came off the now-departed FedEx flight had been opened and emptied. Jay Bruner simply was not there.

Less than a mile north of the airport, two ISIS fighters dressed as construction workers sat on the roof of a half-constructed building and looked through Steiner T42 Tactical 10×42 binoculars stolen from the Iraqi Army.

"They took the cargo into the warehouse almost an hour ago," the first man said. "They should have begun loading the delivery trucks waiting at the gate by now."

"You're right," the second man replied. "Look, our truck is third in line and nothing's moving. Something's not right."

"I'm calling al-Dosari," his partner replied.

"You're sure, Master Guns?" Volner asked.

"I'm damn sure, sir. We opened and emptied every single box. The admiral's not here."

"Could they have left the box on the FedEx flight? Isn't it going to Baghdad next?"

Moore could tell his boss was frustrated. He had to walk him back from the cliff—but carefully. "The refrigerated box was on this flight and all our intel told us the admiral was in it. But he wasn't. And we've been working with these FedEx guys long enough to know they're efficient in the way they pack up and unload their flights. If they ever goon this up—wrong package to the wrong people—their entire business model collapses. I'd bet my mortgage payment he wasn't on that flight."

"Okay, Master Guns; we got it. We'll just wait it out until the next FedEx flight gets here. We think it's arriving in a little less than two hours."

"Roger that, sir."

Dawson made the call to Chase Williams as Laurie Phillips passed the same information back to the Geek Tank. Soon, Op-Center was in overdrive.

"Are you positive?" Mabad al-Dosari barked into his cellphone.

"Yes, I'm certain," the man began. "We have a clear view of the airport. Nothing has come out of the warehouse. Something must be going on."

"Are you sure they're not just having to process more cargo than they did for the other flights? Maybe it's just taking longer."

"There was less cargo on this FedEx flight than on the previous two," the man replied. "And we can see the warehouse. Emad's certain he saw the refrigerated box the man is packed in come off that plane. It has to be the one." The man understood the dangers involved in pressing al-Dosari too hard. But he knew what they had seen and he knew what his instincts told him.

"All right; stay where you are, and tell me everything you see," al-Dosari replied. Then, turning to his number two, he continued. "Get all the men you can get quickly, and load up the trucks. We're going to the airport."

McCord and Bleich sat huddled at the small table in Chase Williams's office as the Op-Center director digested what they'd just told him.

"Where does this leave us?" Williams asked.

"Brian and the JSOC team are going to wait for the next three FedEx flights. We'll hope the admiral is on one of those. If not, we'll start walking this back to where he was loaded on the flight out of BWI."

Bleich hesitated. Things had been moving so quickly he and McCord hadn't had time to regroup. Bleich and his team *had* been walking it back. He had questions, but he didn't want to override his boss. Williams picked it up, "Something on your mind, Aaron?"

"Well sir, we've tried to neck this down from both directions. We think everyone was so focused on the fact that the admiral was in that refrigerated box, we might have lost sight of the big picture," Bleich began. He looked toward McCord before continuing, but his boss just nodded, so he forged ahead. "The FBI HRT never caught up with the van and no traffic cams actually sighted it rolling up to the warehouse, isn't that right?"

"Yes, that's what we know now," Williams replied.

"Well, when Laurie reported what the JSOC team was doing in the warehouse at the Mosul airport, it triggered something for me—" Bleich hesitated again, as he hadn't had time to tell McCord any of this.

"Go ahead, Aaron," McCord urged.

"Laurie said they're using canines to help determine if there's a human in any of the boxes delivered by the FedEx planes. Well, we're all assuming, based on the evidence the FBI HRT has discovered at the warehouse near BWI, that the admiral was packed inside a refrigerated box filled with peaches destined for Mosul. But we don't know that for certain. Do we know if the HRT team used canines after they found that the refrigerated box was gone? Canines would be able to tell if he'd been there if they had some of the admiral's personal items. If that didn't happen, maybe we can contact the FBI and ask them to take that extra step."

Williams considered this a moment. "You're spot on, Aaron. I'll call the director and suggest he do just that. Roger, why don't you ask Jim Wright to start talking with the FBI watch floor, and also tell our team at Quantico they may have to move out soon?"

"You've got it, boss."

"Major Volner, over here, I need you!" Laurie Phillips shouted.

Volner was at her side in seconds. "Whatcha got?"

"Sir, look at the Global Hawk display, right here," she said jiggling the cursor over three closely bunched shapes.

"I see them. When did you pick 'em up?"

"I saw them come out of central Mosul. They came out of a group of densely packed buildings. The fidelity isn't perfect, but they're clearly trucks headed this way. I can't count how many people are in them, but they're all loaded, sir. I make it about two dozen passengers, maybe more."

"I agree," Volner said. "You tell Mr. Dawson and Hector; I've got to call Master Guns and get his guys out of that warehouse!"

"What then, sir?"

"I think these guys—likely ISIL fighters—will head straight to the warehouse. After that, I don't know."

As the three trucks carrying ISIS fighters barreled straight toward the airport, Phillips abandoned her Global Hawk display and, along with Volner, Rodriguez, and other JSOC team members, watched the approaching enemy. Dawson and Volner had made the decision to stay put in their relatively defensible positions on the small bluff overlooking the airport.

Their numbers were perhaps a third those of the fighters on the trucks now approaching the airport, and there was a nearly inexhaustible supply of ISIS fighters in and near Mosul. However, given the punch the JSOC unit packed, backed by the Rangers and on-call drone support, those weren't bad odds.

"Looks like they're about a half mile from the airport, Major. They'll probably just blow through what little security is there," Dawson said.

"Yes, sir; maybe they'll just go into the warehouse, discover nothing, and leave."

"That's what we're hoping for," Dawson replied, his binoculars fixed on the lead truck.

"The high ground" is a term that is used so extensively in the vernacular—in ethics, in business, in competition, and elsewhere—that few remember it's essentially a military term. For millennia, armies have sought to occupy the high ground as the most basic part of operations and tactics. Armies and empires have risen and fallen as a consequence of who has occupied the high ground.

This same terrain feature that attracted the Op-Center men and their JSOC team to the slightly elevated bluff overlooking Mosul airport also appealed to the ISIS fighters. The approaching men were well familiar with the terrain around the airport. Just a quarter mile from the airport, while the lead truck barreled straight for the warehouse, the number two truck headed for the small rise on the north side of the airport. The third truck peeled off and headed south, directly for the Op-Center team.

Contact was unavoidable, and the fight was not a fair one. Volner nodded to one of his sergeants, the one who had a light anti-armor weapon extended and ready. He had been tracking the vehicle as it closed on their position. No one needed to be told what to do. The man with the LAAW waited for the vehicle to come within optimum range, about fifty yards, then applied pressure to the top-mounted trigger detent. With a *whoosh*, a thin smoke trail connected the rocketeer to the vehicle. The warhead hit the driver-side windshield and the shaped charge all but decapitated the driver. The kinetic energy cascaded back into the bed of the truck, pushing shrapnel into those ISIS fighters crowded on the bed. The truck lurched, slewed, and rolled onto its back, crushing many of the already shredded bodies.

As the few able bodies remaining managed to disengage themselves from the wreckage, several of the Rangers began to take aim at the survivors.

"Hold your fire," Volner commanded. "Let's see what develops."

He knew the men in the other two vehicles wouldn't know whether their brother ISIS fighters were taken out by a ground action or a drone strike. Drones accounted for a great many seemingly random fireballs that claimed ISIS lives and vehicles. Volner and his team weren't disappointed; one of the three remaining trucks headed their way while the other stood well off. The second vehicle approached with caution, but it met the same fate as the first. And it was a well-placed shot. Taking out a vehicle at a hundred yards with a weapon as crude as a LAAW is no easy feat. Nonetheless, there were now two smoking hulks laid out before them.

Those few survivors, some walking and some crawling, headed for the road back toward the city. The third truck had the good sense to turn back toward Mosul.

Even though they were scumbags, Volner involuntarily winced at the carnage before him. Phillips didn't say a word, but she was white as a sheet. A few of the young Rangers were high-fiving each other.

It took Volner's JSOC troop and their 75th Ranger escorts less than half an hour to load up their Humvees with all their gear. Phillips's gear was the last to be broken down as the Global Hawk remained in a tight orbit over the ISIS compound. They were looking for more ISIS fighters heading their way.

To their great relief, no vehicles emerged from central Mosul heading south. Still, the American convoy headed back to Baghdad at top speed, the rough terrain punishing the team and their vehicles without mercy.

CHAPTER FIFTEEN

OP-CENTER HEADQUARTERS,
FORT BELVOIR NORTH:
SPRINGFIELD, VIRGINIA

July 20, 0815 Eastern Daylight Time

Williams had asked Roger McCord and Jim Wright to meet him in his office. He had news he needed to share with them.

"A lot has happened in the past twenty-four hours," Williams began. "The FBI is in chaos now that the director has been sacked so abruptly. I talked with his deputy and asked him to revisit that warehouse up near BWI with canines, and he agreed. They're likely on their way there now."

"Thanks, boss. Jim's been talking with their watch-floor folks. They promised to let him know ASAP what the dogs discover."

The three men wanted to ensure they were doing everything they could to rescue Jay Bruner, and they embarked on an earnest conversation and reviewed the bidding. The JSOC-Ranger engagement just outside the Mosul airport gave the FedEx chief executive little choice but to divert the flights destined for Mosul to Baghdad International, and Dawson, Rodriquez, and the JSOC team were poised to intercept those flights when they arrived. But the fact that the admiral wasn't in the refrigerated box they thought he'd be in caused them to wonder if he was ever spirited out of the country.

Wright was in favor of getting Op-Center's domestic component—Allen Kim and his team at Quantico—moving out, and McCord was in agreement. Williams was mindful of not having Op-Center go outside its mandate and tread in domestic areas that should be handled by the FBI. But the chaos induced when the FBI director was sacked, as well as McCord and Wright's urging, moved him to lean forward.

"All right, fellas, I'm listening. How should we do this?"

"Jim can bring you up to speed on where we want to deploy Allen's team," McCord said.

Wright slid next to the Op-Center director and pulled up a map on his secure iPad. "Best we can figure is that the people who took Admiral Bruner have gone to ground, and likely not far from BWI. When they jumped off Route 1 and Berwyn Road, the FBI CIRG lost them. A while after that, we got one fuzzy traffic-cam hit on the van on the inner loop of the Beltway, and several on the BW Parkway, and then nothing. We're guessing—but we feel it's a good guess—that they didn't get to BWI in time to make the FedEx flight they were going to put him on—"

"It's likely they're holding the admiral somewhere

and waiting for instructions from whoever is pulling the strings at ISIL—probably al-Dosari himself," Mc-Cord interjected.

"Do we see them still trying to get him out of the country?" Williams asked.

"It's a possibility, boss, but the people who snatched him and the other guys in the warehouse likely reported everything that happened back to Mosul. They've got to figure we're going to lock airports around here down tight, and given all the preps they had to make to put him into that box, trying to do that all over again and get past our net around local airports, well, it's just not the most likely scenario."

"Aaron and his team have been mining ISIL social media and we think they may go ahead and kill the admiral right here in the United States," Wright added. "I think our main focus needs to be getting Allen and his team deployed so they can start combing the area for the van and the kidnappers."

"I do too," Williams replied. "Now show me where you had in mind."

Wright pulled up an annotated map of the area on his secure iPad and walked Williams and McCord through his recommended deployment plan for their Quantico team.

The text message from Patrick Kissel had been brief, "Call me at 0900; I have news."

Dale Bruner stepped into the backyard of his parents' house and made the call. "Hey, Skipper, whatcha got for me?"

Kissel could hear the excitement in Bruner's voice, which made what he was about to tell him all the more difficult. "Dale, I'm afraid the news isn't good. The Op-Center team in Mosul didn't find your dad on the FedEx flight they thought he'd be on. But they got into a battle with ISIL fighters and they've withdrawn to Baghdad. The remaining FedEx flights that they think could have your dad have been diverted to Baghdad."

"Where are you getting this info, sir—if you don't mind me asking?"

"I told you I've got a pretty good intel network. CENTCOM has the 75th Ranger Regiment providing logistics and other support to the Op-Center team. The Rangers were part of the battle with ISIL and then they were also involved in the withdrawal to Baghdad."

Bruner paused before speaking again as he tried to process what he had just heard. "But if everyone thinks this al-Dosari wants my dad delivered to him, then that's going to happen in Mosul. Why did they withdraw all the way to Baghdad?"

"Dale, ISIL still controls most of Mosul, and they have hundreds—if not thousands—of fighters there. We'd have to go after them with a massive force, far more than Op-Center's JSOC team can muster."

"I get it, and we're doing that, right?"

"Look. I know this is hard. But when they didn't find your dad in that refrigerated box all the intel told us he'd been in, everyone kind of ran out of ideas. The Rangers tell me the Op-Center team thinks they may be recalled stateside—"

"They can't give up like that!" Bruner exclaimed.

"Dale, if I've learned anything during twenty years doing this, it's that there are things that are way above our pay grade. I feel for you and your family, I really do. But it looks like we'll just have to wait it out while this Op-Center organization comes up with another plan—"

But Bruner was no longer listening. He respected his former skipper, but he wasn't getting the answers he wanted or needed. He had calls to make.

At the Baghdad International Airport, Dawson, Rodriguez, and Volner's JSOC team were set up and operating. One of the diverted FedEx flights had already come and gone, and Admiral Bruner hadn't been aboard. The next flight was due in a little less than an hour, and the one after that, three hours later. Captain Jack Larkin had radioed ahead and let the Rangers who remained behind at Al Muthana know that the JSOC team would need billeting, as they might be staying in Baghdad for an extended period.

"Hey, sir, have you spoken with Mr. Williams since we've gotten back here?" Volner asked Dawson.

"I have. Our instructions are to meet the next two FedEx flights. If Admiral Bruner's not on either one of those, he'll make a real-time decision to either leave us here or bring us back to the States. When I know, you'll know. Are you all still getting intel feeds from the Geek Tank?"

"We are. Laurie's getting everything we need."

"Look, Mike, I know this isn't very satisfying for your troops, but the situation is pretty fluid so we just have to be max flex."

"Semper Gumby, sir."

About twenty five kilometers east-northeast of where Op-Center's team was settling in, inside Baghdad's Green Zone, Zack Peters was standing on the roof of his house just south of Oman Square at the intersection of the Qadisaya Expressway and 14th of July Street. He was having a phone conversation with Dale Bruner.

"El-Tee, I get it. This place is even more screwed up than when you and I operated here. The Iraqi Army is no match for ISIL, and the State Department assumes ISIL may have infiltrated the army anyway. That's why my company keeps hiring guys like me. Our embassy here is the biggest and most expensive American embassy anywhere, and there are over 1,500 diplomats who work there. That's more people than the six apartment buildings on the embassy compound can house, so the company I work for must have over a hundred of us assigned here working security."

"And you provide escort for the diplomats who live off-site going to and from the embassy compound?"

"Yeah, and more. State figures every American here is a prime kidnapping target, so we escort them everywhere—shopping, going to a restaurant, going to the doctor, you name it. We've got our own little empire with vehicles, weapons, and everything else. I loved the SEALs El-Tee, but I'm making more than three times as much doing this as I was when I was in the teams."

"I know, Zack. We hated to lose you, but you have what, three kids now?"

"And one on the way."

"You're serving downrange and you're protecting Americans. That's righteous work. And call me Dale."

"Thanks, but to me you'll always be El-Tee—even when they make you an admiral—"

"No chance of that," Bruner interrupted. "I don't think I fit their mold—and this trip would blow that up, even if I did."

Peters paused for a moment. "Look, sir, we've always been straight with each other. I'll give you all the help I can. I owe you that much and more, but Jesus, boss, what you're trying to do sounds crazy. At least let me go into Mosul with you."

"I can't ask you to do that, Zack. He's my dad, and he'd do it for me. Yeah, maybe it sounds crazy, but I'm counting on it being crazy enough that ISIL won't be looking for a lone guy sneaking into their compound. Plus the gear you said you'd get me gives me an edge over them."

"Look, sir, you saved my ass more than once, first in Iraq and then in Afghanistan. I owe you big time. Just 'cause you still wear camis and I'm in blue jeans and T-shirts, doesn't mean we aren't still brothers. If you're hell bent on going on this mission, I'll get you everything you need. How soon do you think you can get on a flight heading this way?"

"There's one out of Andrews midday tomorrow, and

I'm on the manifest. I'll text you my arrival time so you can meet me on the military side of Baghdad International."

"Tell you what, El-Tee, after you do that, leave your cell at home and buy a disposable one for this trip. CENTCOM's cyber folks have the big cities like Baghdad and Mosul blanketed with all kinds of electronic intercepts and eavesdropping. If you want to stay off the radar, you're gonna want to go to ground and stay off the grid once you leave the States. If you bring your own phone, you won't stay covert."

"Good advice, Zack."

"Use your burner phone to call me once you land at Al Muthana and I'll come pick you up. It's best if the next thing I know is you just show up. Fair enough?"

"Good idea. See you then."

Allen Kim was all motion as he reviewed the deployment plans with his number two, Becky Kott. For Kim, this was the second time Op-Center had asked his CIRG team to mount up, and he wanted it to go better than the first time. They had thwarted a terrorist attack on the United Nations Headquarters, but he had lost a Blackhawk and its crew when the terrorists they were chasing exploded their bomb prematurely. Each of the four memorial services he attended had left Kim feeling a profound sense of failure.

For Kim, that had been the first failure in his professional life. The second-generation Korean American had been a rising star in the Army's Delta Force before his father's sudden death had made his near-continuous overseas deployments too much of a burden for his mother and young sisters. The FBI had snapped up the multilingual Kim and he had quickly risen through the ranks to become a CIRG team leader. Chase Williams had done his due diligence in seeking to get the best talent the FBI director could give him, and he asked for—and got—his first pick, Allen Kim and his team.

"Okay, Becky, I think the helos you've laid on should be enough," Kim said. "You gonna have them launch once our ground force gets most of the way up to BWI?"

"That's the plan. Op-Center arranged for us to stage out of BWI on the west side of the cargo terminal. The ground group just rolled out, and it's a seventy-mile trip. At this time of day, it'll take them maybe two hours to get there. We'll each hop in one of the Blackhawks and get there shortly after they arrive."

"Jim Wright gonna meet us there?"

"He's there already. Op-Center's anxious to get this search underway. That's why we mounted up so quickly."

Kim just nodded, and reminded himself why he had lobbied to have Kott serve as his number two. Becky was a former star lacrosse player at Northwestern with an undergrad degree in electrical engineering and an MS in information technology. She had a secure job with General Electric and was well settled in a house in a Chicago suburb with her boyfriend. It was perfect, that is, until she walked in on her boyfriend with another woman in her own bed.

She needed a change—any change that would take her away from Chicago. She found herself at a hiring conference for the FBI, Secret Service, and other governmental agencies. She was warned that applying to the FBI from Chicago would mean there would be no way she could work in the windy city; she'd have to move. She jumped at the chance.

"Do we know yet where they're going to have us set up once we're at BWI?" Kim asked.

"Op-Center's J4, Duncan Sutherland, set something up with the FAA. We got the word from Jim that their air traffic control facility has some unused space we can use as a command post. We'll be able to get real-time intel feeds from the Geek Tank. If the admiral is anywhere in the greater Washington-Baltimore metro area, we'll find him."

"I hope we do, Becky. I don't like his chances if we don't."

At that moment, Jay Bruner was bound and gagged, with a hood over his head and tied to a radiator pipe in a hundred-year-old farmhouse on Dorsey Run Road just north of Jessup, Maryland. Bruner had been brought here by his kidnappers after living in the back of the van for almost two days. He was at the point of despair and was losing hope he'd ever be rescued.

When Amer and his two fellow terrorists had risked being caught by the FBI CIRG only to fail to get their hostage on the FedEx flight departing BWI, they didn't have a backup plan. Amer had first gone to ground and he and the two other kidnappers had taken turns driving the van through rural streets, ensuring they avoided any roads that might have traffic cams. They had also turned off their cell phones, worried those chasing them would be able to track them electronically. Finally, after two days of this, Amer had done the only thing he could think to do: He called his contact.

The man was angry they'd failed to get the hostage out of the country and delivered to Mabad al-Dosari. But now his priority became one of not letting the Americans find the hostage. He knew it was only a matter of time before their van was spotted.

Their contact was a realtor, and he searched the rental listings in Maryland close to Amer's position. He found a furnished farmhouse that had been vacant for months. The small realty company in Jessup was only too eager to rent it to a fellow realtor who paid first and last month's rent, as well as a security deposit, in cash.

The farmhouse had a detached, two-car garage where Amer and the others hid their van. Their two confederates who loaded the refrigerated box on the plane had abandoned their rent-a-car near BWI as instructed and had holed up in the nearby Hampton Inn until Amer had contacted them again. They took a taxi to Jessup and then had walked the two and a half miles to the farmhouse. Now the five of them were in the house on Dorsey Run Road with their hostage and were told to wait for further instructions.

CHAPTER SIXTEEN

July 21, 0530 Arabia Standard Time

"What now, Mr. Dawson?" Volner asked. They were back at the military side of Baghdad International, camped out at Al Muthana Air Base.

"I've called the Op-Center watch floor and let them know Admiral Bruner wasn't on the remaining two FedEx flights. We'll wait until the boss decides what our next move is."

"You think he'll leave us here, or recall us back stateside?"

"Too hard to call at this point. I gotta think al-Dosari wants the admiral in the worst way. I'll recommend we stay here until he's found one way or another."

"I like that idea, sir," Volner replied. "My guys sure as hell don't want to go back to Fort Bragg empty handed."

* * *

While Op-Center's JSOC team was stuck in suspended animation at Al Muthana Air Base, their CIRG counterpart was setting up their command post in an unused wing of the FAA's air traffic control facility at BWI.

Wright was there to meet Kim and Kott as they jumped out of their Blackhawk helicopters. He walked them into the makeshift command post where he had hung a fifty-inch LCD monitor. He tapped the screen and a map of the area popped up.

"You can see the last two traffic cam hits we got on the van here, and here," Wright began, pointing at the display. "It's going on two days since we got those hits and we've been focused on that van big time, so we've got to figure they've stayed off any major highways. And here's where we found their car abandoned—"

"That's a pretty big area, Jim. Anything we can do to narrow it down?" Kim asked.

"We're counting on the fact that these guys haven't been in the D.C. metro area for long, so they're not all that familiar with the local geography. We're linked up with the Geek Tank, and their best guess is these guys have gone to ground somewhere in this radius here," Wright said, pointing to a large circle centered on BWI.

"The good news is most of it's rural," Kott said. "At least we're not going to have to look for them in the heart of a big city."

"You're right," Wright replied. "We're also counting on the fact that the van is their last remaining vehicle and they don't want to abandon it, but they'll likely hole up somewhere where they can garage it or get it out of sight somehow else."

"We can get our Blackhawks airborne at first light tomorrow," Kim began. "And we can roll our vehicles out too if that's what you want us to do."

"Let's plan on that," Wright replied. "But for now, just get your folks bedded down. We'll see what the Geek Tank can come up with before morning."

While the Op-Center team at BWI settled in, the Geek Tank was in overdrive. McCord and Bleich stood in front of a much larger and higher fidelity screen than the one their team at BWI was looking at, but it contained the same type of information. Even with the stress of their mission weighing on them, McCord found a way to lighten the moment.

"Aaron, you're not trying to channel the boss's Navy experience when you tell us your team is standing port and starboard watches, are you?"

"Ahhh . . . well . . . maybe, sir. I just want to cover this with all the talent we can muster until we find Admiral Bruner."

"Fair enough. That means you need to go home too. Are you in the 'port' or 'starboard' watch team?"

"Umm . . . to use another one of Mr. Williams's Navy terms, I'm in 'port and re-port.'"

McCord knew it was useless to argue with his Geek Tank leader. "Okay, Aaron, there's a massive search area Jim and Allen have come up with. Are we still looking for a break, or trying to manufacture one?"

"Actually, we've about got one constructed. Do you want just the time or how we built the watch?"

"How about a little bit of both?" McCord offered.

"Okay, you know how we were a little skeptical about hiring Fred, seeing as how he had those two felony convictions for busting into corporate databases?"

"I know all too well. I used a silver bullet with the boss on that one."

"You'll be glad you did," Bleich replied, and, as he did, he touched the screen and a large number of triangles appeared.

"What are those?" McCord asked.

"Cell phone towers," Bleich replied. "I know there are a lot of them inside this circle, but we can eliminate all these over here, and over here too," he continued, touching the screen in areas north and east of BWI—

"Because?" McCord prodded.

"Number one, because these guys had to be scared shitless after they were chased by the FBI HRT trucks. But even at that, they pressed up toward the airport for a while. But here's where the last traffic cam hit had them—"

"Okay, so what else?"

"Well, we're assuming now the admiral wasn't on any flight out of BWI. And since they were boresighted on the airport, but then left the BW Parkway, we figure the guys packing the box told them they missed the FedEx flight. So they likely left the parkway somewhere between here and here," Bleich said, pointing to the display again.

"And you think they went to ground somewhere to the west of the BW Parkway?"

"Yes, sir. They were pretty new to the D.C. metro area but had to figure if they headed east out toward Glen Burnie they'd wind up on an Interstate like I-97 or I-695, or on a major state road. They had to know—or at least guess—that the FBI HRT chase was triggered by a traffic cam. So the only thing we can suppose is they got off the BW Parkway and went to ground on local streets around this area," Bleich said as he drew his own electronic arc on the screen.

"I don't disagree with any of what you've said," Mc-Cord replied. "But where does Fred come in?"

"Well, boss—now we're prying the back off the watch," Bleich said, touching the screen again in several places. "Even using that process of elimination we just went through, that's a massive area for our CIRG team to search. Maggie ran the numbers, and the population of this area is north of one hundred and fifty thousand, and there are over sixty thousand houses or apartments—"

Bleich hesitated, as he could see the frown forming on McCord's face, so he walked his boss through their analysis. Based on what their anticipatory intelligence was telling them, there were a total of seven cell-phone towers that would service any calls made by the kidnappers. While a typical cell tower can handle thousands of calls in an hour, Fred had hacked into the servers of three different cell carriers to glom onto all the data each cell phone company had, looking for a call coming from Mosul, the Geek Tank leader explained. Once one of those calls hit any of the seven towers—and likely a few of them at the same time—they'd be able to narrow the location of where the hostage was being held.

Bleich's explanation of how they were hacking cell phone companies' databases brought a grimace to Mc-Cord's face.

"Don't worry, boss," Bleich said, smiling. "I gave Fred close parameters to work with. None of this will be traceable to NGA or to us. I've looked at what Fred's built, it's pretty sweet."

"So for now we wait?"

"We wait; but those algorithms will be chugging all night."

The other kidnappers were all asleep as Amer and one of the men who had grabbed Jay Bruner sat at the kitchen table in the old farmhouse. It was close to midnight, but the summer Maryland heat and humidity was still sucking the life out of them, as well as what little patience they had left.

"Why do we have to stay holed up here, Amer? We're sitting ducks. The police or whoever was chasing us will find us eventually, then what?"

"I don't know!" Amer snapped. After his initial call to his contact, he'd been told to wait for further instructions. Several hours later, his contact called him and told Amer to come to this house where he'd find the key under the doormat. He was told to garage the van, get the hostage into the house, and not use their phones again for outbound calls or leave the house until they were told to do so. Amer had even taken the extra step of collecting the phones from the other men and turning them off.

"Look, we'll never get him out of the country now; the Americans aren't stupid. And you've seen the local news reports—every damn police force in the area is going to be looking for us. It's insane to just sit here!"

"I'm just telling you what I was told. If you want to take charge of this and have a better idea, here, you call our contact," Amer said as he pushed his phone across the table.

The other man simply pushed it back, got up, and stormed upstairs.

Twenty feet from where the two men were arguing, Jay Bruner lapsed in and out of sleep. He was all but numb with fear, and he had long ago given up hope of trying to bargain with his captors. Thoughts of rescuers coming to his aid flew in and out of his head, and each time he became more certain they'd never come.

The C-5M Super Galaxy had been airborne for several hours and the constant drone of the aircraft's four General Electric F138-GE-100 engines had lulled Dale Bruner asleep. The Galaxy had been in service in the Air Force for nearly half a century, and the 400-ton behemoth was still going strong. This flight was bringing tons of cargo and a number of passengers to the American military forces operating at Al Muthana Air Base at Baghdad International Airport. An active-duty Navy SEAL who said he had orders to travel to Baghdad was a priority passenger who bumped other pax.

Dale Bruner was traveling in uniform—a require-
ment for all military personnel on the Air Force
Mobility Command flights—but he would shed that
soon after arriving in Baghdad. He knew he was doing
what he needed to do to rescue his dad, but it pained
him that he had lied to his mother and sisters, telling
them he was going back to his command in Coronado.

In their compound in Mosul, Mabad al-Dosari sat with
his number two, Shakir al-Hamdani. Al-Dosari always
counted on al-Hamdani's counsel, and he needed it
now more than ever. Nothing was going right.

After the American airstrike had destroyed his last
remaining SA-15 Gauntlet systems, leaving him naked
to further air attacks, he had had his fighters range
far and wide in areas they controlled, as well as areas
where they could attack successfully, trying to steal
anti-air batteries. But there were none to be had, and
while the Americans and their so-called coalition—
along with the Iran-backed Shia fighters—had been
busy trying to push the Islamic State out of the increasing number of cites they controlled, the air attacks on
Mosul continued. He had had to shift his compound
several times in the last few weeks alone.

Worse, as he retreated to more northerly sections of
Mosul, his ability to threaten the Mosul airport had essentially disappeared. Now many flights a day were
landing there, delivering supplies to the forces aligned
against his fighters. And with few new fighters arriving
from other countries—they were profiling young Muslim men and not giving them visas—the reinforcements

he had always been able to count on in the past were no longer coming.

But what troubled him most was the bungled attempt to get this Admiral Bruner smuggled out of the United States and delivered to him as he had ordered. When he had first cooked it up, al-Hamdani had described the plan as "foolproof." Well, the fools had made hash of it. *That* made him nearly blind with rage. He knew he needed to give his number two a chance to redeem himself, but he wanted to know the details.

"So you see no way we can get our hostage out of the United States?" al-Dosari began.

"I don't think so," al-Hamdani replied. "Our contact has been monitoring police and other activity around the area where our men are holding the hostage. He thinks if they try to get him to that airport again, they'll be caught."

"But what about other airports, or a ship out of an East Coast port? Surely we can come up with another way," al-Dosari countered.

Al-Hamdani knew the ISIS leader was grasping at straws. The original plan—watching the subject's movements so they knew where to snatch him, buying the small packing company at an inflated price, placing the two men in that company, buying tons of peaches—had failed. But the plan had taken time, money, and a dose of patience to put together in the first place. How did al-Dosari expect them to do that again on the fly?

"Look," al-Hamdani began, "we tried and failed to smuggle him out of his country. But we can still accomplish what you want to do—slit his throat on the Internet. It not only extracts the revenge you want, but will strike fear into the Americans, and especially their president. We'll assassinate their man right under their noses. Here, look at this map, the house where they're holding him is less than twenty-five miles from the White House. If we kill him there, it will have a huge impact."

Something about al-Hamdani handing him the tablet and showing him the map calmed al-Dosari and started to bring him around to his number two's way of thinking.

"If we do this, I want your contact to do it. I don't want those five idiots who are holding him to screw it up," al-Dosari said. "Get him there, and let me know when he arrives. Once he's in the farmhouse, I want him to set up our flag, have a good camera, and do this the right way. I don't want Midkiff to see some grainy cell phone picture. I want him to see his man, see the terror in his eyes, and know it's happening right under his nose."

"It will be done; I'll contact him immediately."

Zack Peters liked his new life as a security contractor in Iraq—to a point. He was making what he thought was an almost obscene amount of money for work that was far less dangerous than what he'd done while he was in uniform as a Navy SEAL. But he didn't want to do this forever, as it took him away from his family for extended periods. Even his company's generous package of flying him back to the States for ten days every three months to visit his family wasn't enough for a man who was trying to be a good husband and a good father.

That made his decision to liberate—it was stealing, but that term bothered him—a vehicle and some high-end gear from his company to support Dale Bruner much easier. He'd been in Iraq for fifteen months doing this work, and he had fattened his bank account. If the worst happened and he was caught, fired, and sent back to the United States, he knew he could start over again and find a job close to home in Phoenix.

But the overriding factor that made his decision easy was his loyalty to Bruner. His team leader had saved his life and gotten their small team out of some truly tough spots in the two years they served together. His lieutenant came first; everything else would have to take a backseat.

Amer had faith there was a greater plan that he and his small group were just a small part of. But the concerns the others had expressed were trying that faith. How long would they have to hole up here waiting? And no one had told him what was going to happen next. He wanted to do something, *anything*, rather than just sit here. Amer slept next to his phone hoping for a call—any call—that would tell him what to do next.

The ringing jolted Amer awake. He groped for the phone and finally answered. "Yes?"

"This is Mr. Martin," his contact began, substituting their agreed-upon name for his real one, Masood.

"This is me."

"Do you still have the package?"

"Yes, of course. Do you have instructions for me?"

"Yes, I'll tell you more when I arrive in the morning. I'll be there once I can purchase the material our leader has told me to buy."

"But what will we do then? Are we going to move?"

"That's enough, no more!" the man hissed. "I've only been to that house once, but I remember it fairly well. The curtains do little to darken the living room. Do you have sufficient blankets to cover most of the windows in that room?"

Amer and the others had little need for blankets in the heat of summer, so they'd never opened the up-stairs' linen closet. "I'll go look."

After running upstairs and opening the closet, Amer spoke again. "Yes, there are plenty of blankets in the linen closet."

"Good," Martin replied. "I'll bring everything else we need. Stay off this phone until then."

Amer heard the man click off. He sat and wondered if he should tell the others yet. But what would he tell them?

Several hours later it was first light at BWI airport, and Wright, Kim, and the rest of Kim's HRT team shared similar frustrations to those Amer was feeling just five miles away.

"We're ready to launch," Kim began. "We can start combing the area with our Blackhawks and send our trucks out in a grid search."

"I know your team is more than ready, Allen, but

Mr. Williams wants us to wait," Wright said. "He's confident the Geek Tank will come up with actionable intelligence soon. Then we can make this a precision takedown and we won't have spooked these guys."

"All right. I'll put the team on a ready-fifteen alert. We can sustain that for an extended period."

Wright had been working with his CIRG HRT team leader long enough to read the frustration in Kim's voice and in his body language. "I don't think it'll be long, Allen."

CHAPTER SEVENTEEN

July 22, 0645 Eastern Daylight Time

A haggard-looking Fred Morton burst into Aaron Bleich's office. "Aaron, I think we've got it!"

Bleich looked up at Morton and wondered if he looked as disheveled as the man standing in his doorway. The rest of the Geek Tank was working shifts of twelve hours on, twelve hours off; Bleich and Morton were working port and re-port. Neither man had left their subterranean habitat for the last forty-eight hours.

"Talk to me," Bleich replied.

"You know the program I built was designed to trigger on any call to the United States from Mosul. A call from central Mosul came in a few hours ago, and the program churned through cell-carrier databases narrowing down what cell towers in the United States the call was routed to—"

"How close have you pinned it down?"

"Not close enough yet, but we're in the ballpark. I

think we'll have it nailed down better in a few hours, but I'm pretty sure it's southwest of BWI—"

"Great work, Fred. Are you thinking we've got Allen and his team deployed to the right location?"

"Ahhh . . . well . . . that's not exactly my department, but yeah, I'd say so."

"Okay, let me know as soon as you neck this down."

"You got it," Morton replied as he left.

Aaron Bleich allowed himself a small smile. When the time was right, he'd remind Roger McCord why shooting that silver bullet to hire Morton in spite of two felony convictions was such a good move.

"Quite a place you've got here, Zack. Company pay for this?"

"Yep, they pay for the security guys too, oh, and also a maid."

Bruner just shook his head. They were standing inside the high walls of the compound where Zack Peters lived. The two-story house was bigger than anyplace he'd ever lived, and while it was bare desert outside the walls, inside the compound it was all palm trees, fountains and the like. The two men were standing next to an up-armored Humvee packed with all the gear—and more—Bruner had asked the former SEAL to get for him.

"Do I want to know how you managed to 'borrow' all this gear?" Bruner asked.

"Probably not, El-Tee. But now that you've had some time to think about it, are you sure you don't want a wingman with you? We worked together pretty damn well back in the day."

Bruner had had a long time to think about what he was going to do during the Galaxy flight. He recognized how long a limb Peters was climbing out on to steal this vehicle and the gear from his security company. Peters had done more than enough.

"Zack, you've done me a big solid in getting me everything I need. I can't ask you to do any more. My job is to get all this back to you reasonably intact when I return here with my dad. I'm kinda worried about using your company's gear; you sure this won't jam you up?"

"Not to worry, sir; I've got it covered. You have no idea how much gear we write off when it gets damaged or lost."

Peters paused as he produced a tablet. "Now here's something you're gonna need, El-Tee—"

Bruner arched his eyebrows at yet one more piece of "liberated" gear. It wasn't lost on Peters.

"Don't worry, sir, it's mine, not the company's. I've mapped out the route you should take. It's rough terrain, but I think you'll want to start now so you'll be doing most of your traveling at night. All our intel says ISIL has control of some of the areas you'll be traveling through."

Bruner studied the map, and then asked, "This looks pretty direct. How long?"

"At night, maybe eight hours or so. Here, let me scale this for you. I want to show you where the ISIL compound is in Mosul and where you'll probably want to lay-up—"

"You 'liberate' this intel from your company?"

"Nah, it's all about survival over here. Most of us working for the company are former military, mainly special ops. And there are plenty of U.S. special operators here in Iraq, though they stay completely off the radar, and you never read about them in the press back in the States. If they have good intel, they share it with us; and if we have anything, we share it with them."

Bruner studied the map for a few minutes, asking Peters several questions. Satisfied he was as ready as he could be, he embraced his former SEAL teammate. "Thanks, brother."

"Take care of yourself, El-Tee."

Bruner climbed into the Humvee, fired up the engine and rolled out of the compound. He knew where he was going and how he was going to get there. But unlike the dozens of missions he had planned during his career as a Navy SEAL, he didn't know much beyond that.

"Mr. Martin" had lived in Washington, D.C. for his entire life. He knew where to buy what he wanted. That was the easy part. But Mabad al-Dosari was insistent he get to the house where Amer and his group held the hostage, and get there immediately. He had gotten al-Dosari's order at night, long after stores had closed. He planned his morning shopping trip as best he could, but he knew he'd be fighting his way through the D.C.

metro area's notoriously snarled traffic most of the morning.

His loyalty to the Islamic State leader was absolute, but that didn't keep him from chafing over the fact that it was easy for al-Dosari to dictate to him from thousands of miles away. He didn't even know why he insisted that he go to the house and do this himself. He had trained Amer and the other four; wasn't that enough?

His shopping list was going to fill—maybe overfill— his Lexus SUV. The list included a professional-grade movie camera, high-end tripod, high-intensity lights, lighting umbrellas, a sound amplifier, and a list of other gear. Then he had to haul it all up to the farmhouse outside Jessup. He thought al-Dosari was going overboard with all this—but he dared not question him.

Chase Williams, Anne Sullivan, and Duncan Sutherland sat at the small table in Williams's office on a conference call with Brian Dawson. "We've got you on speakerphone, Brian," Williams began. "I'm here with Anne and Duncan."

"Hey, boss; Mike and his boys are ready to mount up and return—if that's what you really want. Laurie tells us Aaron and his team are zeroing in on where the admiral is being held near BWI."

"That's right. But first, tell Mike and his team well done at the Mosul airport. I read your report, and I know that could have turned out differently. Taking on that group and coming out unscathed is a win in my book."

"I'll do that. But I'd be lying if I told you they weren't more than a little disappointed they didn't get the admiral. But I get what your intel is telling you—they never got him out of the States."

Williams knew this was coming. Dawson was an operator, and he was downrange. Until someone was *sure* the hostage wasn't out of the country, Dawson saw no point in returning home. "It's pretty strong intel, Brian, and we hope to have him in our hands soon."

The ops director knew the decision had been made, and it was useless to continue to press his boss.

"I'm going to put Duncan on, and he'll go over the timeline with you. Looks like we'll be able to get a C-17 to you sometime in the next sixteen hours or so. That going to give you all enough time to get all of the JSOC team's gear ready to load up?"

"Yep, plenty of time, boss. Duncan?"

"Brian, I've already texted Hector the details, so I'll just hit the high notes," Sutherland began in his thick Liverpool accent. A former member the British SAS—Special Air Service—Op-Center's logistics director was part soldier, part logistician, and mostly magician. He was intelligent and he was shrewd and he could finesse any system to deliver what his bosses wanted where they wanted it.

As Sutherland was discussing the details of their return with Dawson, McCord and Bleich appeared in his doorway. McCord was poker-faced, but Bleich couldn't hide his excitement and was beaming.

"You fellas look like you're here to tell me something. Good news?"

"The best, boss," McCord began. "Fred's gotten us the intel we need to narrow the search area. We think the footprint's small enough to deploy Allen and his team. I'll let Aaron walk you through it."

Bleich sat down at the table next to Williams and held his tablet in front of him. "We may have this nailed to a precise location soon, boss, but like Roger said, Fred's program has narrowed the call we were anticipating to somewhere inside this red circle here—"

"That's pretty close to BWI," Williams said.

"Yes, around five miles or so—and if his program does what we think it will, we maybe can nail it to a several-block area soon—in no more than a few hours. But we think we have enough to get Allen's ground vehicles out to start sniffing around. Jim thinks it's a good idea too—"

"You've already spoken with Jim Wright?" Anne Sullivan interjected. Op-Center's deputy director was, for all intents and purposes, Williams's COO. She didn't want the Intelligence Directorate making decisions that should be reserved for Williams.

"Yes ma'am—but just for info. He knows Mr. Williams will make the call from here."

"Then let's make it," Williams said. "Allen's team isn't doing us any good sitting at BWI. Let's get them moving toward—" Williams paused, looking at the tablet. "What's this town, Aaron?"

"It's Jessup, boss. Do you want to call Jim or do you want us to?"

"I'll do that right now," Williams replied. "And, Aaron, good job again recruiting Fred. We had our doubts, but I'm glad you persisted."

"Me too, boss."

As McCord and Bleich left, Williams turned to Sutherland, who had finished his call with Dawson. "All good with Brian and our JSOC team?"

"All's good, boss. We'll get that aircraft to pick them up just as soon as we can."

As Allen Kim and his team got the order to roll their vehicles out of BWI, approximately seven thousand miles to the east, a single vehicle was on the move.

Dale Bruner navigated the jagged topography of the Iraq desert, pushing his Humvee over rocks, wadis, ridges, and depressions. It was slow going, especially at night.

As he drove, he took a mental inventory of the gear Peters had provided. In addition to the Sig Sauer P226 pistol he wore on his hip, he had a silenced .22 caliber automatic in an underarm shoulder holster. His main armament consisted of two Mk17 SCAR Long Barrel assault rifles. One was a SCAR-L that fired the lighter 5.56mm cartridge, and the other was a SCAR-H that chambered the heavier 7.62 rounds. He had ample ammunition for both. For close-in work, there was an MP7A2 submachine gun, several explosive breaching charges, and a supply of M67 hand grenades. For optics, he had a set of Steiner 7×50rc M50rc binoculars and a pair of L-3 GPNVG-18 night vision goggles. The load-out was topped off with assorted sizes of C-4 charges with sticky backing and a variety of timing devices. Dale was familiar with all the weapons, equipment, and explosives. Not that he would need it all, but Peters had covered every contingency.

He was less happy with the garb Peters had given him and insisted he wear, but his brother SEAL had been in-country for a long time and Dale admitted to himself that wearing what he had on now was his best chance to blend in once he got to Mosul. Still he felt odd. The baggy cami pants and oversized cami jacket were bad enough, but the black and gray kaffiyeh he wore on his head seemed unnecessary, and the huge bandolier with dozens of shells just weighed him down.

If there was any advantage to having to make this slow, lengthy, nighttime drive, it was that it gave Bruner an opportunity to build a mental model for how he would extract his dad from the ISIL compound. Sure, he had thought about it on the long flight from Andrews to Baghdad International, but there was something about being in Iraqi territory, having his vehicle with its load of gear and—most importantly— having the detailed picture of the buildings ISIL currently occupied, that helped his plan develop. The tablet Zack had given him was already proving its worth. He was forming the picture, and it was starting to gel.

The unused wing of the FAA's air traffic control facility at BWI was impossibly cramped as Allen Kim and Becky Kott gathered their entire team in front of the LCD monitor. Jim Wright stood off to the side.

"All right," Kim began. "Mr. Wright has spoken with Op-Center, and the Geek Tank has pushed us good intel—plus we're expecting more detailed locating info soon. We've been told to move out to the southwest and comb these areas here . . . here . . . and here," he continued, pointing at the display.

Kim had gone over the plan with the senior ground commander in advance, and now the CIRG HRT team leader stepped up to the screen. "All right, here's what we can do with the assets we have. We figure the kidnappers who have the admiral are holed up somewhere in the area Mr. Kim just showed you. We're all but certain it's a building or house with a garage or shed that can hold a van, so we don't have to look at houses without garages or apartments with outside parking—"

"Do we know for certain they haven't abandoned their vehicle? If they have, could they have hunkered down anywhere?" one of the HRT assault team men asked.

"We don't, but we're operating on that assumption for now. When we roll out, I want two vehicles going down here, along routes 170 and 174 toward Fort Meade," he said, pointing at the screen. "Another two will head out this way, due west, toward Guilford. The final one I want headed west-northwest toward Meadowridge Park," he continued. Then turning to Wright, "That about cover the area your intel says we want to search?"

"Yes, it does," Wright replied. "Let's roll out—" He

paused as Sandee Barron's hand shot in the air. "You want one or two birds up, boss?" Barron asked.

"Two, but no lower than three thousand feet for now, and try not to fly racetrack patterns. We don't want to spook these guys."

Sandee Barron was the command pilot of one of the CIRG HRT helicopters that belonged to Kim's unit. If anyone had lived through career highs and lows, it was she. Barron had been cashiered by the Navy for breaking a half-dozen Navy regs and almost getting herself and her passenger killed. But Op-Center had seen something in her, and Chase Williams had used his influence to get her an assignment with the FBI's CIRG. She wasn't there long before Kim found out about her and recruited her. As a member of Op-Center's CIRG HRT team she had distinguished herself already, stopping North Korean terrorists before they could crash a bomb-laden truck into the United Nations building. Whatever doubts about her abilities some of the veteran CIRG HRT pilots might have had initially were washed away in that operation.

"Got it," Barron replied. The briefing continued for a few more minutes, and then the CIRG HRT team mounted up and moved out.

"Something new, Fred?" Aaron Bleich asked as Morton appeared in his doorway.

"Yes," he replied. "I think we're getting close to nailing the location, but there's a new wrinkle now."

"I'm listening."

"It's like this. While we haven't fingered the precise

location of the cell phone the kidnappers are using, we've found another cell phone they've been communicating with."

"Where?"

"I'm getting to that. I've hac . . . I mean . . . I've looked into who owns that cell, and it's a guy with the last name of Masood. He lives in the District and has been on the move since early this morning. From the one conversation we picked up, we're pretty sure he's heading to where the kidnappers are holding the admiral. We may not have to search that hard—he may just lead us to where we need to go."

Bleich considered this. There was nothing wrong with Morton's logic, and he might be exactly right. But he had to evaluate that against the risk of delaying the search and having the men holding Bruner kill him. But he valued Morton's opinion and felt he needed to bring his idea forward. "Tell you what, Fred. This is a decision the director himself is going to have to make. Let's grab Roger and go see him."

CHAPTER EIGHTEEN

July 22, 1330 Eastern Daylight Time

"Mr. Martin" had just bought the last piece of equipment he needed and was now headed northeast out of Washington. As he passed a vacant lot, he tossed his personal cell phone as far as he could. He had only one more call to make before he got to the farmhouse. He used his burner cell and dialed the number.

David Pierce answered on the second ring. "Pierce here." The disposable cell Masood was using didn't show a name or number, so Pierce was in the dark as to who was calling.

"This is your friend, David."

"My friend?"

"Yes. We have mutual acquaintances, and I assure you that you'll want the information I'm offering you."

Pierce was wary—but interested. Even though he had been in the broadcast news stringer business for only a few years, he had already built a well-deserved reputation as a bottom-feeder. He was adept at finding the most sensational and tawdry stories, getting riveting video, and selling that video to the highest bidder—usually a new cable channel that dealt in the lowest form of gotcha journalism and one that was trying to make its mark in an increasingly crowded field. "I'm listening."

"Do you think one of your clients might be interested in a video that shows something sensational?" he began. Masood then poured out the scene they were about to construct in the farmhouse. He concluded by saying, "The only proviso is this is to be shown on the evening news—tonight."

"I can guarantee it will," Pierce replied as he tossed around dollar figures in his brain. This would be his biggest payday yet.

He had heard from his team—everyone got to weigh in—and it didn't take Chase Williams long to make the decision. "I don't think we should wait for more intel. Let's search. If this other person leads us to the admiral and his kidnappers, so much the better. But for now, let's keep the press on."

"You got it, boss," McCord replied. "I'll let Jim know."

As they left the Op-Center director's office, Bleich pulled Morton aside. "Fred, I know it didn't go your way in there, but that's okay. Keep giving us options, but for now, let's get back on our turf and nail this location down."

*　*　*

He knew he needed to sleep, but the adrenalin pumping through his veins kept Dale Bruner keyed up. He'd arrived in Mosul and had hidden his vehicle where Zack Peters had suggested he stash it.

Now he was hunkered down in his overwatch position in a bombed-out building with a clear view of the ISIL compound. He hadn't humped as heavy a pack since his last tour in Afghanistan, but he had managed to haul all his gear up to the fourth story of the abandoned building in one trip.

He'd decided to snatch his dad after dark, and night had fallen an hour ago. But there was still a great deal of traffic on the streets below, mainly heavily armed men patrolling around the building, as well as trucks loaded with men, coming and going. Bruner was certain this was the ISIL compound, and he was sure his dad was in that building. And he counted on all these men sleeping sometime.

"He's not moving, and he's been stopped for almost twenty minutes," Morton said as Bleich hovered over his screen.

"Where?"

"Right here. It's on the way out of D.C., heading toward the area where we think they're holding the admiral up near BWI. But it doesn't make any sense. It's a run-down area in Northeast, D.C. There's nothing much there except decaying houses and empty lots."

"But you're sure it's his cell phone? There aren't any scrambled signals or anything like that?"

"No chance. This is exactly the same signal we've been following from the get-go. I'm sure of it."

"We're so damn close—we can't lose this guy now," Bleich said, the frustration in his voice hard to miss.

"I'll nail it, just give me a little more time," Morton replied.

At that moment, Allen Kim was airborne in Sandee Barron's Blackhawk helo, one of the two HRT birds searching the area for any sign of the kidnappers or of Admiral Bruner. Once his ground vehicles had rolled out of BWI, Kim felt his place was in the field, not in a building.

His CIRG team was following the most disciplined search plan they could construct, but Kim knew the odds of finding the admiral were still long. Even though the Geek Tank had narrowed the search area, they were still talking several square miles and hundreds of houses and other structures.

Their vehicles were anything but inconspicuous, and he and Jim Wright had had a long discussion regarding the pros and cons of searching the area. While they hoped to find something, anything, that would lead them to the location where the admiral was being held, they also feared spooking the kidnappers into killing Bruner if they thought the authorities were closing in on them. For now, they searched—but carefully.

Jay Bruner was plumbing the deepest reservoirs of his courage and determination. He had heard enough of his kidnappers' conversations to now know that he was going to be killed—and every instinct he had told him it would be soon.

He still didn't know precisely who was holding him, but he had put two and two together and now understood that his death was going to be in retaliation for the strikes he had led as the *Roosevelt* strike group commander. He'd made his peace with God and now he just wanted to get it over with.

While most of Aaron Bleich's focus over the past several hours had been on the work Fred Morton was doing to nail down the location where the kidnappers were holding Admiral Bruner, he hadn't ignored the rest of the Geek Tank. He knew everyone was eager to contribute, and he had dealt out a number of assignments to individuals and groups.

Now one of those assignments might have just paid off. Maggie Scott called him from her workstation. "Aaron, I need you."

Bleich made a beeline for Maggie's cubicle. "Yeah, Maggie, what's cooking?"

"You asked me and my team to look for anomalies— anything in this general area that we thought was different from days ago—"

"And you've found something?"

"I think so. I've had the team cast a pretty wide net, and I've got to tell you, we ran into plenty of dead ends. This area is a throwback to an earlier time. Nothing much happens or changes."

"But?" Bleich prodded.

"Yeah, well, we found out there's this old farm-house; it's a real relic. The place has been empty since the couple who lived there since the 60s finally moved to a nearby assisted living facility several months ago. It was on the rental or sales market for the longest time—"

"And?" Bleich asked.

"I was getting to that. A few days ago a realtor from down in the District contacted the realty company in Jessup that listed the property and said he wanted to rent it. He showed up the next day and paid first and last months' rent and a security deposit in cash."

"Show me where it is, Maggie."

While Scott was walking Bleich through what she'd just found, Amer and his team were unloading Mr. Martin's van.

"What the hell is all this for?" one of the men whispered to Amer.

"Mr. Martin says he'll explain it all once we set it up. For now, he told me we need to haul all this inside quickly, and then he wants to put his SUV in the garage with our van."

The man just shrugged and complied. Soon they were all inside.

It took them just twenty minutes to set up and position all of the equipment to Mr. Martin's specifications. First, they hung blankets over the windows, securing them with generous amounts of duct tape and a few nails. Then they set up all the filming gear, turned on the high-intensity lights, tested the audio gear, and, finally, placed a small rug on the floor and hung the ISIS flag on the wall behind it.

Once they'd finished, Martin walked into the other room and kicked Jay Bruner.

"Wake up!"

As Bruner stirred, Martin untied him, but left the gag in his mouth.

Jay Bruner's eyes went wide with terror as Martin put a gun to his forehead. "Undress."

Bruner stood in shocked silence for only a moment before Martin pulled back the gun's hammer and barked, "UNDRESS!"

Bruner did as he was told and then stood there in his boxers for an anxious moment. Martin reached inside a bag, pulled out an orange jumpsuit, held it in front of Bruner, and said, "Put this on."

Martin shouted into the other room. "Amer, come here!"

Amer walked in and Martin handed him his pistol. "Watch him. If he moves, you know what to do."

Amer just nodded, and Martin added, "Oh, and take the gag out of his mouth. He might want to pray."

Now the real terror began.

It was 1715, and the Washington, D.C. metro area evening newscasts would start in less than an hour.

Martin had walked into one of the farmhouse's empty rooms and called Pierce.

"We'll have this video shot soon and will send it to you. Are you certain you've found a buyer?"

"The best," Pierce replied. "You need to get it to me soon. And the quality needs to be good."

"Trust me, you won't be disappointed."

"We have the location!" Bleich shouted as he burst into McCord's office with Scott and Morton in tow.

"Show me," McCord replied.

"Here, we just sent you a link. Let me pull it up," Bleich continued as he leaned over his boss and scrolled to the top of his e-mail in-box. Soon the map display filled McCord's screen, and Bleich walked him through what they had just learned.

"Great work, Maggie," McCord began. "Fred, does this jibe with what your programs are telling you?"

"It does, sir. It's in the area we were working. Dunno, maybe my program would have ultimately nailed the exact location, but Maggie's good work got us there first."

"Well done, all of you. I'll get this info to Jim immediately. In the meantime, Aaron, send this link to Mr. Williams. We'll go see him in a few minutes."

The meeting with the Op-Center director had gone smoothly, and he'd congratulated them on getting Jim Wright and his CIRG HRT moving. They'd passed the information to the people in the field, and the operators were treating it as actionable intelligence. Williams did say it was times like this when he missed his ops director and hoped he had him back from Baghdad soon.

For most people in the intelligence business, that

was enough, and they could consider their work complete. But it wasn't enough for Fred Morton and soon it wouldn't be enough for Aaron Bleich.

After Bleich, Morton, and Scott got back to the Geek Tank, and as Scott peeled off to head for her cubicle, Morton said, "Aaron, a moment?"

"Sure, what's on your mind?"

"Something's still bothering me. That cell phone that wasn't moving earlier still isn't moving. This Mr. Martin was using it, and now he's stationary in the wrong part of town. I just don't know—"

Bleich could read body language with the best of them, "You'd feel better if you had eyes-on, wouldn't you?"

"You bet."

"I would too. Why don't you grab Erin and the two of you go there? Have Maggie monitor whatever you're covering while you're gone. Call me as soon as you know anything."

"You got it."

CHAPTER NINETEEN

July 22, 1730 Eastern Daylight Time

"I've got Mr. McCord on the line, sir," the woman said. She was manning the phone bank in their command post at the FAA's air traffic control facility at BWI.

Jim Wright rushed over and picked up the secure phone.

"Wright, here."

"Jim, we know where they're holding the admiral. Are you in front of your display?"

"Yes, what's the latitude and longitude?"

McCord passed the lat and long to Wright, and then continued. "It's an old farmhouse outside of Jessup. We think you should get eyes-on immediately."

"Wilco. I've got two birds airborne. Am I authorized to assault once I've got a force in place?"

"Expect that in a few minutes, after I talk to the boss. Let me know when you're overhead. Out here."

The CIRG HRT team members manning the command post knew what to do. One man handed Wright a radio to talk with the airborne Kim, while another punched the lat and long McCord had provided into his computer and then zeroed in on the farmhouse on the LCD display.

"Allen, Jim."

"Go ahead."

"We've got what we think are the exact coordinates of where the admiral is being held. It's an old farmhouse on Dorsey Run Road. I'm sending you a link now. We want you to get a look at it ASAP. How far away are you from that posit?"

In the cockpit of the UH-60M, Sandee Barron had heard the entire conversation and was looking at the map on the display in front of her. "Tell him less than three minutes, boss. I'm bustering that way now."

"Three minutes, Jim," Kim replied. "Can you get the closest vehicles moving toward that house?"

"Will do. Stand by for another link soon. We've contacted the realty company that rented the house. They have a room-by-room description of what it looks like inside."

"Great, we'll need that. Out here."

Dale Bruner had been sitting in his overwatch position for several hours and was frustrated. He'd expected the streets to be empty by now, but there was still a great deal of activity.

He'd used the time to study the information Peters had given him. In addition to the detailed pictures of the outside of the buildings that comprised the ISIL compound, Peters had mined the intel feeds his uniformed friends had provided him and gotten additional information he knew Bruner would need.

In an era where precision-guided munitions could be aimed with incredible accuracy, it wasn't enough to just hit a building or other structure; a smart bomb could literally be put into a specific window of a building. That meant knowing what a building looked like inside was even more important than seeing what the building looked like from the outside.

Soon after ISIL began taking over wide swaths of territory in the Mideast, Joan Hszieh had approached the CENTCOM commander with an idea. His Special Operations component—SOCCENT—was on the ground in Iraq advising the Iraqi Army, especially that army's Golden Brigade of special operators.

They couldn't infiltrate the houses in the ISIL compound in Mosul, but they could move freely about other buildings in the city where ISIL wasn't in control. And given how frequently the terrorist group moved as the coalition bombing raids continued, buildings the Iraqi Army team mapped one day could well be occupied by ISIL the next.

That was precisely what had happened. ISIL's current compound had been mapped—floor by floor and room by room—several weeks ago by a Golden Brigade team. Bruner now had a schematic of that building's interior on his tablet. Once inside the building, he knew where he was going to go.

* * *

From the moment he was grabbed at the Franconia-Springfield Metro station, Jay Bruner had hoped for a chance to talk with his captors, to bargain with them, to try to somehow have them see the value in releasing him. That hadn't happened in the four days he'd been a hostage. But now he got his opportunity.

How many times had he rehearsed what he would say? He'd run it through his mind dozens of times. But now, with his gag off and standing in front of a man who didn't look old enough to vote, he fumbled for the right words.

"Look, you don't have to do this—"

"Shut up," Amer replied.

"What's your name?"

"I said, shut up!" he hissed.

"I won't talk long, I promise. I recognize your voice. I can tell you're one of the ones who've been holding me hostage. But I know you're not the one pulling the strings—"

The idea that he might not be the one to take the fall if they were caught got Amer's attention, and he lowered the gun slightly.

Bruner kept talking. "Someone ordered you to do this. If you let me go, just let me walk out that door right there, I promise I won't tell a soul—" The words weren't coming out exactly as Bruner wanted them to, but he had his eyes riveted on Amer, looking for a sign, any sign, his captor was going to let him escape.

"Jim, we're above the farmhouse at three thousand feet. There's no sign of activity," Kim began.

"Nothing?" Wright asked.

"No. Not at all."

"Are there any vehicles parked there?"

"No, but there's a large, detached garage; it looks like it could hold a few cars."

There was an uncomfortable silence for a few moments, then Kim finally blurted out, "Jim, you're the on-scene commander, what do you want us to do?"

"Does the house have a clear view of the roads around it?"

"It looks like it. Do you want to roll your nearest vehicles this way? How far away is the closest one?" Kim prompted.

Each of the CIRG HRT trucks had a transceiver that reported its position via a GPS satellite. Wright looked at the LCD screen in his makeshift command center. "I've got one over by State Road 174, near Severn, and another one west of Guilford, off of State Road 32—"

"How far, Jim?"

"The one by Severn is the closest to you, just over four miles."

Over the intercom, it was Barron. "Boss, we can fly over there and pick up a team and fast-rope them down to the farmhouse. You see what the traffic is like on the roads down there. It's rush hour, and if our guys do drive over this way and get close to the farmhouse, the people inside will see them no matter which way they come down Dorsey Run Road."

Kim considered this. He knew Jim Wright, and he trusted him, but Wright wasn't processing what he was hearing fast enough. "Jim, it'll take either truck too long to get here. Give us a vector to the one over by Severn. Tell them to find someplace where we can land—a big parking lot, a field, anything—and we'll pick them up there. I've got fast-rope equipment aboard. I can take the team leader plus four."

Hearing Kim spit out this detailed plan roused Wright out of his momentary lethargy. "Will do, Allen. I'll vector our second helo over to Guilford to pick up the team in the truck over there. They'll be your Dash-Two," Wright said, using the common term for the second aircraft in a group of two. "Out here."

Sandee Barron banked her Blackhawk hard and pointed the nose of her aircraft directly at the triangle on her map representing the HRT vehicle she was headed for.

Aaron Bleich picked up his cell on the first ring. The display told him it was Morton. "Whatcha got Fred? You find the cell phone?"

"I did. I'm here with Erin in a big vacant lot. Our info told us it was somewhere here, so we started doing a grid search while we called the number. We finally heard it ringing."

"Can you pull up the display of recent calls—incoming and outgoing?"

"Sure, wait one."

Bleich put Morton on speakerphone.

"Okay, Aaron. I've got all the incoming and out-going calls. There aren't that many of them."

"Good. I've got you on speaker. Read the numbers

out slowly; I've pulled up a program that'll give me contact info for each number."

"Here's the first one," Morton said as he read off the first ten-digit number.

"Got it. Wait."

"Ready for the next one?" Morton asked.

"Wait, Fred."

After seconds that seemed like minutes, Morton said, "Aaron?"

"Whoa, listen to this! The 202 number you read is for a David Pierce. He's a dirt bag investigative journalist; the guy is really pond scum. The sheet on him says he's sold some of the worst crap imaginable to the cable networks—"

"But why would Masood be—" Morton began to ask, but stopped himself, as they both reached the same conclusion simultaneously.

"You know what this means, don't you?" Bleich paused momentarily to collect his thoughts. "I want you to call this Pierce guy, but use your own phone, not the one Masood tossed. Here's what I want you to say—"

As they frog-walked Jay Bruner into the room with the lights, the cameras, the other equipment, and the ISIS flag, Amer and one of the other kidnappers pushed him down on the small rug.

"Unbind his hands," Mr. Martin commanded. "I want him to enjoy his last seconds of freedom."

Amer moved quickly to comply.

At that moment, seeing the setup and knowing

precisely what was about to happen to him, Bruner was unable to keep from shaking, but he tried to put on a brave face. And he had used a great deal of his remaining strength to control his bowels. *I can't let those bastards see me shit my pants,* he thought. But he lost that battle. As he tried to muster saliva from his dry mouth to spit on them, he soiled himself.

"You pig," one of the other kidnappers said as he moved away from the stench.

Martin stood in front of Bruner. He was clad in black with a black ski mask over his head. He held a book.

"Do you have anything to say before you stand before Allah?"

Should he bargain with them? Were they going to ask him to convert to Islam? Should he beg for mercy? Jay Bruner couldn't force any words from his mouth.

Clouds of dust blew everywhere as Sandee Barron landed her helo in the parched field. The assault-team leader and four of his men were already standing next to their truck. With Sandee's crewman already waving the team aboard, the Blackhawk's oleo struts absorbed the weight of the aircraft as it settled onto its main landing gear.

It took less than a minute and they were all strapped in. A thumbs-up from her crewman was all Sandee needed. She pulled an armload of collective, bunted her bird's nose over, and began a turning climb back toward the farmhouse.

* * *

"Pierce," came the clipped reply as David Pierce answered his cell phone on the first ring.

"Mr. Pierce, good afternoon. A mutual friend suggested I call you," Fred Morton began. "Do you have a moment?"

Pierce held the phone away from his face as he looked at the number in the display. While it was a 703 exchange—Northern Virginia—it didn't show a name, so he knew it wasn't from someone on his contacts list, and it wasn't a number he recognized right away. "Do we know each other?" Pierce asked. He was on guard and seconds away from dumping the call.

"Only through our mutual friend—"

"And he or she would be?"

"Mr. Masood."

Pierce's guard was up. He was expecting the feed of the assassination at any moment. Who was this guy now mucking things up in the middle of what was going to be his biggest payday ever?

"And how do you know Masood?" Pierce asked. He was worried; someone clearly knew who his source was.

"That's not important right now. He wanted me to call you and say he was sorry. The operation he planned this evening will have to occur another time—"

"What? No! I've made promises. Put Masood on. Is he there?"

"Just a minute, I'll get him," Morton said as he looked to his partner. Erin was on the line with the

Geek Tank. Bleich and his team had cloned Pierce's phone and were tracing the number.

A few seconds later Erin gave Morton a thumbs-up and mouthed the words, "We've got him." They now knew where his recent calls had gone. One call a short time ago had been routed through the same cell towers that serviced the farmhouse on Dorsey Run Road.

"Mr. Pierce, sorry, I must have been mistaken. Mr. Masood is busy at the moment, but we'll call back soon." With that, the line went dead.

The second CIRG HRT helo landed in the Guilford Elementary School parking lot. The crew took aboard the team leader and five HRT team members.

As the pilots pushed their UH-60M toward its redline speed of 170 knots—almost 190 miles per hour—they heard the same call from Jim Wright that Sandee, her copilot, and Allen Kim heard. So did the crews of the HRT vehicles also heading toward Dorsey Run Road. "Ninety-nine," Wright began, using the standard call sign for all units on the tactical frequency. "This is Wright, quiet on the net."

Double clicks from the operators in each aircraft and vehicle indicated all his forces in the field understood.

"The situation's critical," Wright continued. "We're now certain Admiral Bruner is being held in the farmhouse you're heading for. But we also think the kidnappers are planning on killing him and broadcasting it live during the evening news hour in D.C. That's not long from now. Allen, it's your show; but right now, speed is life."

It took Kim only seconds to make the decision. "Jim, we're less than two minutes out from the farmhouse. Looks like my bird will be first on top. Dash-Two will be just a few minutes behind me. The farmhouse has a number of dormer windows and has porches on the first and second stories. We'll fast-rope either onto the window eves or the second-story porch," Kim said. Then continuing, "Dash-Two, copy all?"

"Roger, Dash-One; Dash-Two good copy."

"Did you both get the pictures of the inside of the house we linked to you?" Wright asked.

"Dash-One, affirmative."

"Dash-Two, roger."

Both pilots bunted the nose of their birds over and ran the engines right up and through their redline speed. As they did, the teams in the back of each bird donned their gloves and prepared their fast ropes.

Masood and Pierce had agreed that the admiral's assassination would be carried live on the evening news on the U.S. East Coast, but "live" was in the eye of the beholder. The networks and cable channels, as well as bottom feeders like Pierce, had been burned before when the promised live video wasn't delivered, or just as bad, wasn't what they anticipated it would be. Once Masood told him how long reading Bruner's "crimes" and the actual beheading would take, Pierce decided a twenty-minute delay was all he needed.

Saad Masood, aka Mr. Martin, stood behind the kneeling and stooped Jay Bruner. Still dressed in all black and wearing a black ski mask, he now wore a large knife in his belt and was holding a book. He looked directly at the man operating the camera and nodded. The bright lights burned in the background. The camera began to roll and Masood began a long diatribe:

> America, you have failed once again. This man kneels before me and before our other lions of the caliphate. You sent him and his assassins to murder us in our homes, but you failed, and we continue to wage jihad against you. But you killed our women and our children in their beds, you heinous infidels, and this man will pay dearly for that crime.
>
> Look at this man, look at him! He fears us so much he has soiled himself. No one can stop us. We snatched him out from under your noses, close to where his family sleeps. Once we kill him, we are coming for them, and we are coming for all of you, including your president, the pig, Midkiff.
>
> Now here are his sins he is dying for . . .

Masood continued to talk, enjoying the high theater, interspacing readings of Bruner's "offenses," with readings from the Koran.

The Blackhawk streaked ahead at two hundred feet, barely above the power lines that stretched along the roads below. Sandee Barron, her copilot, and Allen Kim, who was hunched down right behind the two pilot seats, saw the farmhouse as it came into view. A quarter mile away, Sandee started to pull up the nose of her bird while lowering the collective to maintain altitude as she began to bleed off some airspeed. The Sikorsky bird shook violently, protesting the rapid deceleration.

"Thirty seconds," she shouted to the team in the back.

"There, Sandee, there," Kim said over the intercom. "That portion of the roof above the second-story porch is flat. I say that's the spot."

"Concur," she answered.

Barron drove her bird at seventy knots and eighty feet above the ground and focused on where she'd pull into a fifty-foot hover over the exact spot above the roof the CIRG team leader had pointed to. Kim turned around and duck-walked into the bird's cabin. He grabbed the shoulder of the team leader and led him to the open cabin door. Kim pointed to the flat roof where he and his team would fast-rope onto the farmhouse.

The team leader gave him a thumbs-up.

As they approached the spot Sandee was aiming for, everyone in the aircraft felt the bird shudder as Sandee pulled the nose up—first ten, then twenty, then thirty degrees above the horizon. Soon all they could see was sky. The helo decelerated rapidly, and when all its forward motion had stopped and she could see the flat roof in her bird's chin bubble, she dumped the nose of the helo forward and leveled her aircraft. Then she worked every control in the cockpit to coax the Blackhawk over the exact spot. Once she was in a steady hover, she called to Kim over the intercom, "Now, Allen."

Kim kicked two 40-millimeter-diameter ropes out of the bird, their one end made fast inside the bird and the other descending toward the roof. A nod from Kim, and the assault team leader slid down one rope like an oil drop on a string, landing hard on the flat roof. He was followed seconds later by the rest of the team.

"Dash-Two, I've got five on target now. Pushing off. You'll see a flat roof above a second-story porch. That's your aim point."

"Dash-Two, roger."

Inside the farmhouse, the kidnappers heard the unmistakable sound of an approaching helicopter. Several of the men ran to windows on the east side of the house to try to see exactly where the noise was coming from. They wrestled with the blankets they'd securely taped down over the windows with duct tape, trying to pull them off.

Masood had the presence of mind to shout out, "Amer, run up to the second floor and see what's happening! Take your weapon!"

Instincts took over for Jay Bruner. He needed to buy time for those he hoped were his rescuers.

Bruner rolled onto his side and swept his legs violently, toppling Masood over. The terrorist fell hard and hit his head on the wood floor. The blow momentarily stunned Masood and gave Bruner a small opening. He managed to get himself up onto his hands and knees and got ready to push up and run from the house.

But that was as far as he got. The kidnapper operating the camera had no weapon, but rushed at Bruner and tackled him. Both men went down hard as Bruner grappled with his attacker, buying precious seconds.

While it was chaos on the first floor of the farmhouse, on the second floor, it was precise choreography. The five HRT assaulters had simply swung down from the roof and onto the porch.

They entered the house through two open, second-story windows and methodically, but quickly, cleared each room on the second floor. Then they moved toward the stairway.

A man had just reached the top of the stairway and saw the assault team. He shot wildly at the HRT men closest to him.

The lead HRT man fired his MP5 submachine gun and put two bullets in Amer's head. He dropped like a sack and tumbled back down the stairs.

As Bruner and one of the kidnappers grappled on the floor, Masood had recovered, drew his knife and stood over the two men. "Let him go! Let him go! I'll kill him right now!" he shouted.

Bruner grasped the man he was grappling with as

tightly as he could, knowing his survival depended on Martin not getting a clean angle on him.

Just then, there was a blinding flash and thunderous sound as a flash-bang grenade went off near the bottom of the stairway. Seconds later, a second flash-bang went off, and the HRT assaulters ran down the stairs onto the first floor.

Above the farmhouse at five hundred feet, Sandee Barron drove her helo in tight circles. She could see Dash-Two coming into view from the west, screaming toward the farmhouse at two hundred feet.

"Allen, look, two squirters," Barron shouted over the intercom. "They're headed toward the garage. Do you want Dash-Two to drop its team there and intercept them?"

"Not until I hear from my lead assaulter that the admiral's secure."

It was over quickly on the first floor of the farmhouse. The flash-bang grenades had stunned and disoriented the kidnappers. No hero, Masood had dropped his knife and stood with his hands in the air.

Bruner had disengaged from the man he was grappling with, and two HRT assaulters rushed to him. One subdued the kidnapper while the other one grabbed the admiral and lifted him to his feet. "Sir, are you okay?"

"I think so, fellas. You got here just in time."

"Let's get you outside, sir."

"If you don't mind, could you get me to a toilet first? I've got some business to attend to."

Kim, Barron, and her copilot heard the call at the same time they saw the two HRT men on the ground outside the farmhouse surrounding the admiral and giving them a thumbs-up.

"We've got him. Package is secure. He's a little worse for wear, but otherwise okay," the assault team leader said.

"Got it," Kim replied. Then on the net to the second bird, "Dash-Two, Kim. Go after the squirters; they're inside the garage."

Seconds later, six figures slid down ropes and landed on the ground between the farmhouse and the garage. They deployed in blocking and oversight positions ready to assault the garage and drag out those inside.

Just then, the garage door opened, and a van leapt out. Well-aimed shots took out the driver and the passenger, and the vehicle careened wildly and crashed into a tree.

Moments later, Barron landed her bird in the front yard of the farmhouse, and Kim emerged and headed straight for Bruner. "Sir, I'm Allen Kim. I'm team leader for this CIRG HRT team. We're FBI, but we're seconded to an organization called Op-Center—"

Bruner listened—after a fashion—his ears still ringing from the flash-bangs. But he had a broad smile on his face.

"Admiral, we need to get you out of here and debriefed. We're gonna jump into this bird and fly to BWI; it's just a short distance away. Then we'll get you reunited with your family just as soon as we can."

Minutes later, as Barron and her copilot lifted off with Kim, Bruner, and a few of the HRT team, Kim called Wright, "Jim, we've got the package and he's okay. No casualties for our team. We have all the people who were holding him. Three enemy KIA and three enemy POW. More when we land."

"Roger, Allen, great work. I'll call Op-Center."

CHAPTER TWENTY

July 22, 1845 Eastern Daylight Time

"Jim, that's wonderful news," Chase Williams replied. Wright had given him a complete debrief of the operation and the Op-Center director had listened without interrupting him. "Well done to you and to Allen and his team. I'll contact the FBI director and have him fly a team to BWI to debrief the admiral. If we hurry, we can complete the debrief, get him cleaned up, and return him to his family tonight."

"Roger that, boss," Wright replied. "He's pretty wrung out. They've had him for almost five days, and Allen says it doesn't look like they fed him—plus he was moments from having his throat slit. We'll get him a change of clothes and some chow while we're waiting for the debrief team."

"Good idea. I'll let the president know."

* * *

The call between Chase Williams and President Midkiff was brief. The two men discussed who should call Meagan Bruner with the news and settled on Admiral Eric Oldham. Williams would make the call to the VCNO.

But that wasn't all the two men discussed. The president told Williams that once a new FBI director was in place, he wanted the three of them to sit down and hash out which organization would lead domestic counterterrorism efforts.

Eric Oldham was grateful the president and Williams picked him to deliver the good news to Meagan Bruner and her three children. He had borne up as well as he could when he had gone to their home days ago to deliver the bad news about his kidnapping, and he had left their home with a huge lump in his throat.

"Admiral Oldham, hello. I saw your number pop up. Do you have news?" Meagan Bruner began, hoping for positive news but girding herself for the worst.

"Meagan, it's the best possible news. We found Jay. He's a little worse for wear, but unhurt."

Tears—tears of joy—welled up in her eyes as she processed what Oldham was saying. "Oh, Eric, I'm so thankful. Where is he, and when can we see him?"

Williams and Oldham had discussed just how much to tell Meagan Bruner in this initial call, and Oldham had also consulted with the on-call psychologist at the Navy's Bethesda Medical Center.

"Meagan, Jay's at BWI at a temporary command center being debriefed. But we hope to be able to reunite him with you and your three kids as soon as possible—tonight if all goes well."

"Amber and Katherine will be so happy to see their father. But Dale has already returned to his unit in Coronado. We'll want to fly him home as soon as possible. I'll call him right now."

At that moment, Dale Bruner was getting ready to sneak into the ISIL compound. It was 0200, and the streets were finally quiet. He left the light Mk17 assault rifle and the MP7 in the locked Humvee. He tucked all the gear he could carry into his combat pack and set off for the compound.

He was dressed in the gear Peters had insisted he wear, so he blended in—to a point. Only the Kevlar helmet, NVGs, and his weapon stood out as western military gear, but he had seen many ISIL fighters come and go wearing similar equipment—so that didn't worry him. In deference to moving quickly and carrying a large cache of explosives and ammo, he wore no body armor. He placed a four-pound block of C-4 in an alley close to the compound and set the timer. Then he moved off again, moving easily through the sharp green landscape afforded him by the night vision goggles mounted on his helmet.

He knew he had to move quickly. In spite of his attempt to disguise himself and blend in, he had to bet on the fact that anyone sighting him would suspect he didn't belong there. He had a mental map of the inside of the building burned on his brain.

* * *

Inside the building Dale Bruner was approaching, Mabad al-Dosari and his number two were having a heated discussion. "This should have happened over an hour ago," al-Dosari snapped. "It's past the evening news hour on the U.S. East Coast. Have you called Masood? What's going on?"

"I've sent him texts and left several voice mails. He hasn't replied to any of them."

"But he assured us this would be on the evening news tonight. Didn't he tell you he'd reached an agreement with a journalist who'd sell this to a cable channel?"

"Yes. Maybe there's just some delay—"

"Enough. I knew we should have had Al Jazeera broadcast this. Contact the imam in Minneapolis and ask him how we get in touch with this Amer. I want to know where they have our hostage!"

His number two knew it was useless to argue and he left to make the calls. He was as perplexed as al-Dosari.

Meagan Bruner had texted and called her son and asked him to contact her. She was anxious to tell him the good news and get him back to Springfield as soon as possible so he could reunite with his father.

But when she got no reply, her eagerness to share the news caused her to take a step she'd never taken during her husband's or her son's careers. She called the duty office at the Naval Special Warfare Command.

"Naval Special Warfare Command duty office, Petty Officer Second Class Charles speaking. How may I help you sir or ma'am?"

"Petty Officer Charles, this is Meagan Bruner. My son, Lieutenant Dale Bruner, is an instructor with your training component. I hate to bother you like this, but it's rather urgent. Can you put me in touch with his commanding officer?"

"Yes ma'am; wait one please," Charles replied as he pulled up a command directory on his computer monitor.

Petty Officer Charles had been trained not to reveal information he shouldn't share with unknown callers. Still, the woman sounded sincere—and worried. Rather than dismiss her as a crank caller—something the SEALs had to deal with more than they cared to think about—he took the extra step of calling Captain Pete Cummings.

"Cummings," came the response.

"Sir, I've got a woman on the line who says her name is Meagan Bruner. She's looking for her son and she wants to speak with his CO. I looked in the directory and saw there's a Lieutenant Bruner in your training unit. Do you want to speak with her, sir?"

"Yes, absolutely. Put her through." After a short pause, "Mrs. Bruner, hello. It's Pete Cummings, Dale's CO."

"Oh, Captain Cummings," Meagan began. "I'm sorry to bother you, but I'm having trouble reaching Dale. I have wonderful news to share with him, and I'm afraid it can't wait—"

"Can I ask you if this is about Admiral Bruner, ma'am? Is he . . . has he been rescued?"

"Yes! But please don't tell Dale; I want to tell him myself. But he's not replying to my texts or phone calls. When he left here to return to Coronado he was so worried his dad would never be found, but now he has!"

"Mrs. Bruner, that's wonderful news," he replied. But Cummings's antenna went up. "Ma'am, how long ago did you say Dale left home to come back here?"

"Well, it was several days ago. He wanted to stay with us, but he said he didn't have much leave on the books. Do you have a way of reaching him quickly?"

Cummings was confused. Bruner hadn't returned to the command, and he didn't think he'd flown back to Coronado. He framed his reply carefully. "Mrs. Bruner. There must be some confusion—but I'm sure we can clear it up. Dale hasn't returned to the command yet. Are you certain he said he was coming back here?"

"Why yes, Captain; quite certain," Meagan replied emphatically.

Cummings recalled something his chief in his first team had told him when he was a young LTJG, *If it walks like a duck, and talks like a duck, it must be a duck*. Something was wrong.

"Mrs. Bruner, I'll see what I can find out and get back to you as soon as I can. And Mrs. Bruner, would you mind if I ask you how Admiral Bruner was rescued and who gave you the news that he had been freed?"

"The vice chief of naval operations, Admiral Oldham, told us the good news. He said an organization called Op-Center—I have to confess I don't know who they are or what they do—rescued him."

"Thank you, ma'am. I promise I'll call you as soon as I learn anything, anything at all."

Shortly after finishing the call with Meagan Bruner, Cummings was in his exec's office. "XO, I think we have a problem."

"That's great news, boss," Brian Dawson said as soon as Chase Williams told him about Admiral Bruner's rescue. "And no casualties. That's remarkable under the circumstances."

"You're right: that's the best part. But I have to tell you, you and Hector were missed during this operation. It all worked out in the end, but it would have worked more smoothly if you all were here during this crisis."

"Thanks sir, but you've got a good team there. No surprise it all went well."

"I know that Major Volner and his squad wanted to get their beaks wet, but there'll be other opportunities. And I know you all are tired of cooling your heels in Baghdad. Duncan's working on getting a C-17 to you ASAP. It will be good to have you all back."

"We'll call this one a good practice session, boss. See you soon."

"Someone's trying to track Masood down. He's gotten e-mails and texts from Mosul. I think it's pretty clear who he was taking orders from," Fred Morton said as he stood in front of Aaron Bleich's desk.

"You've got that right. I think we'll know more after we find out what else he says after he's fully interrogated, but Jim says he started spilling his guts as soon as they got him to BWI."

"You think we'll go hard after al-Dosari now that he's taken the fight to us here?"

"Way above my pay grade, that's for sure, but it wouldn't surprise me," Bleich replied.

Pressed up against a back door on the ISIL compound, Dale Bruner figured he would have just a short time to find and rescue his dad once he put the first part of his plan in motion. The building's layout suggested there were multiple rooms his dad could be held in, but some rooms were far more likely than others.

While he'd never had second thoughts about embarking on this mission, it did give him pause and reminded him just what the SEAL brotherhood meant to him. Having a comrade next to you who would literally give his life to save yours was something he had always valued, but he'd never thought about it that deeply. Now he did.

CHAPTER TWENTY-ONE

July 23, 0330 Arabia Standard Time

An explosion some two blocks from the compound shattered the early morning quiet. A moment later, a second explosive device detonated in the street between the building Bruner had left and the building where ISIS was encamped.

Moments later, a blast from the breeching charge stuck to the front door of the compound rocked the building. The door held, but windows all along the front of the structure shattered. As debris rained down along the front of the building's facade, Bruner entered through a back door. Unexpectedly, the door yielded to his shoulder, so he entered with little noise.

The first explosion awakened a few of the fighters sleeping inside the ISIS compound, and the second one had roused more. But when the breeching charge exploded, every one of the dozens of fighters living in the main building—as well as their family members—were shocked out of their sleep. Babies and toddlers started crying and women rushed to protect their children as fighters grabbed their weapons and rushed toward the front of the building. Except for a few flashlights, they were in total darkness. Bruner had set his second explosive device at the base of the power pole that served the compound.

More and more men pushed out into the street, and a dazed al-Dosari quickly joined them. The road was now quiet, and the men looked to their leader for direction. "This may be the prelude to an air bombardment!" he shouted as memories of his son's death welled up inside him. "You take as many men as you need and bring the trucks in front of the building," he continued, pointing at one man. "The rest of you, gather up the families, get them out here, and load them into the trucks. No packing anything; we could be bombed any minute!"

Bruner's diversion couldn't have worked better. Inside, he entered the first room where he guessed his father might be held, his Mk17 at the ready, the infrared flood of his night vision goggles painting the darkened room with a bright green wash. The woman trying to dress two toddlers screamed and stepped in front of her children to protect them from the intruder. Bruner lowered his assault rifle, put his finger to his lips, and quickly exited the room. He headed down a long hallway, following the mental map he had burned on his brain. The next room he wanted to search was just around the corner from the end of the hallway.

More than seven thousand miles away from where a lone Navy SEAL was acting as a one-man army, two senior SEALs had been talking for almost an hour. They were no closer to the answer they sought than when they began their conversation in the late afternoon at the Naval Special Warfare Command training compound.

"Skipper, I know Lieutenant Bruner hasn't been here long enough for us to really size him up, but he came here with a tremendous reputation. I'd say 'this isn't like him' is kind of an understatement."

"I know, XO, but he's got to be pretty torn up over his dad being kidnapped and he was clear when we talked that he didn't think the Navy was doing enough to find him. And there's something else that's been gnawing at me."

"What's that?"

"Bruner's reputation with the teams was stellar. He was a leader and a fighter and a trigger-puller. But the book on him was he was pretty independent-minded. He would have been pulled up short by higher headquarters had they known in advance what he intended to do on some ops he commanded. But in every case, the op was successful, and he brought all his men back. Hard to criticize a leader who does that—"

"But you think he's got enough of an independent streak that he's more inclined to take things into his own hands than not?"

"Exactly; that's what I'm worried about."

"And you said Mrs. Bruner was just as firm that he said he was returning to Coronado? Any chance he came back here and just decided to stay on leave for a while? He flew out of here with two weeks of leave authorized. Dunno, maybe if I were worried about my dad I wouldn't be in the right frame of mind to come back to work right away."

"Maybe, but if it were me, and I wasn't going to go back to work, I'd probably stay with my mom and sisters—that's where I'd be the most useful—not come back to my apartment and stew alone. I don't think he's here."

"That's fine, Skipper, and he sure rates staying on leave for a while. But we texted and called him and said it was urgent he contact us. Even if he's on leave, he'd reply."

"Yeah, I agree. But his life is in chaos right now. He could have lost his cell phone for all we know. What we owe Mrs. Bruner is to find out whether he's in Coronado or not."

"There's one way to find out," his exec replied. "Bruner lives in an apartment over on C Avenue. I'll check the recall roster for the address, but I'm pretty sure it's between 7th and 8th streets. There's no garage, so his Ford-150 should be parked outside. I'll drive over there now and see if his truck is there, and then knock on his door."

"Good idea," Cummings replied, and then paused. "Bruner drives a truck?"

"Single guy, Skipper, what can I tell you? I saw it

when he was leaving work one day. It's all tricked out, and he's got a gaudy Chargers stencil on the back window. I'll call you when I get to his apartment."

"Let's hope he's there."

"Mom, what's a 'debrief'?"

Meagan Bruner climbed off the step stool and put down the streamer she was hanging up to welcome her husband home. "Katherine, do you remember when your dad was still flying? He explained how before a flight the pilots talked about what they're going to do on the mission; that was a brief. Then when they returned, they had a debrief to talk about how everything went and what they could do better next time. This is pretty much the same kind of thing."

"But he didn't sign up for this 'mission,'" Amber said. "Some assholes kidnapped him. Thank God someone—those Op-Center guys, whoever they are— rescued him. He doesn't know anything except they almost killed him. Why can't they just bring him home now?"

"Or we could go get him," Katherine suggested.

Meagan wasn't sure herself why there needed to be a "debrief" or how long it would take. All she could do now was keep her daughters calmed down while she waited for her husband's return and worried about her son.

CHAPTER TWENTY-TWO

July 23, 0340 Arabia Standard Time

Dale Bruner pushed the door open with the barrel of his Mk17 and peered into the room. As he did, two fighters who were trying to gather up their families saw the armed man in the dim light of the room and instinctively reached for their weapons. Bruner saw both figures clearly in his NVGs and toggled his infrared sight, placing a green dot on the head of the nearest figure. He squeezed the trigger of his assault rifle and double-tapped first one, and then the other fighter, the sound suppressor on the Mk17 muffling only some of the rifle's blast.

But the heavy 7.62 slugs did their deadly duty. As blood, skull fragments, and brain matter flew everywhere, the women and children in the room started to scream and wail. Bruner knew it was useless to try to silence them, so he just slammed the heavy wooden door shut. He ran down the hallway, found the stairway he was looking for, and headed up to the building's second floor. He knew he didn't have long to find his father.

At Op-Center, with another successful mission complete, the focus was now on getting Dawson, Rodriquez, and the JSOC team home and on returning the CIRG HRT team to Quantico. The Geek Tank was no longer in port and starboard rotation, and in Op-Center's command center it was back to routine ops.

Chase Williams made a habit of having his teams debrief at Op-Center as soon after an op as feasible. Anticipating Dawson and the others would arrive back around midday tomorrow and would be exhausted after a long flight, he and Anne Sullivan had decided to have a debrief with all players the following day.

"Skipper, I'm at his apartment. I was right, it's on C Street—715 C to be exact—and I've knocked on his door, but nada. There are parking spots designated for each unit and his truck's not here."

"Maybe he's just out getting some dinner, or working out—" Cummings offered.

"Don't think so, Skipper. There's a mailbox next to his door, and it's overflowing, and there are two UPS packages in front of his door."

"Do you want to see if his car is at the airport? He told me he'd park in the long-term lot. You know what his truck looks like. That's the only way we'll know for sure."

"Give me a half hour. I'll call you from there."

* * *

As Dale Bruner got to the top of the stairway on the building's second floor, he revisited his mental map of what rooms were the most likely ones where his dad might be held. There was a dent in his confidence as the two rooms he had entered on the first floor of the compound were small, were clearly bedrooms, and had windows a person could climb out of. They didn't seem like the kind of rooms where a hostage would be held.

As he cracked open the door at the top of the stairway, he saw light and heard shouting. He thought he knew what was occurring—the building's occupants were evacuating because the explosion of his breeching charge had convinced them the building was under attack. As he paused to evaluate his options, he wondered if the ISIL fighters would take his dad out of the compound while they were evacuating their families.

Bruner knew this was the most fateful decision he'd make since he began his lone-wolf mission. He was still considering his options when he heard heavy footsteps, then shouting, and a general commotion on the other side of the door he was pressed up against. He looked to his right and saw a small alcove with a deep sink. He ducked into the tiny space and hunkered down.

"Whatcha got, XO?" Pete Cummings asked as he picked up his phone on the second ring.

"What I've got is a Ford-150. It's here in the long-term lot. It looks like Bruner never returned to San Diego."

"Are you certain it's his truck?"

His exec paused before responding. *I damn well am sure.* "Skipper, I wanted his truck to be gone, but it's not. It's here. And I know his truck; it's definitely his."

"Okay, come on back. We can figure out our next steps as soon as you get here."

Cummings didn't like questioning his exec, but he needed to be sure. And while his XO was driving to the airport, he hadn't been idle. He had done what SEALs are trained to do—hope for the best, but plan for the worst. The "best" would have been not finding Bruner's truck in the long-term lot. Now it was the "worst," and he'd decided what he'd do in the event this happened. He already had the number jotted down.

Within a minute of his jumping into his hiding place, Dale Bruner heard noise and footsteps as the door to the second floor burst open, and people began running down the steps. It was clear to him now that the compound was being evacuated. Maybe the explosions and the breaching charge had done their work too well. He wanted to create chaos and confusion and give himself enough time to rescue his dad. Would his mission consist of nothing more than finding his father in an otherwise empty building? For the moment, he could do nothing but wait.

"Navy Command Center, Chief Petty Officer Hudson speaking."

"Chief, this is Captain Pete Cummings; I'm calling from the Naval Special Warfare Command in San

Diego. May I speak with your watch commander, please?"

"Yes sir, wait one," he replied. Then, turning to the captain sitting at a console across the room, "Captain, there's a Captain Cummings from the Naval Special Warfare Command who wants to talk with you. Line two."

"Got it, Chief, thanks." Then he hit the button on his touch screen and spoke into the mic on his headset. "Captain Duffy here; I'm the watch commander."

"This is Captain Pete Cummings. I'm CO of the Naval Special Warfare Command training component here in Coronado. I'm missing one of my lieutenants, and I need your help. I need to speak with the VCNO."

Duffy couldn't believe what he was hearing. He muted his mic and called out to Chief Hudson. "Chief, read me the number this guy is calling from. I want to know if it's legit."

"Captain, its 619 537-1243."

Duffy had had several tours in San Diego and knew 619 was an exchange in that city. He could press it further and insist on calling Cummings back to ensure it wasn't some kind of crank call or a hoax, but he decided to hear the caller out. He took his mic off mute. "Captain, I'm listening. Would you slow down and tell me a little more. It's late here, and I'm certain the VCNO has already departed for the day."

Pete Cummings poured out everything he knew, and the two men embarked on a lengthy and detailed discussion.

Finally, Duffy said, "Look, Skipper, you're a senior

O-6, and you're in command, and I gotta think you know how the Navy is supposed to work. The VCNO doesn't see one-star flag officers unless his aide and his EA and God knows who else have massaged his schedule to death. I get the urgency of your situation and appreciate that you're worried about your lieutenant. But I am going way, way out on a limb to do what you're asking me to do. You said this guy is single, right?"

"Yes, sir."

"If it turns out that this is nothing more than your guy finding some good-looking honey and shacking up with her for a few days, I'll have your ass for this."

"I know it's not that, Captain. I'll stake my reputation on it."

"You just did. Stay by your phone."

With that the line went dead.

CHAPTER TWENTY-THREE

ISIS COMPOUND: MOSUL, IRAQ

July 23, 0415 Arabia Standard Time

Dale Bruner was torn. He was anxious to find his dad, but he needed the ISIL fighters and their families to clear out of the building—or at least stop moving about. He had been hunkered down for a while and hadn't heard footsteps on the stairway for several minutes. He rose cautiously and walked a few feet until he was pressed up against the back of the door leading to the second-floor hallway.

He cracked the door open several inches. It was quiet. He stuck his head out into the hallway and looked left and right. His NVGs only delivered a narrow field of view so he swiveled his head so he could see the entire corridor. There was no one there. He turned left and began moving.

The U.S. Navy is like most bureaucracies when it comes to senior leaders taking only calls they want to take and being fully informed about who the caller is and what he or she wants before they speak with them—only perhaps more so. It was after 2100 when Captain Duffy had called Admiral Oldham at his quarters in the Washington Navy Yard. As Oldham had him relate the details of his call with Cummings, the VCNO connected the dots instantly and recognized Cummings was Dale Bruner's skipper. With no aide or other assistant at his quarters to place the call for him and get the other person on the line first, Oldham had told Duffy to give Cummings the number of his government cell phone.

"Admiral Oldham here," the VCNO said as he answered the phone on the first ring.

"Admiral, this is Captain Cummings. I'm CO of the Naval Special Warfare Command training component here in Coronado. Sir, thank you for taking my call. I'm mindful of my chain of command, and if this weren't so urgent, I would've used that before calling you, sir. And I'm sorry to bother you in your quarters, but I'm worried about one of my men, and I hope you can help me."

"Captain, to be completely honest with you, I'm not in the habit of taking calls late at night about missing lieutenants. But the command center duty officer said it had something do with Lieutenant Dale Bruner, and that's what got you through to me. Now how about starting at the beginning and telling me what is going on and why you're worried about him?"

Cummings poured out the entire story, telling Oldham even more than he had shared with Duffy. The

VCNO, in turn, revealed what had occurred when he first called on Meagan Bruner and her three children. After an extended conversation, the two men validated each other's fears: Dale Bruner may have embarked on a solo mission to rescue his dad.

Oldham wasn't one to play it safe, but he needed the right trigger. "Captain, I'm going to say this carefully, so please think a moment before responding. Do you think your lieutenant has gone rogue—maybe to go to the aid of his father?"

Cummings didn't hesitate. "Yes, Admiral, I do."

"All right then. I want you to call the duty desk at NCIS there in San Diego," he began, using the well-known acronym for the Naval Criminal Investigative Service. "They're at NAS North Island. Report this to them, and give them all the information you can. I'll call the duty office at their headquarters over at Joint Base Anacostia-Bolling. Once we get the investigative wheels churning, we'll be able to track him down."

"I sure hope so, Admiral."

"Just do your part, Captain, and leave the rest to us."

Dale Bruner tried to not let his creeping doubts immobilize him. He wondered if his dad was in this building at all. What had happened already—his encounter with the two fighters he shot, the commotion of fighters and their families evacuating the building, as well as all the rest—told him this clearly was an ISIL-controlled building. And while he didn't doubt the quality of the intel Zack Peters had given him about the geography of the inside of the building, he reminded himself it was based on a dated Golden Brigade survey of the building before it fell into ISIL's hands.

There were three rooms on the second floor where he thought his dad might be held. Now that the building was empty, he could move quickly from room to room. He looked right and left to ensure no one was lurking in the hallway, and then took off in a trot toward the first room on his mental list. If he couldn't find his dad, he might be able to find some evidence that he had been held in one of them.

Over a dozen trucks had sped off carrying fighters and family members. Now only two trucks remained in front of the ISIL compound, the drivers idling their engines. Mabad al-Dosari and a few of his key lieutenants remained behind, wanting to ensure all the others had dodged the likely air bombardment before they made their escape. Al-Dosari had waved away the urgings of his second-in-command that he be the first to leave.

It had been more than fifteen minutes since the breeching charge had gone off, and there was no sign of approaching enemy aircraft. Soon after the evacuation had begun, al-Dosari had alerted his military commander in charge of the radar batteries they had stolen from the Iraqi Army. Those radars now searched the skies, but had found nothing.

"Do you think it was a false alarm, and there won't be an air attack?" one of his lieutenants asked. "Maybe it was the Iraqi Army, and they're planning a ground assault—and this is just the beginning of that. When the front door to our compound refused to yield, they might have decided to back off and not attack."

Al-Dosari considered this. While the thousands of ISIS fighters he controlled roamed freely through wide swaths of Iraq, Syria, and other countries and struck terror in all those they faced, when it came to defending their own families and dwellings, they were at a decided disadvantage.

"I'm not sure what kind of attack it might be," he replied. "Our first priority is to ensure our families' safety. Have we gotten everyone out?"

"Yes, I think so," one of his men replied.

"That's not good enough!" al-Dosari snapped. "Take three men with you and do a sweep of the building. Once you tell me we've gotten everyone else out, we can leave. Until then, we wait."

Inside, Dale Bruner had cleared two rooms on the second floor and was heading toward the third. The compound had six stories, but the intel Peters had given him strongly suggested that hostages would be held on lower floors. If his dad wasn't in the room he was approaching, there were two rooms on the third deck on his mental map.

The ISIS fighters al-Dosari sent into the building knew they needed to do their job quickly. They had been living in this compound for over a week and they knew the building well, even with only flashlights to illuminate their way. Their plan was to dash up to the sixth floor—there were no elevators—search room to room in teams of two, and work their way down the building floor by floor. They started up the steps of the stairway closest to the front door of the compound on a dead run.

Dale Bruner flung open the door of the room on the second floor—but it was empty. His heart sank. Was his dad in this building at all? ISIL controlled any number of buildings in central Mosul. Maybe they were holding him in a different one. *Get moving, Bruner. The only easy day was yesterday.*

He moved quickly toward the door leading to the nearest staircase. Now that he was convinced the building had been evacuated, he didn't throw caution completely to the wind, but he worried far less about stealth than he did about speed.

He entered the stairwell and started climbing. He had scaled a half a dozen steps when suddenly he heard heavy footfalls below him that sounded like they were moving his way. He also heard men talking. *Decision time, Bruner. Retreat to the second floor or keep climbing?* The need to find his dad overwhelmed all his other emotions. He moved toward the third floor.

But the men below him were taking the steps two at a time, and as Bruner got near the landing on the third floor, the footfalls were right behind him and he heard shouts. He grasped the door handle and was about to pull it open when the light from a flashlight overwhelmed his NVGs and shots rang out.

The wild shots missed, and instinctively Bruner

fired his Mk17 toward the light and the sound as he flipped his NVGs up. He heard a groan and the sound of a falling body, as one attacker was hit and fell down the steps.

More shots rang out from the attackers at the bottom of the steps as Bruner expended his last bullet and reached for another clip. Just then, he felt a hard slap in his left thigh, followed immediately by searing pain—a pain more intense than anything he'd ever felt. Seconds later, a second bullet found his right shoulder, and the force of the shot knocked him down, and he tumbled down the stairway. Then it all went black.

Eric Oldham believed Pete Cummings and wanted to help find Dale Bruner. The SEAL lieutenant was the son of an admiral who was a family friend, but he didn't intend to turn the Navy upside down with the search. He called NCIS at Anacostia-Bolling and talked to the watch commander as he had promised he would. That complete, he did the only other thing he could think to do: he called the Op-Center watch floor. He then returned to the Larry Bond novel he was reading.

Mabad al-Dosari and the men in front of the main compound building heard the gunshots coming from inside the building and rushed toward the front door. They were about to open it, when four ISIS fighters emerged. Two were half-carrying, half-dragging Bruner out of the building, and another man was helping his wounded comrade walk upright.

"I heard the shots. What's going on?" al-Dosari barked.

"We found him in the stairwell. He shot at us and hit Rabah. He'll be all right. But we put at least two bullets in him—"

"His weapons and gear are military. Who is he?" al-Dosari asked.

"We looked through all his pockets but found no ID. He's been lapsing in and out of consciousness. Do you want us to take care of his wounds?" the man asked.

"See to Rabah's wounds first, then his. Tie him up and put him in the truck once you've done that." Then pointing to the other two men, he continued. "You two go back inside and see if there's anyone else there, especially anyone who looks like him."

Fearing an encounter with other armed men, the ISIS fighters sent back into their compound searched more methodically. When they finally returned to the courtyard, the wounded fighter had been attended to and Bruner's wounds had been bandaged. The American was in the back of one of the trucks, with his hands bound, and was drifting in and out of consciousness.

"Is the building empty now?" al-Dosari asked.

"No," one of the men replied. "Two of our comrades are inside, dead. The man we captured must have killed them. Do you want us to bring their bodies out?"

"No, we don't have time. Get into that truck. We'll drive to the safe house where everyone else is. But if there's no air attack by midmorning we'll return here. This guy had explosives and breeching charges on him; it looks like he's the one who set off the explosions and then snuck into our compound."

"We need to know who he is and why he did this," one of his men said.

"We will. But we need to get to the safe house and get the bullets out of him. If we lose him, we'll learn nothing," al-Dosari replied.

As the two trucks left the compound and Dale Bruner bounced around in the back of one of the trucks, he passed out from the pain of his gunshot wounds.

As the black SUV pulled up to the front of their home, Meagan Bruner rushed outside, followed by her two daughters. Jim Wright had remained on scene while Admiral Bruner had been cleaned up and debriefed. His soiled orange jumpsuit had been replaced with a blue one, with FBI stenciled on the back in big white letters. He had talked with the FBI psychologist who pronounced him okay. Wright had called Meagan Bruner when they left BWI and alerted her that her husband would be coming home that night.

As Jay Bruner emerged from the truck, even in the darkness, his wife could see the broad grin on his face. Meagan ran at him and embraced him.

"Oh, Jay; you're all right. Thank God!" she began, tears welling up.

"Hey Megs, it was just a rough day at the office," he replied as he held her.

Bruner looked over his wife's right shoulder and saw Amber and Katherine approaching.

"Dad!" Katherine shouted as the two sisters ran toward him.

But Bruner didn't see who he thought he'd see emerging from the house. He didn't see his son.

CHAPTER TWENTY-FOUR

July 23, 0645 Eastern Daylight Time

When Chase Williams arrived at his office, Anne Sullivan was waiting for him.

"Mornin', boss."

"Good morning, Anne. All quiet last evening?"

"Our watch floor got an interesting call; that's the first thing I wanted to discuss with you."

"Sure. But if you don't mind, first tell me whether we've got Brian, Hector, and the JSOC team headed back this way yet."

"Their C-17 should be landing at Baghdad International soon. I think the schedule slipped a few hours because the aircraft had to take a longer route to avoid some weather, but we're pretty much on track."

"Good, so what is it we need to discuss?"

"Last night, Admiral Oldham, he's the VCNO, called our watch floor with a bit of an odd story—"

"Odd? I knew Eric Oldham from my active-duty days. He's a pretty straight shooter."

"I didn't mean 'odd' as in we didn't believe him. I meant odd in that it involves Admiral Bruner's son, Dale."

"Involves?" Williams asked.

With that, Sullivan detailed the entire story.

After Sullivan had finished, Williams paused to frame his reply. "From what you've told me, Admiral Oldham knows the Bruner family well and is concerned Dale might be desperate enough to take matters into his own hands. I agree we need to look into this; I'll call the VCNO right now."

An hour later, less than twenty miles from where Williams and Sullivan were talking about Dale Bruner, at Joint Base Anacostia-Bolling, two men—the director of the Naval Criminal Investigative Service and his chief of staff—were discussing the SEAL lieutenant.

"The VCNO himself called, not his deputy or his EA?" Jason Gunn asked.

"Yes sir, I got that from the watch team chief myself," his chief of staff replied.

"And this lieutenant's command thinks he's gone AWOL; that's the long and short of it?"

"Yes, sir."

"But he's on authorized leave, isn't that right?"

"Yes."

"And all this was triggered because his mother was worried about him."

"That's what they said."

The interrogation continued, with Gunn sounding more and more incredulous each time his chief of staff related another fact he had gleaned from the electronic log his watch team had compiled regarding the VCNO's call the night before.

Jason Gunn didn't consider himself a bureaucrat—far from it. And if you asked anyone on his core staff at NCIS Headquarters, they would agree: he was an open and even caring boss. But he hadn't climbed to the top of government civilian service by taking risks and ignoring rules. He thought the VCNO was correct in alerting his command, but he didn't see the need to take immediate—or perhaps any—action. And he certainly wasn't about to break any of the rules and regulations that governed the Naval Criminal Investigative Service.

"It's been a while since we had this kind of case. Doesn't someone have to be AWOL for seventy-two hours before they're declared a deserter?"

"That's right, boss."

"And we're not close to that."

"Correct."

"Look, if the second-senior guy in our Navy chain of command says to do something, then we have to do something. Have the ops division open a file on this—what's his name?"

"Bruner, sir. Lieutenant Dale Bruner."

"Bruner, right. Get a file going and do what we normally do in cases like this—nothing more, nothing less.

Come in and give me an update this afternoon, fair enough?"

"Yes, sir."

At Baghdad International, it was still predawn when the Globemaster rolled onto its final approach. Dawson, Rodriquez, and their JSOC team had been awakened two hours earlier by a call from the Op-Center watch floor. They were ready to load up once the C-17 was refueled and made ready for its return flight.

For Volner and his JSOC team, the good news that Admiral Bruner had been found was tempered by their brief, one-sided skirmish with the ISIL fighters in Mosul. It had been little more than a holding action. Yes, they could have been overwhelmed by a large force, and withdrawing to Baghdad was the only sensible option. And they had gotten their beaks wet and taken out a number of the terrorists. But all that said, it was a less than fully satisfying encounter.

Roger McCord and Aaron Bleich appeared in Chase Williams's doorway. "You wanted to see us, boss?" McCord asked.

"Come in, fellas. Coffee?"

"No thanks, sir. Something up—is this about Admiral Bruner's son?" McCord asked. "Last night's watch team put a message in Aaron's queue. It was waiting for him this morning."

"It is. And since you all are up to speed, what are your thoughts?"

"I think, at a minimum, we ought to start sniffing around and seeing what we can find out about the lieutenant," McCord continued. "But isn't this in the Navy's swim lane? Don't they do something when someone is missing?"

"They do," Williams replied. "Admiral Oldham only called me as a courtesy because he knew we were involved in rescuing Admiral Bruner. He said he's turned this over to NCIS. They're the ones who are supposed to investigate these things."

"Boss, you said 'supposed to' but you didn't sound so sure," McCord said.

"I'm not saying NCIS does a bad job, only that they have to live within certain rules and regulations, and that they do things methodically. If the worst concerns about Lieutenant Bruner—that he has taken on finding his father on his own—are true, then I think we'll need to get involved—and pronto."

"We get it, boss," McCord replied. "You don't think he's left the country, do you?"

"I'm not sure, but we have to play worst case." Then, turning to Bleich, he continued. "Start your own file on Lieutenant Bruner, and also get whatever NCIS has on him. Don't ask, they won't give it to you; just get it. And check the records of any MAC flights leaving the country from the time he was last seen until now, Aaron. My gut tells me he might be trying to get to Iraq."

"What about Brian and Hector and our team? They should be leaving Baghdad to come home any time now," McCord asked.

"We're playing worst-case gentlemen. I'll call Brian myself. For now we need to keep them there."

Even though he was exhausted from his days of captivity, as well as mentally drained from his near-death ordeal, Jay Bruner was so stoked up on adrenaline that he couldn't sleep. He and Meagan had sat in their family room for hours after their daughters had gone to bed, talking about everything and talking about nothing.

No matter how many times Meagan had explained their son's disappearance, it didn't track for his father. The fact that the "case" had been turned over to NCIS made even less sense. He wanted to do something, but it was the middle of the night. His wife finally convinced him to go to bed, but it took several Benadryl pills before he was finally able to sleep.

Bruner finally awoke at 1030. Once Meagan had filled him with coffee and a big breakfast, he considered his options.

"Are you going to call Eric Oldham?"

"I'd like to go in and make an office call on him, plus I've been away from OLA—"

"Whoa, hold it there, cowboy," Meagan interrupted. She knew her husband well enough that she wasn't surprised that he wanted to return to work less than twelve hours after nearly being killed. "The doctors from Bethesda said you needed at least several days rest—maybe even a week—before you climbed back into the trenches. I'll be the sheriff if I have to."

Bruner pursed his lips and raised his eyebrows.

"Well, maybe I'll call VCNO. But I need to do *something* Meagan. My son is missing and—"

"*Our* son is missing," Meagan interrupted. "And people are doing something. And I know you don't want to hear this, but what they're doing will probably work best if we don't interfere."

"Okay, you may be right. But after I call Eric Oldham, I want to call Admiral Williams at Op-Center. He was the admiral in charge of Deep Blue during our last tour in the Pentagon. His people rescued me, and I owe him a thank you. If Dale is in trouble and needs help, his outfit may just be the ones to do what no one else can."

"Come on. I bought that great Aeron executive chair for your office. You can sit there and put your feet up and make your calls—that way I can lie to the docs and say you've been resting," Meagan said with a wink.

The object of Jay and Meagan Bruner's worry was sitting in a chair in an otherwise bare room in ISIS's building, his arms pulled behind the chair and his hands and legs bound. After a morning with no air attacks, and convinced all the mayhem at their compound was caused by this one man and was not a precursor to an attack, Mabad al-Dosari had ordered his fighters and their families to return to their compound. Bruner had had the two bullets removed and his wounds patched up soon after they arrived at the safe house. The heavy sedative the doctors had given him had knocked him out and he had just regained consciousness about thirty minutes ago.

Al-Dosari wanted to know who he was and why he was here—and he wanted to know now. He sent in his most experienced—and most brutal—interrogator to extract that information from their captive.

The man was built like a linebacker and stood a foot from Bruner. "We're going to keep doing this until you talk. You clearly know who we are and you know what fate can ultimately await you if you don't cooperate. But I assure you, if you don't answer my questions, what I can do to you will make you beg to have your throat slit. Do you understand?"

Silence, as Dale Bruner just stared straight ahead.

"I said, do you understand?" the interrogator shouted as he smashed his fist into the left side of Bruner's head, knocking his chair over. The man picked the SEAL's chair up and asked again.

"Are you American?"

Silence was met with another fist to the head, knocking his chair over again. His captor righted the chair once more.

"Are you special forces?"

Silence.

The man drew his fist back and smashed it into Bruner's nose, shattering it. Blood gushed everywhere, but the hostage still had a defiant stare.

"Our doctors removed the bullets and bandaged your wounds. This after you killed two of our comrades. I think I need to check on their handiwork," the interrogator said, and, as he did, he wrapped both his hands over the bandage covering the wound on his captive's right shoulder.

The pain was excruciating, but Bruner wasn't going to satisfy his torturer by yelping out. He bit his lip hard and soon a wide rivulet of blood streamed off his chin, joining the flow of blood from his nose.

When no sound emerged from his captive, the frustrated interrogator drew his right leg up then let it fly, knocking the chair and Bruner backwards. As he crashed onto the ground and hit his head on the concrete floor, it all went black.

"Thank you for taking my call, Admiral."

"Jay, don't mention it; we're grateful we have you back."

"Admiral—"

"Jay, it's Eric, please."

"That will take some getting used to. I called to ask two things. First, has NCIS turned anything up yet? And second, I'd like to call Admiral Williams and thank him for rescuing me."

"I'll text you Admiral Williams's direct line; just please keep it to yourself, okay?"

"I'll do that, thank you."

"As to NCIS, I talked with their director earlier today. He's opened a file on Dale and he assures me he'll put his best people on the case."

"I'm grateful for that, Admir . . . Eric, . . . but are we treating this as a criminal case or an act of terrorism?"

Oldham considered this. From his perspective he was doing all the proper things to help find the younger Bruner. He didn't need to be second-guessed by a junior admiral.

"Look, Jay; I briefed CNO on this early this morning. He concurs that we are doing what we need to do to help you find your son. Just give it some time."

Help "you" find "your" son? Jay Bruner didn't like what he was hearing, and his gut told him he wasn't going to motivate Oldham to do any more.

"Thank you, sir, and roger that."

"You rest up now, Jay."

"Will do, sir."

Mabad al-Dosari exploded when his interrogator found him and admitted that he had knocked their prisoner unconscious. "You fool. Did you kill him?"

"No, he's just knocked out. He's breathing and he's okay. When he comes to, I'll continue my work. I'll get him to talk eventually—"

"We don't have time for 'eventually,'" the ISIS leader interrupted. "We need to know who he is."

"He hasn't said a word in response to anything I've done. He may never say anything, no matter what we do to him."

"I want to know who he is!" al-Dosari shouted.

"There may be a way," the man replied. "We have equipment to take an adequate set of fingerprints. And we can take a DNA sample just as easily—"

"What does that get us?" al-Dosari asked. "We don't have the equipment to test DNA samples, and we don't have access to databases where we can screen fingerprints—especially the fingerprints of Americans."

"I know that, but the Saudi General Intelligence Directorate does. We've cooperated with them before, and they've been helpful."

"Do it then!" al-Dosari barked. "But do it quickly."

Jay Bruner had called Chase Williams and the Op-Center director had listened to his story from start to finish. He expressed relief that Bruner had been rescued and gave all the credit for it to his CIRG HRT team. Once those pleasantries were done, Bruner got right to the point.

"Admiral, I'd be lying if I told you I thought the Navy was going full bore trying to find Dale. It seems like they're treating this as a criminal case—and he's the criminal."

"I don't believe they think he is, Jay. They just have to follow procedures; I know I had to during my thirty-five years in uniform."

"I know your outfit can bend the rules when they have to, sir. All I'm asking is for you to jump in if need be."

"That's more than fair. We're running our own trap lines as we speak. If Dale pops up on our radar, I'll let you know immediately."

The call complete, Williams headed for the Geek Tank via Duncan Sutherland's small office.

"Hey, boss, anything new?" Sutherland asked.

"Only that I'm more sure than I was earlier that we need to keep Brian and the team in Baghdad and maybe move them north like we did before. You'll know more when I know more, but for now, work your magic with CENTCOM and the 75th Ranger Regiment. They're our wheels."

"I'm on it."

Mabad al-Dosari's number two knew his leader would brook no delays. He called his contact at the Saudi General Intelligence Directorate and told him what he wanted. His contact said he understood his urgency and would get him what he needed.

They took Bruner's fingerprints with a simple machine liberated from an Iraqi notary company some time ago. His Saudi contact told al-Hamdani that if the hostage was U.S. military, as they suspected he was, then his fingerprints would be on file in several databases, all of which were laughably easy to hack into. The man scanned the fingerprint sheet and e-mailed it to the address the Saudi provided.

The Saudi contact told him he could take a DNA sample if he wanted to, but it wasn't really necessary. If he was an American, he was certain the fingerprints would tell them all they needed to know. Al-Dosari's man didn't want to leave anything to chance and stuck a swab in Bruner's mouth, put the sample in a plastic jar, and arranged for it to be flown to Riyadh. Now all they had to do was wait.

Aaron Bleich barely had the presence of mind to collect Roger McCord as he made a beeline for Chase Williams's office.

"Roger? . . . Aaron?" the Op-Center director said as they stood in his doorway.

"Boss, Dale Bruner is out of the country; we're sure of it."

"Tell me more, Aaron."

"We hac . . . ahhh . . . checked the MAC flight databases like you suggested. Lieutenant Bruner was manifested on a flight out of Andrews headed for Baghdad several days ago. He's in Iraq, boss!"

"Damn; that's our worst fear," Williams replied. "I doubt Lieutenant Bruner flew out of here to hang out in Baghdad. Roger, get with Duncan and contact CENTCOM. Have him tell them we need to get our JSOC team moving toward Mosul ASAP. Then call Brian and tell him what's going on. Ask him to let us know how soon he can get moving toward Mosul. I've got to call the president."

CHAPTER TWENTY-FIVE

July 23, 1830 Arabia Standard Time

Shakir al-Hamdani had been pacing most of the day, waiting for the call from the Saudi General Intelligence Directorate. He knew the DNA sample they had taken from their hostage was still en route, but his man in the directorate had told him the fingerprints would be enough and al-Dosari's number two was counting on that. He didn't know who wanted the information more—he himself or the ISIS leader.

The call had come minutes ago, and now al-Hamdani climbed the stairs to his leader's second-floor office as quickly as he could. As he walked into al-Dosari's simple space he had a broad smile on his face.

"So have you heard from our friends in the General Intelligence Directorate?" the ISIS leader asked.

"I have. You thought he was American and might be special operations; and you were right. He's a Navy SEAL—"

"I knew it!" al-Dosari exclaimed. Then he caught his number two's body language. "You have more?"

"I do. Our hostage's name is Dale Bruner."

"What? Is he linked to the man we tried to capture in the United States and bring here?"

"Yes. After our Saudi friend told me his name, I asked him to find out just that—and he did. He's the admiral's son."

"But his father was rescued. Why would he come here if that happened—to avenge an attempted kidnapping?" al-Dosari asked.

"When we captured him, he had no identification, and he didn't have any communications devices—no phone, no radio, nothing. He must have wanted to stay completely off the grid."

"I understand," al-Dosari replied. "It's not hard to believe he'd abandon all his radios and phones, but I still don't understand why he would come here in the first place."

"Remember, we had his father hostage for several days and we would have gotten him out of the country had the people who had him not bungled what should have been a simple mission. The son must have assumed we were going to bring him here and decided to come to get him. But now we have the best of both worlds."

"I see where you're going with this," al-Dosari replied as he smiled.

"Good! The father attacked our old compound and killed your son—as well as many others. Now you have his son and you can extract revenge and broadcast it for the father to see!" al-Hamdani replied emphatically.

"You're right; but I want to know more. I want our interrogator to confront him with what we know, and I want this American to understand precisely what we're going to do to him."

"It will be done. Do you want me to alert our contact at Al Jazeera?"

"Not yet. We want them to broadcast his death, but let's tell them later. We don't want any leaks."

Brian Dawson and Hector Rodriquez were in the back of the lead Humvee of the convoy as they pounded north through the Iraqi desert toward Mosul. "We're about ninety klicks north of Tikrit, boss," Rodriquez said. "At this rate we should get to Mosul a little after dark. We get any more intel on where we should lay up when we get there?"

"The Ranger regiment is working on it," Dawson replied as he pointed at the electronic tablet. "There are a few places we can stage just outside the city. We're heading for this one right now," he continued, tapping the screen. "For now, Laurie's just trying to get us close to the city without being detected."

Several Humvees back, Laurie Phillips rode with Major Mike Volner and Master Guns Charles Moore. The CENTCOM commander had dedicated one of his two Global Hawks to this mission, and Laurie saw what the bird was seeing on her secure iPad. One half of the screen had the video the RQ-4B was piping down from its position about twelve klicks north of their convoy. The other half of the screen displayed the chat window she had open with the Air Force's 13th Intelligence Squadron at Beale Air Force Base. As their convoy snaked its way north across the desert, avoiding major roads, she was giving the controller constant instructions, and the Air Force captain controlling the bird kept it flying just ahead of their convoy at an altitude of fifty eight thousand feet.

"This doesn't look so good up here," Volner offered as he tapped the screen. "Looks like several trucks. It could be an ISIL patrol. We may want to turn to avoid them."

"I agree. I'll recommend that to Mr. Dawson."

In the lead Humvee, the tactical net crackled in Dawson's ear, "Mr. Dawson, Phillips on tactical."

"Go ahead, Laurie."

"Sir, I've got the Global Hawk flying about a dozen klicks north of us. I've picked up what looks like several vehicles heading south. Don't know if they're ISIL, but whoever they are, I don't think we want them seeing our convoy."

"I don't either. What's your recommendation?" Dawson asked. There was an unmistakable urgency in his voice.

"If we head east, the terrain rises pretty quickly and it gets rugged real fast. That would slow us down. I recommend we head west a bit, and then head north again. It's flat and it doesn't look like we'll hit any towns—"

"Concur. I'll have our driver slow down. Have yours speed up and take the lead. You're our guide now."

Laurie tapped their driver on the shoulder. "Sergeant, Mr. Dawson wants us to be lead vehicle. Jump ahead of his Humvee. Once you're in the lead I'll give you a vector. We need to head west to skirt around some trucks up ahead."

Al-Dosari had given his interrogator specific instructions to soften their hostage up and gave him almost an hour to do it. The man had done his job, and as the ISIS leader entered the room, he saw a face covered in blood. One of Bruner's eyes was almost swollen shut and his broken nose jutted sideways at a precarious angle. Their hostage's head was bowed, and it looked like he was about to lose consciousness.

"Stand over there," al-Dosari barked at the interrogator, as he glared at him and shook his head in disgust. The brute had done his work too well.

Al-Dosari stood inches from Bruner. He grabbed his hair and pulled his head up. "Look at me!" he shouted.

Bruner complied and held his head erect.

"Do you know who I am?"

Silence as Bruner just stared straight ahead.

Al-Dosari grabbed Bruner's bloody face in both hands and shouted, "I said, do you know who I am?" as spittle hit the hostage's face.

Still silence.

The ISIS leader smiled and bared his teeth. "I am the caliph and I will lead my followers on a crusade to ultimately destroy everything that you hold dear."

When there was no reaction from his prisoner, al-

Dosari continued. "Now that I've told you who I am, perhaps you can return the courtesy. Or would you like me to leave you alone with him again?" he asked, gesturing toward his interrogator.

Bruner stared at the ISIS leader for a few seconds, and then looked down again.

"You pig!" al-Dosari shouted as he balled his fist and delivered a blow to Bruner's head. "We know who you are, Lieutenant Bruner, Lieutenant *Dale* Bruner."

The shock of hearing his name registered on Bruner's face and caused al-Dosari's smile to broaden. "Surprised? You underestimate us. We know who you are, and of course we know who your father is. So what are we to do with you?"

Bruner was still processing the fact that they knew who he was. He was certain he hadn't brought any kind of identification with him. How could they know this?

"You want to ask me how I know this, but your code of conduct says you can't. But you are military, a Navy SEAL, and that code says you can tell me your name, rank, and serial number. Shall we start with that?"

Bruner continued to stare ahead in stony silence.

Still smiling, al-Dosari turned to his interrogator. "It's still several hours until the evening news broadcasts on the United States' East Coast. You can work on him for about an hour longer, but then I want his face cleaned up and I want him put in an orange jumpsuit."

The man just nodded.

For the first time, fear registered on Dale Bruner's face.

Eric Oldham was the person who knew the Bruner family the best. As Op-Center's JSOC team closed in on Mosul, Chase Williams called Oldham. The VCNO had told his senior staff to put Williams through to him immediately without the usual skirmishes that EAs and other horse holders usually engage in.

"Chase, thanks for calling. I got your e-mail, and you said you'd have more to share when you phoned."

"I do. All the intel we have says Lieutenant Bruner flew into Baghdad on a MAC flight. After that, the trail is cold, and he's completely off the grid—or he was."

"Was?"

"We're working on the assumption he didn't know his dad had been rescued and that he thought he had been brought to Mosul. Based on what you told me about the family and especially what his skipper at the Naval Special Warfare Command told you about Dale, we feared he might have decided to take matters into his own hands."

"And I guess finding out he was on a flight to Baghdad pointed in that direction," Oldham replied.

"It did, but then the next step was trying to figure out how he could get from Baghdad to Mosul. I had our J4 shop run their trap lines. Turns out, there's a contractor in Baghdad that provides security for State Department and other U.S. officials working there. Part of their contract requires them to have GPS trackers in all their vehicles. Seems they were doing their normal inventory of trucks in their motor pool last night, discovered one missing, and traced it to Mosul."

"That pretty much squares the circle, doesn't it?"

"We can't be certain Bruner is the one who took the vehicle—and it was never signed for—so there's no one in that outfit we can question. But I've got my JSOC team headed to Mosul right now. I want them to be in position to snatch him if he falls into ISIL's hands."

"Got it. Is there anything I can do to help?"

"There is. If the worst happens and ISIL captures him, we all know what'll happen. I think your best place right now is with the Bruner family."

"I do too. I'll head over to their home right now."

As their convoy steered a wide arc around the suspicious vehicles, Laurie Phillips was able to keep them in her sights. She typed furiously as she worked the chat room window with her Beale controllers and they flew the Global Hawk over the suspect three-truck convoy. Brian Dawson, now in the number two truck, was active on the tactical net talking with the 75th Ranger Regiment contingent in Baghdad. The Rangers knew where the ISIL compound was, but they were still struggling to find the best lay-up spot for Dawson and his JSOC team once they got to Mosul.

"Those trucks south of us now, Laurie?" Dawson asked.

"They are, boss, moving south and opening. I think we can pick up our original route again."

Just then, the Iridium satellite phone Hector Rodriquez was monitoring came alive. "Rodriquez."

"Hector, it's Duncan. Are you all still moving toward Mosul?"

"We are. We had to take a little detour, but we're back on track now, about thirty klicks south of the city outskirts."

"Good. The boss says keep going. We've located the vehicle we think Lieutenant Bruner used to get from Baghdad to Mosul. He may be with it. We want you to head there now. I've got a lat-long for you. You ready to copy?"

"Ready," Rodriquez replied as he wrote down the latitude and longitude of the GPS fix. Then he turned toward Dawson. "Duncan's located the truck Bruner took to Mosul. Here are the coordinates," he began. As he read them, the ops director punched them into his tablet. "We heading there now?" Rodriquez asked.

"Yep, straight shot," Dawson replied as the triangle appeared on his screen. "I'll tell Laurie we're jumping back into the lead."

Maggie Scott appeared in Aaron Bleich's office with the rest of her team in tow. "Got something, Maggie?" he asked as they all filtered into his small space.

"We do, and it's not good. About twenty minutes ago, the ISIL Twitter feeds started buzzing. They were elliptical as they always are, but there's a crescendo building and references to YouTube and Al Jazeera 'later today.' "

"Tell me more."

"Well, it's like this. The analysis points directly to the fact that ISIL has a hostage they intend to kill and they are getting their followers—as well as others—all spooled up to watch."

"How about their hostage?" Bleich asked. "Is there any reference or even an allusion as to who it is?"

"I was coming to that. Several feeds have mentioned 'special operations.'"

Bleich stole a glance at the lower right-hand corner of his computer screen. "It's less than two hours until the evening news here. I'll grab Roger and we'll go see Mr. Williams. Maggie, I want you to tell Fred to stop whatever he's doing and hack into Al Jazeera and see what he can pull down. We don't have much time."

Mabad al-Dosari had told his number two to give him at least forty-five minutes in his office alone. He needed to write down precisely what he was going to say before he slit his hostage's throat. This execution was an important one, and one that would continue to rally followers to his cause. It wasn't going to be about how he would appear or how he would speak his words—it was strictly about what he was going to say.

They had enough lead time to activate their social media networks and had promised Al Jazeera a story that would give their ratings a significant bump. Millions would see this, and it would be broadcast at precisely the right time, when Americans living in some of the country's most prominent cities—Boston, New

York, Philadelphia, Atlanta, Miami, and especially
Washington, D.C.—were getting their nightly news.

Al-Dosari tried to keep his emotions in check as he
recalled why he was doing this. He had dedicated his
life to establishing a caliphate throughout the Middle
East. That was his destiny and he was Allah's instrument. His zeal had already cost him the life of his only
son. Some men would have shirked their duty and
given up. But he was not like other men. He had a sa-
cred duty. After a number of stumbles with crafting
just what he wanted to say, he finally had the words
he wanted:

> America. Listen to me. In the time it took you
> to go about your business today, our caliph-
> ate has continued to expand. We have taken
> over more territory, and nations you once
> knew—Iraq, Syria, Yemen, Libya, Tunisia,
> and others—will soon no longer exist. There
> will be just one nation, the Islamic State. This
> I can promise you.
>
> But while your politicians rail against us
> and your public-opinion polls say we must
> be stopped, few of your decadent citizens do
> anything. That is because they are cowards
> and tremble before our mighty fighters. So
> you send your military to try to defeat us. But
> all they do is kill our women and children as
> they sleep in their beds.
>
> You sent your admiral named Bruner to
> bomb our homes and kill our mothers and

their children. We sought retribution on this man and have not killed him yet—but we will eventually. But do you not have enough fighters in your military? Look who we have here. We have this cursed killer's son, a military man himself! And we caught him sneaking into our compound to kill our families in the middle of the night. Have you no honor?

This young Bruner will pay the price not only for what he tried to do, but for what his father did. And we will do the same thing to whoever else you send to challenge us. Look, America, and get used to seeing this. We are coming for all of you and we are coming for your so-called leader, the pig, Midkiff.

You Christians know an eye for an eye, a tooth for a tooth, do you not? Then hear this. The murderer, Bruner the elder, killed my son. So it is by your own decadent religion that I kill his son. Praise be to Allah.

Satisfied that what he had written down conveyed what he wanted to say, al-Dosari pushed his chair back from his desk. He wanted to see how al-Hamdani was progressing in getting his fighters and their families ready to evacuate their compound. He knew that soon after he decapitated this man in front of an international audience, the bombs would start falling again. This time they would fall, but they'd accomplish nothing.

They would all be in the wind and would continue the fight.

Brian Dawson knew Chase Williams trusted him completely to carry out his mission and that the Op-Center director would never micromanage his operation. But as their mission became more complex, he also knew Williams was working on getting him more support from the CENTCOM commander. He needed to continue to communicate with him in real time, and he needed a constant stream of intel from the Geek Tank.

"Boss, Brian here."

"I have you four-by-five," Williams replied.

"I'm about five klicks from the outskirts of Mosul. The intel Aaron and his team have pushed to us says that ISIL social media is buzzing, and they likely intend to kill Lieutenant Bruner at 1800 Eastern Standard Time—"

"That's right; less than ninety minutes from now."

"If that's the case, we don't have time to lay up and make this a deliberate attack. We need to storm into town at full speed and head straight for their compound. We've geo-located the truck we're pretty sure Lieutenant Bruner used to drive from Baghdad to Mosul, and it's close to ISIL's main compound. That makes sense; if he was coming to rescue his dad and shoot his way into their building to get him, he wouldn't want to be on foot for long."

"I take it you're certain you know exactly where their main compound is located?"

"We do. The 75th Rangers have this place mapped out pretty well. And we've got the Global Hawk to give us eyes-on surveillance. We'll know what we're getting into—"

"I know you will, Brian. We've worked together long enough that I don't need to tell you the safety of your men is paramount. We want to save Lieutenant Bruner, but if it gets too hot, you wave off, hear?"

"Loud and clear, boss."

"I've talked with General George about what else the 75th Rangers can provide for you. I know the exact route you take into the city will depend on what the Global Hawk sees ahead. We're having the same feed from Beale piped in here and General George is seeing it in his command center in Tampa too. Here's what I want you to be ready for—"

Williams provided the details about the added support their team would get for their mission. When he finished he simply said, "Questions?"

"None. I've got it. And thanks; we'll take all the help we can get."

CHAPTER TWENTY-SIX

July 24, 0030 Arabia Standard Time

As the convoy approached the southwest outskirts of Mosul, Brian Dawson knew their chances of remaining completely covert—even in the early hours of the morning when most of the city was asleep—were remote. He understood ISIL's strategy and knew Mosul was not only Iraq's second-largest city, but the one the group considered most valuable as they tried to expand their caliphate.

Their Humvees forged ahead with their headlights off, the 75th Ranger Regiment drivers navigating by the dim green light of their NVGs. Once Dawson had decided the need for speed trumped trying to remain undetected for as long as possible, he had Laurie position their Global Hawk over Highway 1, just west of Mosul's airport. That's where they'd rejoin the main road and speed into the city. They were minutes away from the juncture, and he anticipated resistance almost immediately.

"Carnival, you up on the net?" Hector Rodriguez asked over the tactical frequency Williams had provided them.

"Roger, we're up."

"We're about to join Highway 1. The RQ-4B shows it quiet up ahead, but we don't expect that to last long. Can you take up about a three-mile trail behind us?"

"Wilco."

Mabad al-Dosari had entrusted his number two to make all the necessary preparations for their hostage's execution while he worked on what he would say in front of the camera. Shakir al-Hamdani had done just that. There was little guesswork or need to create anything from whole cloth. ISIS had executed so many prisoners that it had perfected the morbid process to the point where the disgusting ritual was routine.

While the executions of multiple prisoners simultaneously were always carried out outdoors, the time of night and the fact it was a lone person who would be slaughtered, drove al-Hamdani to use the large room on their building's first floor as their "studio." It had been several weeks since they had beheaded someone in this room, so he gathered a few men and ensured all was as it should be. In short order, the cameras, lighting, sound equipment, and most importantly, the ISIS flag, were in place.

* * *

He was too small for the Global Hawk to pick up, but the man standing guard at the Wadi Hajar Gas Station was the first to hear—and then see—the convoy. He immediately called his commander. Within minutes, trucks full of ISIS fighters were rolling out of their compound in the Hayy Al Uraybi neighborhood in northern Mosul and heading south through the mostly darkened city.

They had just passed the Mosul Mansour Gas power plant when Dawson's radio came alive. It was Phillips. "Mr. Dawson, looks like we've got company. The Global Hawk's picked up trucks—lots of 'em—flowing south, just north of where Highway 1 takes a turn to the west. That's just where we're heading."

"Got that. Keep me posted on how many trucks the bird picks up, and tell me where it looks like they're deploying. For now, we'll keep our speed up."

"Roger that, sir."

"Hector," he said, turning to his number two. "Tell Carnival to close our posit and take up a loose trail on tail-end Charlie."

"You got it, boss."

"Major, we've got company up ahead," Dawson said on the tactical net. "I won't drive us into a buzz saw. If they take up blocking positions and Carnival can't clear 'em, we'll pull back. If we do get through, your troops ready for a full-on assault on the compound?"

Volner looked at Master Guns Moore, who had heard the same transmission.

"Yep, that's what we came here to do," came the laconic response from Moore.

"Yes, sir," Volner replied over the net.

The ISIS leader's ashen-faced military commander, Akram al-Nahas, burst into his office and delivered his breathless report. Now he stood in front of al-Dosari's desk, almost slack-jawed.

"What do you mean, 'trucks are approaching'?" the ISIS leader shouted.

"Our sentry at the Wadi Hajar Gas Station sighted them first. He counted almost a dozen trucks, all with their headlights off, traveling at high speed up Highway 1—"

"What are they? Are they Iraqi Army? Are they American?" al-Dosari asked. But he knew the answer. The Iraqi Army—even buttressed by increasing numbers of American special operations advisors—had long ago given up trying to retake Mosul. No, these had to be Americans and they had somehow sniffed out that he had this SEAL hostage and were coming to rescue him.

"Tell me where you're deploying your men. We need to stop them!"

Flying at two hundred feet above the desert, and about five hundred yards behind the last Humvee in the JSOC convoy, "Carnival," in the person of Warrant Officer Alex Purvis, was piloting the lead AH-6G in a flight of two Little Bird attack helicopters. The Little Bird, in use by U.S. Army special operations units for over three decades, had been continually upgraded for attack and other missions. The CENTCOM commander was backstopping Op-Center's mission with the best assets he could provide.

With a fully loaded weight of little more than three thousand pounds, the Little Bird was aptly named. But what it lacked in weight, it made up for in offensive firepower. Most of the multiple attack versions of the AH-6 helicopter could be loaded out with various types of guns—either chain guns, mini-guns, or the fifty-caliber GAU-19—as well as Hydra 70 rockets, the AGM-114 Hellfire missile, and Mk19 forty-millimeter automatic grenade launchers.

Purvis knew little, and cared less, about the conversations that had gone on between the director of someplace called "Op-Center" and his CENTCOM commander. All he knew was the order had flowed down from CENTCOM, through the CENTCOM Special Operations component—SOCCENT, to the Army SOC in Iraq, to his four-aircraft unit that shared the Al Muthana Air Base with the Iraqi air force. He was told to take two Little Birds and fly to a FARP—a forward area refueling point—four miles east of al-Shirqat. There would be Army SOC Chinooks to provide gas to his thirsty AH-6Gs so they could cover a JSOC convoy heading into Mosul.

Fully gassed and now loaded out with fifty-caliber GAU-19 guns and all the AGM-114 Hellfire missiles their two aircraft could carry, Purvis had waited for the "go" order from someone named Dawson—whoever he was. That order had come, and

Purvis and his wingman were now riding shotgun for the convoy.

Dale Bruner had been cleaned up and put in an orange jumpsuit, but not without a struggle. Each time the two men al-Hamdani had assigned to the task tried to take off an item of his clothing, he had gone limp, making their job as difficult as possible. Afraid to hit him in the face and anger al-Dosari even further, the men encouraged him to comply by kicking him in the ribs.

Now, as he sat bound to a chair in the same room he had been interrogated in, Bruner heard shouting and a general commotion. He had learned enough Arabic during his tours in Iraq that he thought it sounded like fighters streaming out of the building, likely in response to an approaching enemy. He prayed that someone was coming to his rescue. At the same time, he was overwhelmed with shame that he had put others at risk because he *needed* rescuing.

Akram al-Nahas was al-Dosari's most capable military commander. He had ably defended Mosul from multiple attacks over the past several years, pushing back coalition surges into the city outskirts. He had led the attack on Ramadi in 2015 and had routed an Iraqi Army force composed of four times as many soldiers as he mustered.

But now he faced what might be his greatest challenge—beating back an armada of what were probably American special forces bore-sighted on Mosul and, most likely, the ISIS compound in the north of the city. Worse, he had little time to prepare. Now in the lead truck streaming south, he put together his defensive plan on the fly.

"Mr. Dawson, we've got company, less than two klicks ahead. I'm sending you a link now!" It was Laurie Phillips's voice on the tactical net. The Global Hawk had done its work as it looked ahead along their intended route.

Dawson looked at the picture for only a second, and then turned to his number two. "Hector, looks like a big group of trucks ahead. They're bunched together—so it's impossible to count them—but they're massed around the traffic circle right here north of us. Their posit is just a klick south of where Highway 1 takes a jag to the north-northeast."

"I see it, boss. They've probably got a lot of firepower; there's no way we can break through unless Carnival can blast 'em out of there."

"Carnival, you up?" It was Dawson on the tactical net.

"Right here, sir," Purvis replied.

"I've got a bunch of enemy trucks on my nose, less than one klick. I need you to jump ahead of me and engage."

Two clicks of the mic was all Dawson heard, followed soon by the distinctive growl of the two six-bladed Little Birds zooming over them at close to their redline speed.

At the traffic circle, Akram al-Nahas hadn't had time to engineer an elegant or even a complex defense. He had simply massed all the trucks he could muster and strung them out bumper to bumper along the southern end of the traffic circle on Highway 1. His fighters, armed with rocket-propelled grenade—RPG—launchers, heavy machine guns, and a few light anti-armor weapons, crouched behind the vehicles, ready to take on the approaching convoy.

While al-Nahas had massed the bulk of his forces at the traffic circle, he had kept a few trucks and fighters back guarding the two turnoffs from Highway 1 that led directly to the Hayy Al Uraybi neighborhood where their compound was located. In the unlikely event the enemy convoy broke through, they would be his goal-line defense.

Purvis, his copilot, as well as the pilots of the second Little Bird, saw the outlines of the ISIS trucks ahead of them in the green glow of their helmet-mounted NVGs. As they closed at one hundred fifty knots, they armed their weapons pods. "Steady, steady," Purvis called over the tactical net, "wait for my command—"

They heard the approaching helicopters before they saw them in the black sky. The up-Doppler sound of a helo's blades compressing the air as it rushed toward them was a familiar sound to the ISIS fighters manning the roadblock. They knew what to do.

First one, and then a second fighter fired an RPG at the approaching noise in the sky. Then one of the machine gunners began firing his weapon, the tracer rounds arching into the night. All al-Nahas could do was run from man to man, trying to help them adjust their fire.

"Flash!" Purvis's copilot called out over the tactical net as he saw the rocket motor on the RPG fire off.

"Deploying chaff and flares!" Purvis's wingman shouted.

Purvis deployed chaff and flares as well, and, as he did, both Little Birds dropped down to fifty feet above Highway 1.

"Weapons now!" Purvis called. Each Little Bird crew felt successive jolts as, one by one, the four Hellfire missiles each bird carried dropped free of the launchers and headed for the massed trucks.

The AGM-114L "Longbow" Hellfire air-to-surface missile is a "fire-and-forget" weapon, first used by the U.S. military in Operation Just Cause in Panama, in 1989. In the decades since that first use, it has been one of the premier air-to-surface missiles used by the U.S. military, as well as by over two dozen countries allied with, or friendly toward, the United States. The reason so many other nations have purchased the missile is the same reason the U.S. armed forces have thousands of Hellfires in their inventory. It is extremely accurate and completely deadly.

The eight Hellfires launched from the two Little Birds streaked toward their targets at Mach 1.3, close to one thousand miles per hour. Each missile's millimeter-wave radar seeker locked on to what it saw straight ahead: the boxy chassis of the trucks strung along the highway traffic circle. As each missile closed its target, its semiactive laser homing guidance system took over.

The integrated blast fragmentation sleeve warheads all hit within seconds of each other, shredding the trucks and taking out most of the fighters as hot shrapnel cut through their bodies. A few moments later, secondary explosions turned the massed trucks into a towering inferno.

"Great shooting Carnival," Rodriquez said as he saw the explosions and fires less than a thousand yards ahead of where their lead Humvee and the rest of the convoy were temporarily stopped.

Both Little Birds had made a 180-degree turn to stay out of the blast pattern, had done another one-eighty after a minute, and were now just south of the JSOC convoy, and heading north along Highway 1 again. Both aircrews were ready to take out whatever enemy fighters had survived the carnage, their fingers on the triggers of their fifty-caliber GAU-19 machine guns.

"Sir!" It was Purvis on the net. "We saw lots of secondary explosions and there will likely be more. Maybe you want to jump off Highway 1 and take another route—"

"Quiet on the net. This is Phillips!" came the loud shout over the tactical net. Seconds later, "Mr. Dawson, the Global Hawk's picked up a large number of men, probably at least two dozen, fanning out in an arc of about one hundred eighty degrees from the ISIS compound, going down most of the major streets leading south. A few are in trucks. They're stopping every so often, digging, and then moving south again—"

"Shit!" Rodriquez exclaimed. "I'll bet anything they're laying down IEDs to guard the approaches to their compound. Once Laurie sends us the link we'll have to swing way around to the east or west and approach the compound from another direction."

"There isn't time, Hector. By then they'll have killed Lieutenant Bruner. We've got to find a way to break through—"

"Mr. Dawson!" It was Purvis. "Sir, we can take out the trucks on the main thoroughfare leading to the ISIL compound and then rip up the road with our GAU-19s. That should take care of all or most of the IEDs sir."

"Negative, Carnival. The first group of trucks had a lot of RPGs and these backstop trucks likely have them too. If you had more Hellfires, it would be a close fight anyway. But their RPGs outrange your GAU-19s. You know that—"

"But sir," Purvis protested. "We're about out of options."

"We may be, but sending you and your wingman into a meat grinder isn't one of them. Stand off and take station behind our convoy."

The convoy remained stopped, their Humvee engines idling, as Dawson and Rodriquez looked at the Global Hawk feed and just shook their heads. The minutes until the evening news ticked down inexorably. But four Humvees back, Laurie Phillips typed furiously, writing a message in the chat room window she had open with the 13th Intelligence Squadron at Beale Air Force Base.

She waited only a few minutes before the 13th IS controller responded to her request to pass what she wanted them to do with the Global Hawk up his chain of command. What popped up in her chat window wasn't encouraging. It said: "Ma'am, are you shitting me?"

Shakir al-Hamdani was out of breath from the exertion of running down four flights of steps. He burst into al-Dosari's second-floor office and rasped, "I can't raise al-Nahas. But I climbed up the roof and looked toward the traffic circle where he set up blocking positions—"

"What did you see? We heard the explosions. What's going on?" al-Dosari asked.

"The entire area is ablaze. The Americans must have attacked our fighters."

"Can you see anything else? Is their convoy still approaching?"

"I can't see it. They're probably waiting for the fires to die down before proceeding—"

"Have your men finished their work? If they destroyed that barrier we set up, the few trucks we have left guarding the roads leading here won't be able to stop them."

"My men should be nearly finished. I sent them out with scores of IEDs. Anything trying to drive over any of those roads will be blown to bits."

"Good, we don't have much time left before we broadcast our hostage's execution. We need to hold off our attackers at least that long."

Al-Hamdani paused to frame his reply. He had wanted to suggest this earlier and didn't, but now the situation was critical. "We can carry out the execution now and then send the feed to Al Jazeera and post it on YouTube later. Everything is ready and we can do this immediately. It will make no dif—"

"NO! And don't bring this up again," al-Dosari barked. "I want to do this live to show the Americans we control their news cycle, not them."

Al-Hamdani didn't reply and began to leave al-Dosari's office, but the ISIS leader called out to him. "Have the remaining trucks pull back from the blocking positions. We'll need them to help us move out of this building immediately after the execution."

Al-Hamdani just nodded. He felt no need to tell the ISIS leader he had already begun doing just that, using their few remaining trucks.

"Mr. Dawson, Phillips here."

"Go ahead, Laurie."

"Sir, you can wave this off if you want to, but I can't see any other way to clear a path to the ISIL compound. I'm working with the controllers at Beale and they're going to push my idea up to their higher headquarters. But to be honest sir, they weren't warm to it, even after I explained the urgency of the situation. I think we may need Mr. Williams to weigh in on this— and quickly."

"Weigh in on *what* Laurie?" Dawson asked, sounding exasperated. Phillips had a role—an important role—in this operation, but she couldn't help him with his current crisis.

"This is what we can do, sir," Phillips began, "and I think it will take Mr. Williams to make it happen," she continued as she poured out her plan to a stunned Dawson.

Williams considered himself blessed to serve the nation and the president as Op-Center's director. But if he had one regret, it was that unlike his Navy career, where he was leading from the front—as a ship's captain multiple times, as a carrier strike group commander, and finally as a numbered fleet commander later in his career—at Op-Center his role was not to lead from the front. Here, his role was to send other men and women forward while he remained behind at his headquarters.

The call from Dawson had charged him. He banged out a short POTUS/OC Eyes Only memo and then reached for the phone. His first call would be to the Air Force chief of staff, and the second one would be to the CENTCOM commander. Both calls would be to their private lines.

CHAPTER TWENTY-SEVEN

CENTRAL MOSUL, IRAQ

July 24, 0145 Arabia Standard Time

On the ground, just south of the traffic circle, the convoy was still stopped when the call from Carnival crackled in Hector Rodriguez's headset. "Go ahead, Carnival."

"The trucks north of here we spotted earlier are all pulling out of their blocking positions. It looks like they're heading back toward the ISIL compound."

"Roger that, Carnival."

His number two looked toward his boss as Op-Center's ops director considered their options. Finally, Dawson spoke. "Okay, Hector, that's good news . . . but it doesn't solve the IED issue. There haven't been any secondary explosions for several minutes. Think there will be any more?"

"Don't think so, boss. I think we can push forward a bit. Maybe as far as here," Rodriguez said as he pointed at his tablet, indicating a position where Highway 1 turned due west.

"Let's move out then," Dawson replied. Then tapping their driver on the shoulder, "Sergeant, head for that smoldering truck on the far left. We'll push through the wreckage right there."

The RQ-4B Global Hawk is the premier unmanned aerial vehicle (UAV) used by the U.S. military for large-area surveillance. Taking over the missions provided for decades by the U-2 manned aircraft, the Global Hawk uses a high-resolution synthetic aperture radar as well as long-range electro-optical/infrared sensors to provide all-weather eyes in the sky. Able to survey as much as 40,000 square miles of terrain a day, it's little wonder the U.S. Air Force considers the RQ-4B its best unmanned aircraft and has invested well over ten billion dollars in this capable UAV.

Most people think of UAVs as small craft—and many of them are. But the Global Hawk is a beast. Almost fifty feet long and with a wingspan of over one hundred and thirty feet, a fully loaded and fueled RQ-4B weighs in at over sixteen tons—close to the weight of a similarly outfitted U.S. Navy F/A-18C/D Hornet. Nor is the Global Hawk cheap. A single RQ-4B costs over a quarter of a billion dollars.

The cost of a Global Hawk—as well as the unprecedented nature of the request—gave those at the Air Force's 13th Intelligence Squadron and 548th Intelligence Group pause, and all they could tell those trying to rescue Dale Bruner was that they would forward the request up their chain of command. Unbeknownst to them, there'd soon be orders flowing down that chain.

A short time later, the Global Hawk was ten miles south of the JSOC convoy, lining up on a long straight-away and descending rapidly out of 58,000 feet.

Shakir al-Hamdani knew they could only hold the Americans off for so long and that his leader wanted their hostage executed precisely when the U.S. evening news programs began their broadcasts. After he left al-Dosari's office, he hurried down to the room where the execution would take place. All was in order, and his fighters who would operate the cameras and sound equipment lounged casually and smoked cigarettes. Then he went to the room where two of his fighters were standing guard over the bound, gagged, and hooded Bruner.

"Take him into the room now. Leave him as he is, but put him on the carpet, kneeling. We don't have much time."

As the convoy snaked its way around the smoldering wreckage of the ISIL trucks, the 75th Ranger Regiment driver of the last Humvee heard the Global Hawk's Rolls-Royce AE 3007 turbofan engine first. Dimly, then more clearly as it passed just west of them, the RQ-4B came into view, bore-sighted on the road leading directly to the ISIS compound. The bird streaked by the convoy at less than two hundred feet altitude at close to its top cruise speed of three hundred fifty miles per hour.

As they moved slowly up Highway 1, everyone in the convoy watched as the massive bird touched down precisely where the road they were heading for jagged north from the east-west-running Highway 1. They watched the bird disappear between buildings as it mowed a path through the exploding IEDs, each blast slowing the RQ-4B only slightly as it careened ahead at high speed.

Overhead, the two Little Birds watched from an altitude of five hundred feet. Finally, the Global Hawk ground to a stop as it impaled itself on a building. The massive UAV was near the end of its mission time and had but a small fuel reserve—just enough to get it back to its secret aerodrome in Qatar—so there were no fuel-induced secondary explosions.

"What can you see, Carnival?" Rodriguez asked.

"I'll get a bit closer if I can, but it looks like the bird got to within a few hundred yards of the compound. It cut a hell of a swath along that street. It'd be hard to believe any IED along the way wouldn't detonate. I'd say it's safe to drive up to where it stopped and maybe to go on foot the rest of the way."

"Roger that, Carnival." It was Dawson. "This is Dawson on tactical. You all heard Carnival's report. Will drive up to right behind where the Global Hawk's stopped. Major, it's your show from there—just like you rehearsed."

"Roger that, sir; we're ready," Volner replied.

"Carnival, can you cover the assault and clear us a path with guns?"

"That's what we do, sir," Purvis said.

"Great. How much time can you give us on-station and still have enough fuel to get back to your FARP site?"

There was a long pause before Purvis replied. "Forget the FARP site sir. We'll give you all we've got until the fans stop turning," Purvis said. "Seeing as how we don't care much about destroying aircraft this morning, we'll do what we came here to do, and then we can blow our birds up once we rescue the lieutenant. Then we'll just catch a ride back with you folks."

"Damn, I love these guys," Rodriguez said to no one in particular.

Dawson overheard him and replied, "I do too, Hector; I do too."

The Global Hawk crash was enough to drive Mabad al-Dosari out of his office and send him running up to the roof of his compound. When he arrived, there were a half a dozen of his fighters pointing and gesturing at the hulk of the Global Hawk. Al-Dosari took one look at the wreckage and headed for the stairway.

The Humvee convoy drivers had maneuvered around the burning wreckage in the traffic circle and were now ready to work their way up the road along the path the Global Hawk had cleared. "This is Dawson. We think the Global Hawk has detonated all the IEDs along the road to the ISIL compound, but we can't be certain. I want the second vehicle—that's Major Volner and Master Guns Moore—following no closer than twenty yards behind me; after that, the rest can bunch up. I want each driver to follow my path as exactly as possible. Questions?"

There were none.

"Carnival, cover us as we press forward. I know we're going to attract attention."

"Carnival, roger."

Al-Dosari ran into his office to grab the screed he intended to read as he executed Bruner. Al-Hamdani was there to meet him.

"What happened?" al-Dosari asked. "This aircraft was aimed right at our compound. Was it an American suicide plane?"

"I don't know," al-Hamdani replied. "But the American convoy is coming this way, up the same street where this suicide plane tried to land—"

"They won't get far; you told me your men seeded the street with IEDs," the ISIS leader interrupted.

Al-Hamdani knew his leader was under enormous stress and wasn't thinking clearly. He had heard the explosions as the American suicide airplane—or whatever it was—caused multiple detonations of IEDs as it careened up this street. But now wasn't the time to correct him. "Perhaps," he began. "But I've ordered most of my remaining fighters out into the street with all the heavy weapons they can gather. They'll pick off those vehicles before they get far."

"Fine!" al-Dosari barked. "But we still need to evacuate this building right after we kill our hostage. Do you have enough men here to drive the trucks to our safe house?"

Now al-Hamdani thought the Islamic State leader was losing it. There were scores of family members living in the compound and only a few trucks remaining. "I . . . I've begun shuttling them there already. We should have most of them moved in less than an hour."

"Good."

"Let's go do what you mean to do," al-Hamdani said. "I have him in the studio under guard, and it's almost time."

As he led the convoy forward, Brian Dawson heard the Little Birds zooming overhead at low altitude.

"Oh, we got a lot of 'em," Purvis said to his copilot.

"Roger, target-rich environment."

"Carnival trail, Carnival lead, you take the right side of the street, I'll take the left."

"Roger that, lead."

The two AH-6G helicopters dropped down to fifty feet off the deck and slowed their speed to eighty knots. As they picked up men on the street, they shot short squirts of their GAU-19 three-barreled machine guns. Capable of firing one thousand fifty-caliber rounds per minute, the GAU-19 is a deadly anti-personnel weapon. As the intense fire began to cut down their comrades farthest south along the road, the remaining fighters scrambled for cover wherever they could find it.

"What's that?" al-Dosari shouted as he heard the roar of the Little Birds and the bark of their machine guns.

"I don't know," al-Hamdani replied. "Our men will handle it. We just need to finish our job here."

"Carnival's wheeling around for a second gun run." It was Purvis.

"Roger, Carnival, we're pushing forward," Dawson replied, his hand on the shoulder of the Ranger driving the Humvee. "Stay in the center of the road, sergeant . . . Keep your speed up . . . That's it . . . Steer a bit this way," he coached, trying to trade off speed in an effort to avoid any IEDs that might have survived the Global Hawk's crash landing.

"Mr. Dawson, we're ready to move out on foot on your order." It was Volner calling from the second vehicle in the convoy.

"I want to push forward a little farther—" Dawson began to reply, when a deafening explosion rocked his Humvee. The vehicles in trail screeched to a halt as they watched the lead truck leap into the air, come crashing down, and roll over on its side.

"Lead's down," Volner shouted over the tactical net. Then turning to Moore, "Master Guns, we need to dismount now. You know the assault plan. The driver and I will take care of Mr. Dawson and the others in the lead truck."

"Moving out now," Moore replied. Then, "This is Moore on tactical. We're moving out on foot now. Form up on me."

"You all dismounting?" It was Purvis.

"Carnival, the lead vehicle hit an IED," Volner replied. "We're going the rest of the way on foot. Can you see any more fighters in the street?"

"Nada. Looks like the few we didn't get retreated back toward their compound."

"Good. Got plenty of ammo?"

"Roger."

"I want you and your wingman to slow and fly right over the downed Humvee. Then I want you both to paint the street with rounds from your guns. We need to explode any remaining IEDs. Don't save too many rounds."

"You got it, sir."

As Mabad al-Dosari entered their "studio," he looked at al-Hamdani. "I heard a large explosion, what was it?"

"It was one of their trucks hitting an IED. I think we're holding them off for now."

There had been no secondary explosions in the lead Humvee. Volner and their 75th Ranger Regiment driver rushed up to the broken vehicle. It was lying on its left side and all was still.

As they looked in, Volner saw their driver struggling to get out of his seat belt and harness and the other man extracting himself from the passenger seat, climbing up and out of his window. Both were blood-ied from shards of glass from the shattered windshield, but otherwise looked okay.

What he saw when he yanked open the right-side back door was a different story. A dazed Dawson just mumbled, "Hel . . . help . . . Hector." Then he tried to raise himself up, but he passed out.

They reached in and lifted the unconscious Daw-son out. Then Volner lowered himself into the back cab. Rodriguez wasn't moving. Volner shook him, "Hector . . . Hector!"

There was no response. Then he held his fingers against his neck.

"This is Carnival on tactical."

"Go ahead, Carnival," Phillips replied. She knew that with Dawson's vehicle destroyed and Volner and Moore otherwise engaged, someone had to communi-cate with Purvis.

Purvis paused, momentarily surprised to hear a fe-male voice. "We hosed down the street pretty good. I think we got a few detonations, but not sure exactly how many. Dunno if the street is completely free of IEDs now, but it's a lot better than it was."

"Thanks, Carnival."

"Orders ma'am?" Purvis began, still trying to sort out why he was hearing a female voice.

Phillips flashed back to her career in the Marine Corps. She had done several tours in Afghanistan with the Marine Corps Cultural Support Team where she had served on the front lines and had been decorated for heroism. Instinctively, she surveyed the tactical situation.

"Carnival, the roof of the building we're headed for has the clearest field of fire no matter how we approach it. Hold south at an altitude where you can see what's going on up there. If you see any activity, hose the roof with all you've got."

"Roger that, ma'am; it'll be just like spraying ants off a picnic table."

"Exactly," Phillips replied. "Still got plenty of ammo?"

"Ahhh . . . I wouldn't exactly say 'plenty' ma'am, but we'll get the job done."

Master Gunnery Sergeant Charles Moore had "been there and done that." A seasoned veteran of indeterminable age, he had joined the Marine Corps Special Operations Command at its inception and was one of the first MARSOC team members to serve at JSOC. With multiple tours in Iraq and Afghanistan, he had been on the raid into Pakistan that led to the killing of Osama bin Laden. He knew how to lead men into battle.

They had rehearsed what they were about to do scores of times in shoot houses at Fort Bragg, and had done walk-throughs in Baghdad while they waited for further orders. Now it was the real thing, and time was of the essence. Moore gathered the two dozen men around him. "You fellas don't need a pep talk. Here's the way we're gonna do this—"

Finished, he asked, "Questions?"

There were none.

Dale Bruner was kneeling down on what he thought was a carpet, his hands bound behind his back, with a gag in his mouth and a hood over his head. He heard men whispering off to his left, and then voices in front of him and a rattling of some kind of equipment.

The Bruner family's religious tradition was Episcopalian. Their family attended Sunday services regularly while the Bruner children were growing up, and it was never a question as to whether Dale and his two sisters would attend church with their parents; they just knew it was expected. But once he was in college, Dale never made church attendance a priority. And, he had to admit, God was not someone he thought much about any longer. But now he did.

A few voices seemed to move closer, and he thought he recognized one of them. It was the man who had held his face in his hands.

The ISIL fighters on the roof of the compound didn't have NVGs, but they didn't need them. Once the Global Hawk had crash-landed, every light in every window along that block had come on. They were ready to open fire on the approaching enemy with RPGs, machine guns, and their personal weapons as soon as the men came into view.

They didn't see the approaching helicopters, but they heard the clatter of the blades and the roar of the

T63-A-700 turboshaft engines on both birds. Instinctively, the men dropped their weapons and rushed toward the door leading back into the building.

It was no use. The carnage was unimaginable as first Purvis's bird, and then his wingman's, sprayed the roof with squirts from their GAU-19s. In less than thirty seconds, there was no movement.

"This is Carnival; you folks are cleared in!" Purvis said.

"Good shooting!" It was Phillips on tactical.

"Let's go!" Moore commanded. "Form up on me. We're moving forward; easy trot."

The JSOC squad covered the two hundred yards from their position to the compound in less than two minutes. A few wild shots rang out from several windows in the compound, but none of them found their mark.

While Moore and his core JSOC squad made directly for the ISIL compound as they had planned and rehearsed, most of the men of the 75th Ranger Regiment—along with Phillips—stopped short and clambered into an abandoned building just south of where Moore and the rest were heading. They took up positions to serve as a security element and blocking force should any fighters emerge from the building's entrance. There was only one way out of the front of the building, and soon they had that door under their muzzles.

Volner had kept two of the Rangers with him—one of them a medic—as he tended to Dawson and

Rodriguez. The JSOC team leader wanted to get his gun in the fight, but right now taking care of these two men was his top priority.

Moore's men were pressed against the back of the building between two doors. He yelled, "Fire in the hole," and the two breechers triggered their Nonel firing systems, and almost simultaneously moved to the side and squeezed against the building with the rest of their comrades.

The blasts knocked one door completely off its hinges and blew it back inside the building, while the other door hung on for a moment by its top hinge until gravity took over and it crashed down. The first men through each door tossed a flash-bang grenade well into the building and instinctively covered their ears and simultaneously closed their eyes. Seconds later, each assault squad poured through their respective doors like a football team emerging from their tunnel and coming out on the field. The last man in the second squad put a long burst of fire into the transformer that served the building. Everything went dark. Now it was game on, special operations style—act and react, move and shoot.

Al-Dosari stared at al-Hamdani in the light of an emergency lantern for a moment, and then shouted, "You said we could hold them off, but now they're here!"

Al-Hamdani was initially too stunned to reply. He looked at al-Dosari, then looked down at their hostage, then looked at al-Dosari and finally said, "Kill him now!"

"No, it will gain us nothing if we don't broadcast it, and the power's out!" the ISIS leader replied. Then turning to one of his men, he barked, "Where is your truck parked?"

"It's right outside, on the east side of the building."

"Good, let's go. You drive and al-Hamdani and I will take the hostage with us." Then, pointing to another man, he said, "Take everyone else and hold off whoever's coming."

The man stood frozen, refusing to move. "This . . . this is insane. Leave the American; we have to escape while there's still time!"

Al-Dosari pulled a pistol and shot the man in the head. He gave the same instructions to another man who immediately complied. Then al-Dosari grabbed the kneeling Bruner and jerked him to his feet, yanking his hostage's hood off as he did. "Up—and if you go limp and try to make us drag you, I'll kill you right here."

CHAPTER TWENTY-EIGHT

The JSOC team moved through the building with the same precision and choreography as a Broadway musical. The teams surged forward deeper into the building, stopping at preplanned positions to toss flash-bangs and then clearing the areas they were responsible for. There was no shouting, just quiet statements on their tactical net.

"Clear right!"

"Moving forward!"

"Clear left!"

"Moving up!"

"Right behind you!"

"Clear left and right!"

"Wait!" Moore said over the net. They had begun to clear the first floor, but had encountered no resistance. Had the breeching charges and the flash-bangs made the enemy run off? All of Master Guns's professional experience told him that couldn't be the case. He was about to split his force and have half of his men move into the one remaining wing of the first floor they hadn't cleared and have the other half push up to the second floor, when shots rang out. They had engaged the ISIS rear guard.

The two ISIS leaders followed their driver out the side door of their compound, dragging the handcuffed Bruner with them. The driver jumped into his seat as al-Dosari and al-Hamdani began to shove their hostage into the truck's backseat. As they did, al-Dosari shouted at the driver, "We'll go to the safe house, and you need to hurry! Take that road to the right!" he continued, thrusting his arm into the front cab.

The man paused a moment to frame his reply. He knew the penalty for angering al-Dosari, but he didn't want to die this way. ISIS fighters are fanatical, but they're not stupid. "But that will take us along a road we seeded with IEDs. One of them will blow up this truck and us with it."

Seated in the back of the truck with Bruner squeezed between him and his number two, al-Dosari couldn't believe what he was hearing. "Shut up and do as I say!" the ISIS leader shouted. "You were one of the ones seeding the IEDs; you must know where they are. Just drive around them."

But the driver just sat there, his hands frozen on the steering wheel. The key was in the truck's ignition but he hadn't fired off the engine.

"I said start the truck and drive!" al-Dosari bellowed as he hit the man on the shoulder.

The driver was frozen for another instant. Then he was all motion as he flung his door open, leapt out of the truck, and ran off.

"STOP!" al-Dosari shouted, but the man kept running.

Al-Dosari looked at his number two who was about to run after the driver. "Let him go. I'll drive. You stay in the back with him. We'll go directly to the safe house; they won't find us there."

The ISIS leader hoisted himself out of the backseat of the truck and climbed up behind the wheel. He fired up the ignition and started to creep forward.

"Stop!" al-Hamdani shouted.

"What?"

"Don't go that way. We need to turn right. I know they seeded a number of IEDs on that main street. We need to head for the alley over there," he said, pointing at their escape route.

One squad was pressed against both sides of a long hallway while the other squad moved carefully up a stairwell to clear the other floors of the building. The JSOC team had studied the building's layout, and their best guess was that the hostage was being held on the first floor. When they heard the shots, their guess became a near certainty.

Master Guns Moore was crouched down right behind his lead assaulter with his hand on the man's shoulder. In the green glow of their night-vision goggles they couldn't see exactly where the shots had come from.

"Now," Moore said on the tactical net in a low, conversational voice.

The lead man in each line tossed a flash-bang grenade forward as every squad member closed their eyes to keep the white-hot light of the flash-bangs from overwhelming their eyes.

Seconds after the flash bangs went off, it was all violence as both teams surged forward down the long hallway. A few wild shots rang out as Moore's squad shot at fleeing figures. They heard a cry and a loud thump as one of the enemy went down. As the JSOC team looked far ahead, they could see the ISIL fighters running away ahead of them. They seemed to be heading for a large doorway. The fleeing men poured through the open door of the ISIL studio and out into the next corridor. The room was empty, but a door on the far side of the room remained open. Moore held up his hand as the rest of the squad filled the large room. They saw at a glance it was the set of an execution.

"We have to catch them," one of Moore's men said.

"No, let them go. They ran out of here at full tilt. They wouldn't let trying to drag along a hostage slow them down. He must be somewhere else in the building."

The ISIS leader had no trouble sending men—and even women and children—into danger, and even commanding them to be suicide bombers. But when it came to his own safety, and especially the fear of being blown to bits by one of the IEDs he had ordered sown or shot by the approaching enemy, that was another matter.

"If we go into that alley, we might be ambushed as we come out the other end," al-Dosari shot back, rejecting his number two's suggestion. He sat in the truck, the engine idling, frozen in indecision.

"Then don't," al-Hamdani replied. "Turn around and go the other way. It doesn't—"

He stopped talking as both men saw several of their fighters emerge from the building's doors, running from the compound.

"Let's go!" al-Hamdani shouted. "The enemy must be in the house. They'll be out soon, and they'll see us!"

As he tried to urge his leader to drive somewhere, anywhere, away from where he was sure heavily armed Americans were about to find them, al-Hamdani loosened his grip on the handcuffed and gagged hostage. It was a small opening, but it was all Bruner was going to get.

As al-Dosari put the truck into gear, Bruner twisted his body ninety degrees so his back was pressed against al-Hamdani. Using the large man as leverage, he aimed his feet at the door's handle and kicked with all his might. Nothing.

Bruner reared back and kicked again. This time the door popped open.

As the truck lurched forward, the stunned al-Hamdani flailed his arms in an attempt to corral their hostage. Bruner half jumped, half rolled out of the truck and hit the ground hard.

Al-Dosari looked over his shoulder just in time to see no hostage, but his number two groping for the door. He slammed on the breaks and jerked to a stop several yards from where Bruner had left the truck. "Get out and catch him!" he bellowed.

Moore's squad searched the room and a few adjoining rooms but didn't find the hostage. They did find a hood on the floor near the carpet. One of Moore's men suggested, "Master Guns, maybe he's in another part of the building and they were going to bring him down here soon."

"Maybe," Moore replied. Then he continued, "This is Lead on tactical. What floor are you on, and have you found the hostage?"

"We've just cleared the fifth floor and are headed up to the sixth. No hostage and no enemy fighters, Master Guns; just a few remaining family members huddled in rooms scared shitless. Looks like these assholes ran away and left some of their women and kids behind."

"Roger," Moore replied. "Call me once you've cleared all the floors and then come down. Looks like we may have to cast a wider net to find Bruner."

Dropping out of a moving car had stunned Dale Bruner, but with adrenaline coursing through his veins, even with his hands cuffed behind his back, he had managed to right himself and stand up. In the darkness he swiveled his head, looking for a way to run. He was still evaluating his options when he saw a hulking figure lumbering toward him. He instinctively fled from the approaching threat.

Bruner looked over his shoulder and saw he was outdistancing the man, but as he did, he saw, then heard, a truck bearing down on him from behind his pursuer.

Still wearing their NVGs they used to explore the upper floors of the ISIL compound, the second squad reached the roof. They knew Carnival had cleared the roof of fighters before they assaulted the building, but they thought other fighters might have retreated to the roof once the assault had begun. They checked the roof in the same disciplined fashion they had cleared the floors of the building.

"Clear." It was the squad leader on tactical. He continued. "Master Guns, we've cleared the building as well as the roof. Lots of EKIA up here. We're coming—"

"Staff Sergeant!" one of the JSOC men who was peering over the edge of the roof shouted. "There's a figure down on the street running south. He looks like he has his hands bound and he's running for all he's worth . . . Wait . . . There's someone running after him and a truck closing in on both of them."

In an instant, every man on the roof was looking over the same edge. The squad leader quickly assessed the situation. "That must be the hostage, Lieutenant Bruner. He's heading toward where the Ranger

Regiment is holding the blocking position. Who has comms with them?" he asked of no one in particular.

"Master Guns, we see our hostage," the squad leader said. "His hands are bound and he's running toward the Rangers and there's a vehicle in pursuit, but we're not in position to engage. I want them to hold their fire, repeat, hold their fire, and not shoot the man on foot. Tell them there's a truck that looks like it's after him. They should open up on it when it comes into range."

"Roger, copy," Moore replied. Then on his radio, "Raven, this is Moore. Our hostage is heading toward you. Send some of your men down to grab him and then fire on the vehicle pursuing him."

"Copy all." The captain leading the Ranger team looked at Phillips. "Laurie, you've got the best optical sight. Let me know when he comes into view and then get eyes-on that vehicle." Then turning to the closest man, he continued, "Take a few men and go down to the street and grab the man running toward us. The rest of us will take out the vehicle chasing him when it comes into sight."

Three men ran down the several stories of the bombed-out building, their NVGs lighting the way. They had just begun moving north along the street when a man in a jumpsuit came into view. His hands were bound and he was gagged. The men grabbed him and held him upright.

"Lieutenant Bruner?" one of the men yelled as another one pulled the gag out of his mouth.

"Yes!" Bruner replied, relief lighting up his face.

"Sir, I have to ask you some questions. It's hostage protocol."

"Ask away!"

The Ranger paused, at a loss for words, and then said, "Sir, just what the fuck are you doing here, anyway?"

Al-Dosari was at the wheel of the truck, and al-Hamdani was in the passenger seat. The ISIS leader had picked up his number two as he drove after the escaping hostage. They were worried about IEDs and al-Dosari pressed the truck as close as he could to building facades, knowing the IEDs his men had seeded were placed more toward the middle of the street. He drove so close to the buildings that the passenger-side mirror had been torn off.

They heard the first "plink" on their truck before they heard the gunshot sound. Then more plinks, then the dirt of the street being torn up, and then automatic weapons fire. They looked ahead and couldn't see the fleeing hostage.

Al-Dosari was no hero. He jerked the wheel to the left, and tires squealing, did a rapid 180-degree turn. Once pointed north, he picked up speed and sought the safety of the other side of the street, careening the truck against the front of buildings. Soon, fewer and fewer bullets were hitting the back of the truck.

Two blocks away, Master Guns Moore and his team were working their way south. They moved slowly, wary of IEDs.

"Raven, this is Moore."

"This is Raven, go ahead."

"We're about four blocks from your posit, heading your way. We've cleared the compound. About two dozen EKIA. We didn't get the package. Repeat, we didn't get the package."

"We have him here!" the Ranger captain shouted over the radio. "We have Lieutenant Bruner!"

"Is he okay, sir?" Moore asked.

"He's been through the ringer, but otherwise all right. Get here as soon as you can. We need to withdraw in a hurry. Who knows how many fighters they're trying to muster to counterattack."

"Roger that, sir, we'll be there in ten mikes."

CHAPTER TWENTY-NINE

July 24, 0315 Arabia Standard Time

A bit south of where most of the Rangers were clearing out of the bombed-out building and were waiting for Moore and his team to reach them, Volner and two Rangers were standing guard over their comrades whose Humvee had been hit by the IED. Volner had followed everything that had gone on over the tactical net.

The fact that Lieutenant Bruner had been rescued meant their mission was a success. And when Master Guns Moore had told him he hadn't lost any of his men when they stormed the ISIL compound, that provided more good news. But none of that was enough to allow Volner to be joyful. He called Moore.

"Master Guns, I heard our Ranger escort, and I agree. We need to pull back fast and withdraw. I'm close to the downed Humvee. Once you and your men join up with the Rangers, meet me here."

"Roger that, sir."

While a few of the 75th Ranger Regiment men—along with Laurie Phillips—maintained overwatch positions in their building, scanning in all directions for a possible ISIL counterattack, the rest of the Rangers, as well as Moore and his squads, converged on Volner's position. They all were worried about Dawson and Rodriguez.

Volner, now the senior man and the de facto mission commander, wasted no time. "Gents, gather 'round and listen up. We need to mount up and get out of here soon, so I'll be quick."

All of the men shuffled toward him until they were in a tight circle.

"First, well done on rescuing Lieutenant Bruner. Master Guns, you and your teams did a great job and I think we got him out just in the nick of time. One of the Rangers' medics has him in a Humvee and is looking after him. He went through a hell of an ordeal, but he's basically okay."

Volner paused to frame his thoughts. "I know you're worried about the men in the Humvee that was taken out by the IED. The driver and the JSOC trooper in the front passenger seat made it out with just minor injuries. But the good news ends there—"

The men surrounding him could tell Volner was struggling to control his emotions. "Mr. Dawson was pretty banged up and suffered a concussion. He's been lapsing in and out of consciousness." Then turning to the Ranger Regiment captain, he continued. "Your medics say he's otherwise okay, but we need to get him to a field hospital ASAP. A fresh section of Little Birds are inbound to help with our extraction. We'll be putting him, as well as Lieutenant Bruner, in one of the birds so we can get them to Baghdad as soon as possible. The other bird will ride shotgun for us on the way south."

Volner paused for a long moment before delivering the news everyone there feared. "Men, we lost Hector. The captain's medic did heroic things to save him, but the shrapnel from the IED that tore into him cut too many arteries and we couldn't stop the flow of blood. He died quickly and he died a hero's death."

The men surrounding Volner reacted in various ways, but most were stoic; they'd lost good men before, and they'd probably lose good men on future operations. It was what made the brotherhood of arms what it was.

While the JSOC squad and the Rangers continued to process what they had just heard, one of Volner's men said, "Roger that, sir. Are we going to destroy the Global Hawk before we pull out?"

"No, there's no time, plus there still could be IEDs in the street. I've passed its coordinates up the chain. They'll have to deal with it another way."

"Questions?" There were none.

"All right, let's mount up. Captain, pull your remaining men out of the building. Everyone will head south in the Humvees. When we get to a secure LZ, the Little Bird will medevac Mr. Dawson and Lieutenant Bruner."

As the Rangers and the JSOC component moved out to carry out his orders, Volner walked a short distance away and punched a number into his Iridium satellite phone.

It was almost 0400 in Mosul, which meant it was 2100 on the U.S. East Coast. Volner didn't expect Chase Williams to be in his office, and, as he anticipated, his call was routed to the Op-Center watch floor. The watchstander told him that Williams was at home in the Watergate. He asked to be connected to Williams's cell phone and within a minute, the Op-Center director was on the line.

"Sir," Volner began. "We have Lieutenant Bruner—"

"That's fantastic news!" Williams interjected.

"Yes, sir. He's been roughed up by his captors, but he's otherwise okay. I'm afraid the rest of the news isn't all good—"

Volner gave him a quick overview of the action, including the loss of Rodriguez. He knew how a loss like this would impact the Op-Center director, and he didn't interrupt the extended silence as Williams processed what he'd heard. Finally, the older man spoke.

"Major, well done again. Please pass along my congratulations to your men as well as to the 75th Rangers. Do I need to ask General George for any additional assets to cover your extraction?"

"No sir, but thank you. The Little Birds he sent have

it covered, and the Rangers have a way to pull more assets up if we need them."

"All right then. Safe travel south, and we'll get you back to the States just as soon as we can."

"Yes sir, Admiral. And sir, I'm sorry about Hector."

"I know you are, Major; I am too. He was one of the best."

Sitting in his Watergate apartment with only family pictures—including those of his late wife—Williams was alone in his grief. In his few years as Op-Center director he had lost both JSOC and CIRG heroes in conflicts but had not yet lost one of his core staff—someone he saw and talked with almost every day. Now he had.

Shake it off, Chase. This is a tragedy and something you need to process, but now isn't the time. You have work to do.

Williams sat upright in his chair at his small desk in his condo. He scrolled through the contacts list on his iPhone and found Eric Oldham's number. As he hit "Call," he framed his thoughts.

"Oldham here."

"Eric, it's Chase. Are you still at the Bruners' home?"

"I am."

"I have wonderful news," Williams continued. Once he had told him everything he knew he concluded, "Please tell Jay and Meagan how happy and relieved we are and that we'll get their son back to the States as fast as possible."

"I'll do that," Oldham replied. "And thank you, Chase. Thank you to you and your people."

The next call he made was to the one person he needed to lean on in this difficult time.

"Sullivan here," she replied to the ring on her Op-Center secure cell phone.

"Anne, this is Chase. We've had a loss and I need you. Can you be dressed in a half hour?" Williams began. He told her they had lost Hector Rodriguez and that he wanted—no needed—the both of them to drive to the Rodriguez home that evening and break the news to his wife.

"Absolutely, boss."

EPILOGUE

Alerted by his 75th Ranger Regiment that they were in a firefight in Mosul and would likely be exfiltrating soon, the CENTCOM commander had sent a C-17 with a medical evacuation team to Al Muthana Air Base on the military side of Baghdad International Airport. The aircraft was there when the two backup Little Birds delivered Dawson and Bruner, and the medics immediately went to work on the two wounded men.

The Humvee convoy had sped south at top speed and arrived several hours later. Volner, Moore, and four of the more senior JSOC men carefully loaded Hector Rodriguez's body onto the C-17 with quiet dignity. Within an hour of the convoy arriving, the Globemaster was heading west.

The USS *Wayne E. Meyer* (DDG 108), one of the Navy's newest Arleigh Burke Aegis destroyers, steamed at bare steerageway in the northern reaches of the Arabian Gulf. Her captain had put her in the launch basket and only awaited the order from higher authority. Unknown to *Wayne E. Meyer*'s captain, the debate as to whether to alert Iraqi authorities had been intense and ultimately had to be adjudicated by President Midkiff. Finally, the order came.

The sound was deafening and the fiery flash intense as a single Tomahawk cruise missile leapt out of *Wayne E. Meyer*'s launch tube and soared into the night sky. The BGM-109D Tomahawk Land Attack Missile—or TLAM-D—armed with cluster munitions, unfolded its tiny wings and exposed its air-scoop seconds after it emerged from the ship. Ascending and heading north using inertial guidance, it soon picked up the GPS satellite signal. Minutes later, as the missile made landfall on the southern tip of Iraq's Bubiyan Island, the Tomahawk's terrain contour matching navigation system took over, comparing terrain contours built into the BGM-109D's electronic brain with the route it was programmed to fly.

Flying at five hundred and fifty miles per hour, it took the TLAM-D almost an hour to reach Mosul. Once over the city, its highly accurate Digital Scene Matching Area Correlation system took over, providing terminal guidance as the missile homed in on its target. It hit the hulk of the Global Hawk with tremendous kinetic energy, but it was the explosive force of the 166 bomblet submunitions that ripped the downed UAV to shreds and made it unrecognizable and of no value to any enemy.

*   *   *

Chase Williams and Anne Sullivan sat in companionable silence in front of her Georgetown brownstone near Dupont Circle for a long time. Like Williams, she too felt the loss of one of their core staff in a profound and personal way. Finally, Sullivan spoke.

"Chase, this is the first time I've had to do something like this. I . . . I hope I was helpful. It was all I could do to keep from losing it."

"I've done it more times than I care to remember. It doesn't get any easier. You being there was important to me, and I could tell it was important to Mrs. Rodriguez."

"She took the news so stoically; it was almost like she was expecting it."

Williams paused a long moment before speaking again. "It takes a strong woman to be a warrior's wife. They all hope the worst never happens, but if it does, they know they have to deal with it. Those with children focus on helping their kids get through it and worry about dealing with their own grief later."

"I almost felt like she was consoling me."

"She was. I'm certain she's dealt with this before, helping the families of Hector's comrades who've been lost in battle. Now she knows she has to deal with all the details this loss brings with it: notifying family, getting her adult children back home—they have six kids and they're scattered all around the country— arranging the wake and the funeral service, even ensuring Hector is buried in his best dress uniform."

"She said they attend Our Lady of Angels in Woodbridge."

"They do," Williams replied. "And we'll all be there for his service; we can keep just a skeleton crew on the watch floor. And as soon as Brian gets back, I know he'll want to take lead on this; Hector was his guy, and he'll want to make sure everything is handled with class and dignity."

"He's done this sort of thing before I suspect."

"You can bet he has. Sadly, our military—and especially our special operators—are good at this."

After an extended silence, Williams spoke again. "There's one bit of business I want us to attend to first thing tomorrow. Before that young SEAL we rescued returns to the West Coast, I want to have a talk with him."

"I'll see to it."

They talked for a little while longer, and it was close to midnight when Williams walked Sullivan up the steps to her front door. For the first time in their professional association he hugged her and simply said, "Thank you." Then he got back into his car and navigated his way through D.C.'s streets to the Washington Nationals baseball park.

Hector had been a huge New York Mets fan, while Williams rooted for the Nationals. They had taken in many Nats-Mets games together and their rooting rivalry was well known to everyone at Op-Center and was a source of constant chatter and ribbing between the two men. There in the shadow of the darkened ballpark, Williams reflected for a long while, and then he wept unashamedly.

* * *

Two days later, there was a somber reunion at the Bruner home in Springfield, Virginia. There were no welcome home banners or streamers or signs. Instead, there was just a profound sense of relief the five family members shared together. Williams and Oldham had intervened and ensured that Dale's debriefing was expedited, and he was returned home without delay.

Late in the evening, when the Bruner women had finally gone to bed, father and son sat alone on their screened-in porch, each man holding a glass of Irish whiskey—the good stuff, as Bruner senior called it. Even long after sunset, the July heat and humidity in Northern Virginia felt like a sodden blanket covering both men.

The elder Bruner knew what needed to be done, but it pained him to do it. He sat struggling to form the words, but they finally came.

"Dale, your heart was in the right place trying to come rescue me, but at the end of the day, none of that's going to matter—"

"I know," he interrupted, "I know I screwed up big time, but I didn't think the Navy was doing enough to save you."

"I understand that, but you know how many regulations you broke and how you let down your command," he continued. "And beyond that, Dale—" The older man paused before continuing to ensure his son was completely focused on what he was about to say. "You put men at risk, and one man died trying to rescue you. You have some serious questions to answer. I'll support you one hundred percent, but at the end of the day, you will have to stand tall and take whatever accounting comes your way."

"I know."

"It pains me to tell you this, but I've made inquiries with some of my fellow flag officers. Even under these exceptional circumstances, your commanding officer is going to have no choice but to bring you up on multiple charges of violating the Uniform Code of Military Justice. This may even go to court-martial."

The younger man was silent for a moment as he took a gulp of the Johnnie Walker Black.

"What should I do?"

"Look, I know you love the SEALs, but under the circumstances I think you should write your letter of resignation and fly to Coronado and deliver it to your skipper in person."

"I will, Dad."

At Op-Center, Chase Williams sat with his ops director. He was mindful that Hector's death had affected Dawson even more than it had impacted him. He knew the former Green Beret needed to decompress, but sending the divorced Dawson to mourn alone in his condo in Tysons Corner wasn't the answer. He allowed him to stay at Op-Center virtually around the clock while he attended to all the details of helping Gianna Rodriguez through Hector's death.

Now it was business, and he needed his de facto chief of staff's input on changes they needed to make in future missions. The two men agreed that when they sent their JSOC team downrange, it needed to have a bigger footprint and an on-call aviation component. Had the CENTCOM commander not had the Little Birds available in Baghdad, their mission would not only have failed—it would have failed spectacularly, likely with more loss of life.

The domestic situation was more complex. Once again, in spite of the personnel and material resources they could muster if needed, the FBI's CIRG HRT had tried to intercept Admiral Bruner using far too few assets, and only serendipity kept him from being spirited out of the country on a FedEx flight. They both knew they needed to tread carefully and not bash another federal agency, and Williams had his work cut out for him. He would try to use "peer suasion" to reach an amicable solution with the attorney general and the incoming FBI director. If he couldn't, he'd have to approach the president and get Op-Center involved on the domestic front sooner.

Several days later, Dale Bruner was back at the Naval Special Warfare Command. He had reported back to his commanding officer, Captain Pete Cummings, immediately. Cummings had dealt with a full spectrum of emotions over the past week: concern when he couldn't locate an officer in his command, terror over what might happen to him if he fell into ISIL's hands, anger that the man had done such a damn-fooled thing, and then resignation that, as Bruner's commanding officer, he would have to impose discipline. He told him that they both would have to appear before Rear Admiral James Green, the Naval Special Warfare Command commander, for admiral's mast.

The next day, Bruner and Cummings, both in their starched white uniforms, stood at attention in front of Admiral Green as he read the lieutenant's letter of resignation. Green's face was emotionless as he held the letter in both hands. Finally, he spoke.

"Captain Cummings, you've read Lieutenant Bruner's resignation letter. What do you think?"

"I hate to lose a good man, Admiral, but under the circumstances, I think he's doing the right thing."

Green sat in silence for an extended time before he spoke. Now his face was contorted in anger as he rose. As he did, he tore the letter to shreds. "Well I'm not letting you off that easy, Lieutenant. You cost a good man his life and you need to pay for what you've done—you can't just walk away!"

Both men standing in front of him stood up a little straighter but couldn't hide their shock.

"Lieutenant Bruner, you will stand before me at 1000 hours tomorrow morning for admiral's mast. At that time, I will impose summary discipline. There are people who want you taken to court-martial, but all that would do is give this command and your fellow SEALs a public black eye. Your record downrange buys you another chance and you'll continue to serve at this command, but you will be under probation."

"Yes . . . yes, sir, Admiral," Bruner stammered.

"Now both of you get out of my office."

The assault on their compound had shaken Mabad al-Dosari. The ISIL leader had thought himself invincible and out of reach of the Iraqi Army, the American coalition, or anyone else who might try to stand in the way of his dream of establishing a caliphate throughout the Middle East.

While his fighters still controlled most of Mosul, al-Dosari no longer felt safe having a large compound that was an easy target for coalition airstrikes. He dispersed his fighters throughout the city, and he moved his family to the western outskirts of Mosul. He had been humbled, but he remained committed to his cause and found new resolve. *I will be back, and I will never rest until we prevail.*

Trevor Harward entered the Oval knowing the president was once again intently focused on the Middle East—and that was good as far as it went. But he also knew stopping ISIL had become the cause de jour, and it was going to be difficult to get the president—or anyone else for that matter—to look beyond the borders of the areas ISIL controlled or threatened.

The national security advisor had prepared as thoroughly for this meeting as for any meeting he had ever had with President Midkiff. As the two men who had weathered so many crises together sat in the Oval's conversational area, Harward powered up his secure iPad, brought up a map of Europe and began, "Mr. President, this is what is worrying our national security staff." As he spoke, the national security advisor scrolled eastward from the heart of Europe.

AFTERWORD

As this book was being written, edited, copyedited, printed, and distributed, it was difficult not to be inundated by news about the Islamic State. Therefore, it would be easy to think of this book in the same way many think of television police procedurals that are "ripped from the headlines," and give it the same degree of interest—passing at best. That would be a mistake.

Scorched Earth is much more about the future than it is about the present. ISIL is a steadily metastasizing cancer that can draw on almost unlimited resources. It recruits fighters from around the globe—all eager to join the fight. As a panel of national security and military experts noted in testimony to the U.S. House of Representatives Armed Services Committee recently, "This is going to be a long fight and likely will continue for another decade."

ABOUT THE AUTHOR

George Galdorisi is a career naval aviator. His Navy career was capped by four tours as commanding officer and five years as a carrier strike group chief of staff, including two combat tours to the Arabian Gulf. He began his writing career in 1978 and has written eleven books, including the *New York Times* bestseller *Tom Clancy Presents: Act of Valor* and *The Kissing Sailor,* which proved the identity of the two principals in Alfred Eisenstaedt's famous photograph. The Tom Clancy Op-Center series is his latest effort, with the first two books of the series (*Out of the Ashes* and *Into the Fire*) achieving bestseller status. He is the Director of the Corporate Strategy Group at the Navy's Command and Control Center of Excellence in San Diego, California. He and his wife, Becky, live in Coronado, California. Contact him via his Web site: www.georgegaldorisi.com.

Read on for an excerpt from the next book
by Jeff Rovin and George Galdorisi

TOM CLANCY'S
OP-CENTER:
DARK ZONE

Available from St. Martin's Griffin

CHAPTER ONE

June 2, 11:25 am

"It is said that a diplomat is someone who is able to deceive his friends but never his enemies."

Douglas Flannery brushed windblown strands of gray hair from in front of his sunglasses as he looked up at the speaker. The sixty-two-year-old former ambassador was sitting on a bench near South Street Seaport, watching the late-morning sun play on the East River, mesmerized by the shards of light leaping and stabbing constantly as water taxis and ferries shot by. He was thinking back to the last time he had sat beside a river, waiting for her. It was on the older, western right bank of the Dnieper River, in a park with winter-bared trees and lean squirrels emboldened by hunger. There were squirrels here, too, but they were well fed.

He stared briefly at the woman who had spoken, took her in with surprising equanimity—surprising, given how they had parted—before turning back toward the hypnotic water. She looked well, and he was glad of that; but it was the woman's accent that had stirred an immediate and overpowering rise of emotions. The inflection was Ukrainian, starting far back in the throat and possessing a somewhat nasal quality. It was an accent Flannery had grown accustomed to during the eight years in which he served as the United States ambassador in Kiev. Though he was fluent in the language—he held a master's degree in translation from NYU—he had never quite mastered a precise accent, since most of his contacts had been in writing.

"I have heard that said," Flannery replied. "Which is why, after thirty-plus years, I've learned that a good diplomat treats everyone equally—as a potential adversary."

"Even an old friend and ally?"

"Everyone," he said, his body tensing, the word sounding harsher than he had intended. He relaxed his shoulders. The conflict in Crimea had done that to all of them—made them callous, or worse.

"I see," the woman replied quietly.

"Events change us, alliances challenge us," Flannery said in an apologetic tone. "In our work, 'old' doesn't mean settled. You still have to start over again."

"What is the saying? 'Everything old is new again'?"

Flannery nodded and took another look at the familiar figure as she sat easily on the opposite end of the bench. The woman was in her late thirties. She had dark eyes, a long neck, and a broad, open face framed by black hair worn in twin ponytails. Her powder-blue jogging suit was speckled with perspiration. Swallowing a mouthful of water, she began to text as she spoke.

"I suppose even friends and allies want something, often without knowing it," she said.

"Inevitably," he said. "Though I continue to believe that there may be rare exceptions. People who just want to say hello or reconnect. Otherwise, I might become a cynic."

She gave him a sidelong look. "You know what I remember best, Douglas? I remember watching you with the Australian ambassador when he called after Malaysia Airlines Flight 17 was shot down. So many of his countrymen lost, and you could not have been more sincerely compassionate. You will always be a humanist."

"That was three years ago, another life," he said. He met her glance, and then they both looked away.

In 2011, three years before the hostilities began in Crimea, Galina Petrenko—who had been relocated at age two from Chernivitz after the Chernobyl nuclear disaster—had secured a mission position as an ADC, an arrivals and departures coordinator who helped orient and acclimate American staff. Flannery had been impressed by her work ethic, her patriotism, and her courage: after two years at the embassy she had been drafted, but was turned down when a medical exam revealed Stage 1 thyroid cancer. She went back to the mission, missing only a few days of work to undergo treatment. Risking her job and her freedom,

Galina had spied on her employers to transmit any potentially useful scrap of information to the ZSU, the Zbroyni Syly Ukrayiny—the Ukrainian military. Flannery was forced to have her dismissed, though he checked on her through mutual acquaintances. He heard that she had gone to work for a lieutenant general at the Sluzhba Zovnishn'oyi Rozvidky Ukrayiny, the Foreign Intelligence Service, and was now working as a translator for the Permanent Mission of Ukraine to the United Nations. He was not surprised to hear from her after his appointment as a fellow of the York Organization for Peace had been announced two weeks before. The think tank was located on Pearl Street, in a three-story-tall manor-style building from the Revolutionary era. Financed by wealthy Eastern European expatriates, York was deeply involved in analyzing and guiding the politics of the region.

"How is your health?" Flannery asked.

"Two years in remission, three to go," she said. A brow went up. "Unless you're referring to something else?"

"I meant the . . ." He touched his throat as if he were loath to say the word. "Though there is a rumor that you are involved with Russians here," he added. "Buying information?"

"We buy from them, they buy from us—it is an honest arrangement, no one is deceived," she said.

"That also lets you watch each other," Flannery said.

"Yes, which is why I asked you to meet me on the river," she said. "A short walk from your office but a decent run for me, and it will take a monitor at least another ten minutes to catch up."

Flannery made a point of not looking north. It would indicate a level of confidence that could put him in jeopardy. "Do you have any backup?" he asked.

"Not today. He is pursuing his own contacts."

Flannery felt an old, familiar feeling. The Galina he once knew—warm, smart, attentive—was still very much in evidence, though those qualities had a newly burnished edge. They were not enough to be off-putting, but they were enough to make him wary.

"So what do *you* want, Galina? I'm due back at a symposium at noon."

"For lunch?"

"For peace."

"Most of the people are there for the free food," she said. "You know, Douglas, I never knew which you disliked more in Kiev, the borscht or the small talk."

"Neither. As much as I dislike a slow verbal massage like the one I'm getting now," he said. "You and I did not part on the best of terms, but I always appreciated your directness."

"Fair enough," she replied, setting her smartphone in her lap and taking another swallow of water before continuing. "I phoned, Douglas, because we need someone inside Suhoputnye Voyska Rossiyskoy Federatsii. Our people undercover in the Kremlin have disappeared amid rumors that six armored columns are being readied as the spearhead for a renewed invasion force. The ZSU wants information on the tanks and their deployment to make a preemptive strike."

Flannery turned to her abruptly. "You want to attack Russian troops and tanks *in* Russia?"

"We don't want them setting a foot deeper in our soil," she replied.

"How—*where* have you been preparing for this?" the diplomat asked. As far as he knew, his own nation's Department of Defense was unaware of any such preparations.

"Do you really want to know?" she asked.

"If I'm to believe you, yes," he replied.

"All right. It's very ingenious," she said. "We use VRS in a secret facility. Only a handful of people know of this training center's existence."

"Virtual-reality simulations?" Flannery said, openly astonished.

"It's the boot camp for the next generation of soldiers," she said. "You'd be surprised. Some of our new recruits suffered PTSD without ever leaving their chairs. They had to be replaced."

" 'New recruits,' " he said. "Are you talking about regular military, or paramilitary?"

Galina was stubbornly silent.

"And this facility," he said. "At least tell me where it is?"

"I'm sorry, I cannot do that," she replied.

"That is madness," Flannery said. "All of it. You understand that this will provoke a *massive* retaliation."

"We understand that if the ZSU never takes the fight to them Putin wins by attrition," she said. "And— there are other precautions we are taking. Please. Before we can do anything, we need intelligence."

"Then count me out," he told her. "I don't want to expedite a reckless suicide."

Galina stared thoughtfully out at the river. "Douglas, if you won't help, then our people will be forced to proceed under the assumption that such an attack is being readied," she said bluntly. "Participating, you have the ability to prevent needless bloodshed."

"Or help trigger it by confirming your fears," he said.

"In that case, helping us end this quickly may save lives."

If Flannery had possessed an appetite, he would have lost it. Imagined scenes of combat filled his mind, the grainy green tint of night-vision goggles sparked by the crisp cries of gunfire and screaming—shouted commands, agonized injuries. The region had never been a bed of tranquillity, with ancient ethnic and religious strife, two World Wars, and then the decades as Soviet Socialist Republics. But York was working hard with the heads of local governments and relief groups to try to sow at least the seeds of peace.

"I have to think about this," Flannery said. "How much may I share with my colleagues?"

Galina checked the time on her smartphone and stood. "As much as you see need to, though time is obviously critical."

"How soon do your people plan to move?"

Galina briefly looked down at him. "It will be this month," she said. "That is all I can say." She waggled the phone she was holding. "I have a burner the Russians haven't hacked. Call me on it? You have the number."

Flannery nodded noncommittally.

The woman sent the number to Flannery's phone and, with a lingering look at him—an expression of resolve—ran off to the north, back toward the United Nations.

Be careful, he thought, not daring to speak aloud in the event someone was nearer than she suspected.

The toot of a tugboat brought the diplomat back to the moment, and he rose on suddenly unsteady legs. He stood for a moment, smelling the salty sea air of the harbor. He didn't want this responsibility, but it was his nonetheless. Redacting and forwarding intelligence that helped forge U.S. policy in the region had been stressful enough, which was why he'd left the diplomatic corps. But this . . .

He didn't feel like attending a symposium on the real and existential risks facing Belarus, Lithuania, and Latvia, but he had to get through that before he could discuss this with his colleagues.

And, as if to underscore the fact that even a man of nearly three score years could still learn new ways, the idea of small talk suddenly seemed vitally appealing.

His lean face pulled in a familiar scowl, his careful eyes tired and itchy from the high morning pollen count, Andrei Cherkassov was definitely ready to go home.

When he left Moscow in 1986, it was expensive for a young man—even a former *kapitán* who had been an honored Spetsnaz officer in Afghanistan but who had been retired due to tinnitus, of all things, a six-foot-three-inch young man who could only get work as a security guard at the Cosmonautics Memorial Museum, where he didn't have to hear very well because most of the visitors didn't speak Russian. All he had to do was make sure no one touched the space capsules and satellites.

That job had lasted a year. One of his former superiors, Polkóvnik Birman, had been leading a group through the facility and recognized him, asked him to come and see him at his new post in the Main Intelligence Directorate. Eighteen months later, after a shakedown period in South Africa, Cherkassov was assigned to London, then New York. He remembered, with a smile, the jealousy of his colleague, Georgi Glazkov, who had really wanted the post. Instead, he was sent to Mongolia to keep an eye on the many members of the Mongolian Revolution of 1990, the "Democratic Revolution," which threatened the country's extensive border with southern Russia.

"You may be killed in a very dangerous position," Glazkov had said, "but at least, Andrei, you will not die of boredom!"

His job was surveillance with occasional *zvetchenya*—termination up and down the Eastern Seaboard. It was just like being back in Afghanistan, only civilized. The truth was, Cherkassov preferred assassination to the Spetsnaz or to working at the CMM. The hours were shorter and the clothes were less restrictive.

But now, after more than twenty-five years in New York, that city had become much too expensive. Even Moscow was preferable, especially since he could get into one of the flats open to individuals over sixty-five. In just a few days, he would turn sixty-six. Birman was gone, but his successor had promised Cherkassov a plane ticket . . . and a big party. Cherkassov hadn't had a birthday party since he was six, living in what was still Leningrad.

After receiving the call from Olga confirming the route his target was apparently taking, Cherkassov had taken an Uber to South Street, just north of the Brooklyn Bridge and below the FDR Drive. The highway cast the area in darkness and the columns that supported it provided ample cover. He had arrived in time to see Olga pant her way south, after her quarry—the woman was in very good shape, but she was not young—and then he saw Olga again, running the other way. A look from her told him that the other runner had finished her meeting early and was already on the way back. The runner would see Olga, of course. Olga was there to be seen. She would not, however, see Cherkassov.

The killer was dressed in jeans and a New York Mets T-shirt. Both had been freshly laundered; she couldn't see or hear him, and he certainly didn't want her to smell him. Many homeless people lived under the highway. People who ran here were alert to odors, the scent of potential danger.

Cherkassov had chosen this particular spot across from Beekman Street because the road to the west was little traveled and there were parked cars to block the view of anyone to the east. Traffic passing overhead created an irregular, rattling beat; he wouldn't be able to hear her footsteps, but he would see her shadow. The sun was over the harbor and would throw her elongated shape well forward, right in front of him. As it happened, he saw the shadow, heard the footfalls on dirt left over from a recent street excavation, and saw a cloud of that dirt preceding her. His hand went into his pocket and he took out his wallet. He used two fingers to remove his preferred weapon—one that never tripped alarms, attracted the attention of the TSA, or broke any laws: an American Express card, one corner sharpened to a razor's edge. He pinched it between the thumb and index finger of his left hand.

As the woman jogged past the large, slightly rusted stanchion, Cherkassov's right arm shot out toward her. It stretched across her breastbone, circled her throat, pulled her toward him back first. She did what everyone did: she reached up with both hands to try and dislodge the biceps that were thicker with flesh than muscle but still held her fast. In the shadow of the highway, the credit card flashed across her throat, drawn firmly and steadily across the arm that restrained her. It was a guide, a way of making sure he sliced both her windpipe and her carotid artery. As soon as the blood began to shoot out, he leaned her forward so she'd bleed out on the street. She gurgled and gasped, but only for a moment, as her throat filled with blood and drowned her—which caused her to lose consciousness that much quicker. The hands stopped struggling within moments. She was unconscious within seconds. Though blood continued to flow and pool, she was dead when he let her flop to the asphalt.

It was a relatively clean kill: there were only a few spots on his jeans and shirt. The denim quickly turned those speckles brown so they wouldn't attract attention. The shirt was blue and, to anyone who had ever been to Citi Field, the splatters looked for all the world like smudged ketchup.

Crouching and wiping the credit card on her jogging suit—where the blood did look very red—he put it back in his pocket, retrieved her smartphone, and pressed her dead thumb on the screen. The phone unlocked. Then the killer slipped deeper under the highway and headed south for several blocks before turning toward the sunlit streets and the omnipresent security cameras.